Speakeasies and Spiritualists

Curated by Nicole Petit

Speakeasies and Spiritualists
An 18thWall Productions book published by
arrangement with Nicole Petit
verba mea in minibus
desiderium meum
Cover by Johannes Chazot
Text Copyright
Imposture, Coincidence, or Mistake © James Bojaciuk
All That Jazz © M.H. Norris
Gabriel's Trumpet © Jon Black
Double D © Donald J Bingle
Hoodoo man © John Linwood Grant
Moses Callahan's Last Chord © Brendan Foley
The Uninvited Guest © Josh Reynolds
Moving Pictures © William J. Martin
The French Communication © Aaron Smith
The Unbearable © Peter Rawlik
Rose Mackenberg material is public domain.

Table of Contents

Preface

Rose Mackenberg has been unjustly forgotten.

In an era when spiritualists were preying on the grief created by the Great War, Rose Mackenberg was one of the premiere investigators debunking them. She was chief of Harry Houdini's "secret police," and would often present her findings about local psychics while onstage. More than that, she was a master of disguise—essential in a field where exposed mediums could attempt murder. She even testified before Congress.

Speakeasies and Spiritualists is our homage to Rose Maceknberg's life and career.

We're proud to present what is, so far as we're aware, the first two pieces of historical fiction starring Rose Mackenberg. James Bojaciuk looks at her early days, and writes a case that shows how she b and a case that could have brought Houdini's notice. M.H. Norris examines how Mackenberg's careful notice would benefit a murder investigation. We will also present two of Mackenberg's own articles.

After that, we have a selection of stories set in Mackenberg's 1920s, spiritualist-filled milieu. But are the ghosts real now, or still trickery?

That is for you to investigate.

DWARF INSIDE "PSYCHIC" DRUM
CAUSES EXPOSÉ OF MYRA'S MESMERIC MUSIC
Rose Mackenberg

Ever since the ancient Egyptians learned how to make their statues "sing," the terrifying power of sound has been a valuable stock-in-trade of magicians and miracle-mongers. When to that power is added darkness, it is exceedingly stout-nerved person who, under "Mystic" circumstances, can remain unmoved.

The fake "medium," on impressing clients to bleed them of ready cash, would find a singing statue impractical; he has, therefore, perfected and exploited sound for his cabinet séances in another way—he has devised a series of tricks with trumpets that have been, in the long run, hugely and unholily lucrative.

I want to take you with me, in this chapter, behind the curtains of an average cabinet hoax, and show you how really profound the effect of a musical instrument is, when it is apparently sounded by ghostly lips. And I want to also prove to you that such "manifestations" as this can readily be duplicated by any intelligent stage performer, with a little practice.

MYRA'S SÉANCE "TOO PERFECT"
The same affirmation holds true—at least, so far as my professional experiences go—without forms of sound, including the beating of tambourines, the playing of violins, cornets and drums.

And, speaking of the last-named instrument, I want to tell you an amusing episode in which I participated during my work as a special investigator in attempting to ferret out

6

"mediumistic" frauds. This was just prior to my association with Harry Houdini as his special detective, and it may have been that he engaged me on the strength of my reputation, slight though it was at the time, won by my exposure of this particular hoax.

Always interested in psychic investigation, though openly skeptical about most of the "phenomena" I have witnessed, I was one evening invited by a friend to attend a cabinet séance. She was not, by the way, an extremely gullible girl, and at her suggestion that the séance would be "good, clean fun," I agreed to accompany her.

Since the young "spiritualist" who put on the show—the clientele would have been horrified to hear it referred to in that way—was eventually exposed, reformed, and is now living happily as a married woman, I shall not divulge her identity, but merely refer to has as Myra. Gifted with remarkable beauty, intelligent, magnetic, and clever, she had every natural factor to aid in her exploiting the "supernatural."

Myra was a cabinet working; that is, she permitted herself to be bound, hand and foot, to a chair in a curtained recess. The draperies were then closed and the sound of cornets and other instruments could be plainly heard by the auditors outside. But Myra's trump card was a really adroit bit of inspiration.

As you doubtless know, most "mediums" never work with the curtains drawn back and the lights turned on—it would be obviously impossible.

No Aid from Darkness
But Myra, for the finish of her stunt, had an assistant pull back the curtains and turn on the lights. This time there was no sound of brass or reed instrument, but a very large bass

drum that had stood on the stage throughout the "séance" began to give forth muffled, steady, rhythmic reverberations.

As a piece of clever psychological showmanship, the effect of this was very imposing; for the true believers in the audience, their appetites whetted for further marvels by the demonstration in the darkened room, never once thought that the bass-drum finish could be anything but "immaterial."

I had my suspicions of Myra from the start. It was too perfect, too suave and well built up. I didn't confide my skepticism to my friend, who was plainly impressed, but a few nights later, effectively disguised as a respectable bespectacled old maid, I gained admission to the circle again. This time I determined to do a little "materializing" on my own, and when the lights were first extinguished I "Broke" the circle of hands—a simple trick—and crept around to the back of the cabinet.

Cautiously lifting the curtain, I stretched out my fingers tentatively in the direction of the base drum and encounter— human flesh! His deformed little body compressed into an arc, a tiny dwarf was preparing to emerge. His never was marvelous, for he uttered no sound though he must have known that someone was wise to him. I decided to leave well enough alone for the time being, and returned to my seat in the circle.

Trickery Apparent

Myra's trickery now became apparent. Her "routine" was as follows: with the lowering of the lights and the drawing of the curtain, the midget—she "rented" him from a circus—would creep out—beat or blow the various musical instruments, then return to his hiding place. Then, for the grand finale, with lights up and Myra exposed to full view of the circle, he, screen from scrutiny, would add the artistic finishing touch by pounding like a fiend on the inside of the big drum.

Confesses Fakes, Retires

Myra did a flourishing business with this chicanery, though I warned everyone I knew that she was a skillful faker: but eventually her exposure came about and she withdrew from public life after a full confession of her misdeeds. We are good friends to this day, and I get an occasional letter from her.

Most trumpet "mediums" have not Myra's skill. The bulk of them—I do not refer to men and woman who actually believe in "trumpet voices"—are clumsy frauds, and their clients are, for the most part, credulous and stupid.

Imposture, Coincidence, or Mistake

James Bojaciuk

"I am perfectly convinced that I have both seen, and heard in a manner which should make unbelief impossible, things called spiritual which cannot be taken by a rational being to be capable of explanation by imposture, coincidence, or mistake." ~ Augustus De Morgan, *From Matter to Spirit: the Result of Ten Years' Experience in Spirit Manifestations* (1863)

"Science" is overstatement.

Left hook. Jab—to the kidneys, jab—to the kidneys, her head is bowed—so jab to the temple. The blow is off: some misshapen punch that can't decide if it's an uppercut or a right hook smashes into her chin, and she staggers back to her canvas corner. On the first punch, she collapses against it. On the second punch, she tries to fall. On the third punch, she throws her hands up—but they're smashed away...

Heavy with breath, her opponent collapses back to the center of the ring.

With an updated record of 29-1, Mildred Divoso, champion-in-waiting of the Brooklyn Women's Welterweights, is dead.

"It's disgusting, unwholesome—and, further—unladylike."

Mac spared her half a glance, then turned her attention back to a little street sweeper who worked his way down the street. In the half hour they'd been there, leaning against Miss Esmée's railing, he had worked his way down the street, then up the street, then down the street, then up the street in a frustrating, tennis-ball fashion.

10

The street should be very clean.

It was, perhaps, dirtier than any New York street.

Mac kept her gaze on the sweeper. "And *male* boxers?"

Betty shrugged. "At least you expect men to kill each other for money. That she died before the championship—that all sounds like a message, doesn't it?" A righteous tongue-click.

In that half-hour, the little sweeper'd been nearly run over twice. Each time, he waddled up to the driver's door, they shouted at each other with the expected New York language, then passed a half dozen whispers between each other.

Mac squinted. Another unmarked car nearly ran him down.

They shouted at each other again.

He said something the city swallowed up in its unending noise.

Betty hadn't noticed.

"What time is it?" Mac finally looked back.

She took a belated, brief glance at her watch. "Seven forty-five."

"Hrm," was all she heard back. Roughly every fifteen minutes, then.

Moments passed. The sweeper passed.

And when the sweeper threatened to pass again, Betty tapped Macs arm and pulled her through the brownstone's doors—to quite another world. The entryway was designed to deny your senses—deny that New York, with all its dirt and inefficient sweepers, was immediately behind you.

Betty looked about, an *ahhhhh* caught in her throat. It finally came out in a wheeze.

Real magic is attended to by a certain unmistakable touch. Dusty scholarship graced by the bric-a-brac that's built-up over millennia of manuals, rumor, and folklore. Esmée's lounge featured none of that, hushing it away in favor of a flamboyance which would be quite at home on the stage.

Embroidered stars festooned every surface, from the divan to the carpet. Crescents, stolen from the nearest magician's dunce-cap, broke up the night skies, and seemed to be applied almost randomly.

"Don't look so suspicious. It's good, clean fun." Betty caught her arm again, sensing a flight risk, and pulled Mac deeper.

"Cotton Mather would disagree."

But Betty was not wrong. The decoration presented magic without acknowledging the sinister. Stars, moons, wands, charms, a crystal ball placed prominently in the entrance, in the fashion of a pawnbroker's Lombard. Mac smiled. No skulls. No knives. No animals for the sacrifice.

"Oh, perhaps it is all *good* and *clean*."

"And fun."

"That, Betty, remains to be seen."

An assistant, stately and assured enough to comfort anyone from the upper reaches of the upper west, ushered them into a waiting room dominated by catoptromancy. Every wall was a mirror, and glancing above the wainscoting invited a dizzying look into infinity. Mac blinked, then looked at everything except the walls—this was evidently a waiting room. Chaise lounges were arrayed to encourage conversation, and others were already seated.

The Mrs. Costervelt and *the* Mrs. Coquine, their society heads raised in the society manner.

A large woman, hedged into a corner by a man who had, sometimes decade ago, been large. Mac shook her head at the word. "Large" implied fat. This young woman was anything but. She was built well enough to knock a boxer cold, and the old man had gone to slackness in a way that suggested he had forgotten his muscles at home.

A few men were scattered about, all with anonymous faces

pasted above anonymous suits.

Mac leaned back. To pass the time, she judged who could be Esmée's floor-workers. To pass the time, Betty watched her own expression.

It was all perfectly calculated, of course, to heighten the sense of the uncanny.

Betty twitched. The society heads fell to whispers. The large woman flexed her hands, unkinking muscles.

It was at this moment, where someone must break the tension, a new man opened the waiting room's curtain. He was a white man. But this had not stopped him from dabbing...*something* brown across his hands and face, and mounting a loosely bound turban on his head. Betty gasped. Mac followed suit—if only to keep her face straight.

"The preparations have been made. The spirits wish to speak. Rise. Follow."

And so they did, following until they arrived in a large, dark room. The only light was from a candle at the center of a round table.

"Sit."

And so they did. Mac found herself between the large woman and Betty—who had already taken her hand and clung to it. Mac gave it a squeeze as she stared.

Moments passed. That careful pacing showed itself once more, and just as Betty's squeeze became white-knuckled, Esmée appeared.

"Welcome, explorers of the afterlife. Tonight we shall journey to beyond." For all the suggestion of the otherworldly, Esmée dressed in a simple—but handsome—gown.

She sat, extending her hands for a circle.

"The spirits are excited tonight. We must contact them swiftly, yes?" She looked across them, gaze lingering on the large woman and the anonymous men. Perhaps one nodded.

"Some spirits are quite impatient, I hardly—"

The candle winked out.

"As you see."

Society heads let out the society sigh.

A trumpet spoke from the far wall, distinct against the dark. It glowed, dim; the pistons flowed, worked with a jazzman's grace and the air behind it played with a jazzman's lungs.

Betty's hand had to be numb by now.

A tambourine rattled.

The candle flared up, back to life.

Esmée permitted herself to fade, drawing up her charisma as she let her shoulders slide and a slight stoop into her back. Soon there was very little of her left—all except her voice, which raised in a room-filling chant.

The chant cut off.

The room fell to emptiness.

But with Vaudeville's sense of timing, she spoke, her customary control returning. "Mrs. Coquine. Ah. Miss Betty. Would you please take the rope from that table? Ensure it is of good quality. Absolutely free from any imperfection. Totally ordinary rope as sold in any store."

They did so.

"Please, tie me. However you like—either tie my arms in my lap, or, more securely, to the arms. The arms are more secure, but the option gives every assurance the chair has not had any clever carpentry."

They did so.

The next statement was delivered all in a gasp: *"They're coming!"*

Her eyes blinked up, vacant, and a rush of strange syllables tumbled out of her lips. Mac smiled, and leaned in. Leaving the audience to finish the set-dressing could open all sorts of room for trickery. Betty and Mrs. Coquine soon got the message. Mac counted to three. The timing demanded some turn.

1: Nothing

2: Mrs. Coquine and Betty made their awkward way back to the circle.

3: The circle closed once more.

The lights, electric or not, were snuffed with all the efficiency of a bell crushing a wick.

Mac smiled, straining her eyes against the dark. Oh, anything for strong eyes. It was near total black.

Betty gripped her hand, again. Mac gave it a gentle squeeze, a reminder there was still something sane, and tried to lean back. Anything to get an unintended view of the show.

The lights returned.

Esmée began to stir from her trance. First with a shiver, then with a blink, and slowly pulled herself to her full height. Mac approved of the performance. It pulled an observer in like drama. If anyone was expected to take *Romeo and Juliet* seriously, this is how Juliet must awaken.

"I have made contact with a specific soul, tonight. One of you has recently lost your mother. It is your habit to speak to mediums, such as myself, to learn what insights she can bring you from the spirit realm."

She pierced the large woman with her gaze.

"You have been long disappointed. There is an edge of falsehood in other medium's reports. Well. I tell you the truth, she has told me she would *physically* appear, in her old form, and speak to you tonight."

She began to convulse, gagging.

Mac sat straighter in her seat. None of this was traditional. None of this was like the thousand other "funny little magic shows" friends had dragged her to. The form was off. The cadence was off. It was as though this has been stapled onto an ordinary show. Betty was aware as well, and she clung to Mac's hand with a rigor mortis grip.

But Mac's attention was on another hand entirely. Across the hall, barely peeking out from the doorway's curtain, was a hand. It showed for a moment in the gap between the doorway and the wall curtain. The hand went below the second curtain. Only an angle of tuxedo was still visible. She wondered what the man would trigger. More spectral instruments? Ectoplasm? She smiled to herself, considering the final option. Another dwarf in a drum?

"SPEAK."

All of Esmée's words were swallowed up in her chant. Louder now, more insistent.

The lights shorted out. They did not cut off, suddenly, with the flash of a turned switch, or pulled fuse.

Instead…

An electric wail cut through the room. Sparks burned out of the far chandelier.

At the moment of climax, *something* swung down from the ceiling. It blazed above the table, a tang of ozone everywhere, words seeming to radiate forth. Its pitch was too high to be (undoctored) human speech.

"Maud, you have upset the balance. You have committed a great sin. You *sent* someone here. She is so…angry."

As it spoke, another ball raced toward it. Seemingly *through* the window and across the hall, shattering the first ball and dissipating. It left a white streak across her vision. She blinked. Over and over. It hurt to open her eyes.

Esmée screamed, thrashing against her bounds, and her chair fell over on its side. Esmée did not stop screaming.

The boxer had no reaction at all. She sat, stupefied, starring at nothing at all. Her only reaction, at long last, was to start crying.

"Mama! Mama!" Her voice cracked. She fell back from the chair, onto the floor.

Where her mother floated was only scraps of…ectoplasm? They burned as they floated. Cinders flaring from their ends and blazing a path to the other. They were consumed. Ashes were consumed. Soon, nothing floated.

That is, nothing except a length of…something. It was about the length of Mac's thumb. It met the table just before her.

She covered it with her hand—glanced left, then right. When she was sure no-one watched her, she extended her other hand and picked it up. The distinct touch of lace. She slid it up her sleeve. Everyone sat dead as the boxer cried and the medium screamed.

They only spoke again in the taxi. No magic can long survive the scent of oil, gasoline, and a night-time taxi.

Mac leaned over, slid her fingers up her sleeve. "I discovered something."

"Yes, so did I."

Mac finally smiled.

Betty leaned back, hand hanging out the window. "I was right. It's all like a sign, isn't it? Not a week before she can murder someone else for the attention…well. It's a sobering lesson." Her expression was anything but. "The sins of the father are not only visited on the son, but the son's on the father. It's all very interesting. I told you. Séances grant perspective."

Mac pushed the scrap of fabric back up her sleeve.

She held it to the light above her desk, hours later. It was crinoline, lacy enough to suggest any mother. It had a faint scent. When she held it to her nose and breathed in, however, it was obvious. Salt. Oil. Something below that—metallic? The fabric was absolutely soaked in oil.

From there, she supposed the "ghost" had been nothing but soaked scraps. This one largely escaped the fuel, hence how it survived. She chewed on her cheek.

"Poor girl. You're being taken for a fool."

The street outside Parkin's Gymnasium was about as dirty as any she could name, even Esmée's, and yet a street sweeper still worked his way up the asphalt with lazy strokes. Then the realization hit. It was the same little man, with the same ineffectual sweeping. She stopped awkwardly on the pavement, watching him.

He looked up at her. Stopped sweeping. Something trigged in his memory, and he tilted his head.

But Mac knew this was trouble. She stepped inside quickly, holding the door behind her and trying to control her breath.

"Can I help you?"

"Oh. Yes." She glanced through the pane. The sweeper stared at the door for another moment, then returned to his "work," shoving dirt across the street without even pretending to clean. "I would like to see Maud Emerick."

If the man seemed to have left his muscles at home, his eyes had not forgotten their shine. He stared through her. He was more aggressive with each question.

"Reporter?"

Mac shook her head.

"Bookie?"

Mac shook her head.

"Another medium?"

Mac shook her head.

"…Moll?"

Mac paused. "No. Certainly not. I attended last night's séance and—"

Anger is the most sudden emotion. His face suddenly tightened, cheeks molten; he captured her shoulders and walked her back. *Thrust* her back until she was running backward, only upright by his grip.

"You wanna make her go crazy?"

They were just about at the door.

"You think—"

"It was fake!"

He stopped, eyes nearly lost in a squint.

"I have proof. Someone is trying to—"

He dropped his hands—hid them behind himself. "You got proof?"

She half turned to see out the door. The street-sweeper was watching them, leaning down on his basket, right ear inclined their way.

Quietly, "Do you have somewhere private?"

He let the crinoline go slack, then yanked it taut, then slack, then taut. His jaw worked, grinding.

"If you're lying, you got one I wanna hear."

When he met her eyes, his gaze was exhausted.

"Mr. Novik. Would anyone—"

"It's boxing. That means it's more crooked than a crossword. Dead mom. Killed an opponent."

"It all makes her seem an easy target?"

"Better'n a bullseye."

Mac reached out, taking the crinoline before he ripped it apart.

"If I wanted a name?"

He shrugged. "The Zappas. The Gambino. The Genovese.

19

Any of 'em. She's good. She's clean." He paused, summoning up a word. "Independent. Good way to take her out of the title without the cops getting interested."

With nothing to do with his hands, he splayed them out on the table, limp.

"Because next week is the—"

"Title match, yeah. Odds dark horse, too. She wasn't supposed to beat Divoso." Silence. "It'd be bad enough if she beat her. The mob'd wanna make sure she's under their thumbs. But...*like that*, it's all personal now. They want the investment back. They lost a lot. In bets, and all they spent establishing Di."

Whatever light had been in his eyes was gone.

"If I could see her, Mr. Novik..."

He began to curl his fingers toward his palms, then pushed himself upright.

"Yeah."

Perhaps Mac expected something sparse. A champion's gym room which existed only for naps, robes, and perhaps trophies—all carrying the distinct punch of sweat.

But if that is what she expected, Maud Emerick's room would have taken her by surprise.

Overturned books.

It's unnecessary to say more. The room was overtaken by overturned books. Moran. Blatvasky. Morgan. Sigsand. Doyle. Steiner. Some were well-thumbed. Others had the too-fresh sent of books acquired at the last minute. Dog-ears dominated, and paged were often bent over at bottom and top. The books spilled open around her, well-underlined passages visible on every page.

Maud looked up at her.

She clearly had not slept, eyes gritty with caffeine.

She didn't say a word.

"My name is Rose Mackenberg, and I—"

Professionalism faltered. She was by Maud's side, holding her hand (both of hers hardly big enough to cover Maud's).

She tried to speak now, shaking off the sleeplessness.

Mac cut in. "I was there last night."

"Get out. I don't need more sympathy."

"I have eviden—"

She rose up, deadlier than she ever was in the ring, hands sealed into fists. "What the hell do I care? She's gone, and you want to prove things? She's gone. *Her soul is dead.* Doesn't that matter more?"

"I...have evidence for the opposing point of view. It was fake. An elaborate fake to take you out of the ring."

Maud sagged. Fifteen hours driving herself to find a loophole, any out in her library, and she was presented with one. She still squinted at Mac.

"Evidence?"

Mac produced the crinoline. She explained.

Maud continued to sag. "I'm not convinced."

"But—"

"It's not..." Maud threw her hand up, pressed it into a fist. She grunted, trying to find the words that fit. "I killed Di. I murdered her. It doesn't matter if the cops don't care. I murdered her." She picked up a particularly tattered book, one swallowed up by her hands, and paged through it. "*I* broke her. Who do you think mom's..."

She stopped on a particularly tattered page of this particularly tattered book. A page that had been half-crumpled, and half-torn. The binding hung loose. "...annihilation is on? Who do you think's got that on their soul?"

"I can help ease your conscience. That was not your doing.

Your mother is…fine, wherever she may be."

"And? Even if it's fake? That's *one* less murder on my head."

She looked at Mac. Mac imagined this was the same look her opponents saw from the opposite corner.

"And however many people I murdered, I've got to go out and do it again. Nothing else's gonna feed my sisters." She pressed her face into her hands. "And I can't even fight."

"It was an accident." Mac tried to meet her eyes.

"I was angry. That's not an accident."

Mac reached out, put her hand on her back.

"It's gonna kill all of them." Maud's back shook.

"You can feed your family. You won't worry about…this awaiting them. Come with me to Esmée's. I'll prove that something isn't waiting to kill your family's souls."

Maud took her hands away, crushed them into fists, and held them against her face.

"You'll be there?"

"I'll be right beside you."

When she exited to the street, the sweeper was gone.

A black sedan followed her home, no matter how many turns she took or how long she stopped in shops.

At her doorstep, the sedan honked and drove away, slowly, haughty.

Mac sat with her hand in her head, fingers knotted in her hair, tugging. She could hardly show up now. They could shoot her, or stab her, or…sweep her streets. She gnawed her cheek, but that would simply leave Maud in the same state, imagining her mother's soul was murdered and career in ruin.

This would give her grey hairs.

Then, she grinned.

There was a trick to age.

Mac was painstaking with her hair. A costume party could do with baby powder dumped on your head. The color is uneven, the grain is visible, but you'll pass as an "old woman" until you dunk for apples. That wouldn't do. She partitioned her hair into layers, as though preparing for the fanciest style. She tried to gauge exact distances in her bathroom reflection.

Then, working from the roots down, she powdered each partition a shocking white. The sort of graveyard white only undertakers should have.

She shook her head, smiled at the cloud, and shook harder.

Then the comb. Long, straight strokes working the grains into each individual group of hair.

That done, she dabbed a washcloth in the basin and patted her hair down. Not enough to wash the white—but enough to blend it, temper it, and hide the obvious grain.

"I'm about ready for my pension."

She shrugged her shoulders, leaned forward. It was almost believable.

Now she sagged her knees. Perfectly believable.

She stood straight again, and leaned into the mirror.

"Curse my complexion."

Well, there was nothing to be done about that. She stared at herself, chewing on her cheek.

"Of course…"

She scattered makeup across the dresser, until she reached the bottom of any woman's bag of tricks. The very bottom. The *very* bottom, where unwanted Christmas gifts and grandmother's recommendations languish. She splayed her finds out between her fingers: powered lipstick, and thick face cream.

Balling up a washcloth, she dabbed off her lipstick and began again. The bee sting was gone, replaced with a line of powder that followed the line of her lips without flourish, without dip, and without crest. Perfectly boring. Perfectly out of date.

She slathered the cream across her cheeks, chin, nose, and forehead until she resembled a china doll more than anything else.

Now she sagged and drooped again, settling her face in such a way she led with her lips.

She looked *ancient*.

"Ah, yes, I knew Victoria in her youth."

No, she sounded like a child mimicking her grandmother. A little lower.

"Ah, *yes*, I knew Victoria *in her youth*."

No, crack her voice here and there.

"AH, *yes*, I knew Vic-toria *in her youth*."

That was it.

No-one would believe she was the girl who raised so much hell the mob had to trail her.

It was a crumpled leaf of an old woman who sat, impatiently tapping her cane, in Esmée's reception room. Now and then she was wracked with a shuddering breath, and held a bit of lace to her mouth, before once more looking out over her eyelids defensively. The boxer sat across from her. The anonymous men were gone—and it was the general mix of social heads, thrill-seekers, mild men, and true believers.

"She has to." Maud did not turn her head, nor did she look into the mirror. She addressed Novak blind.

She pressed her right hand into her left, squeezing. Her knuckles burned. Her voice was small.

24

Mrs. So-and-so looked at her with the kind of sympathy that only comes from people directly involved in a matter—and prying old ladies.

The curtain shifted.

When it was pulled aside, the old woman began to gather herself up to stand.

But it was not the assistant.

It was Esmée. She took quiet steps across the room, pausing at the boxer, and knelt down to take her hand. All her muscles were taut.

"I am not sure I can now offer you any comfort. Not after what happened. But…" She seemed to sag. "You are welcome to come, and see what you will see. Remember, people are not always responsible for their own actions. Do not…blame anyone. You never know."

She seemed to realize she was speaking nonsense, and stood. Turning, she was the hostess once more, and approached Mac.

She tried to sit more like an old lady, tried to speak more like an old lady, through a blur of a conversation. She was under direct, well-lit examination. That could not end well. She expected the assistant again. But he was nowhere to be found.

But then Esmée moved on, greeting the others, and Mac resisted the urge to show relief.

This walk was shy. They were unattended by mystery. Esmée led them with confidence, the convivial host every step, and Mac began to suspect this was her usual mode. The mood set, Esmée stood with a flow of skirts and sleeves, not so much walking as undulating to her cabinet.

"The preparations have been made."

Her eyes widened.

"The spirits wish to speak."

She raised her hand to her mouth.

"Rise, spirits! Tonight, we shall journey beyond!"

A gentle, enraptured gasp.

"Hold your partners' hands. The spirits will only emerge from a sense of universal brotherhood. Attend to your souls, let go of ought you have against your fellow man—and woman—and let yourself stand aside your brothers and sisters."

The hush fell over them, as it had before, and Elise pressed her eyes shut. Hands were held. Heads were bowed. And Mac held hands and bowed heads among the best of them, every motion the so-dull-she-disappears old woman.

There is nothing easier than breaking the circle in darkness. Tremble your right hand, pulling your rightmost partner's hand closer to your center. Begin to slip, sweaty, in your leftmost partner's hand, pulling them toward your center as well. The moment you slip out of the hand entirely, tremble your right partner's hand closer. They'll cradle each other's hands, hardly paying attention in the darkness.

Mac slid out of the chair. The chair did not move.

"Spirits dance in time to the music of the spheres. Attend, listen."

The trumpet emerged from seeming nowhere, beginning at the horn and receding to the tip. It seemed suspended in air, before. But from this perspective, a system of levers, all painted black, held it up. A man blew into it. Thanks to the drapes, he was all but invisible from the perspective of the table.

"Be still, be still."

The tambourine surprised her. She jumped. There was no hand—merely pullies that flung it out across the room, shaking, clinging, as a wooden support held it just still enough to seem like a human hand supported it.

This is all a sham.

But all her instincts and knowledge couldn't dispel the malignant sense that arises from standing alone in a dark room as a wordless chant surrounds you.

She took a step.

Then another.

Relying on memory, she made her way to the curtain.

She peeled the curtain back and felt the wall.

Cold plaster.

Keeping herself calm, she ran her hand down the wall in a straight line.

Still, cold plaster.

She moved over a few inches, *you're wrong, you're wrong, you're wrong* cascading in her head.

Smooth plaster.

But she cracked a grin that the demure, ossified Mrs. So-and-so would have clicked her tongue at.

It was not *cold* plaster.

It was warm.

She swept her hand to the right, and collided with a button-switch.

She bit her lip.

A series of switches, so rush-installed she felt that brassy taste in her mouth as her fingers brushed over them.

"Focus on your loved ones. Send them your love. They can feel it, even as the veils begin to close once more."

She froze. Out of time.

What switch would swing down the mother's "ghost"?

She pressed her eyes closed, hard enough her vision blurred red and green. All to remember the assistant's hand. How far away had he stood? She tried to picture the hand. How far had it extended from the next room? Did the tuxedo conceal his true reach?

She sprayed her arm against the wall, guessing a moment, and pressed a switch.

She felt a vibration from deep inside the wall. It was soundless. That was the only indication machinery had caught.

The mother's "ghost's" carriage did not swing down. She heard the rush of fright over the séance, saw Esmée turn in her seat, and felt her stomach twist in preparation of some assistant grabbing her.

The sweeper and the sedan stood at the forefront of her mind. What would be done if she were discovered? She prepared to press another switch. In spite of herself, she prepared to run.

A glow began to gather by the windows, suggesting the otherworldly. Silent steps took her back to the table.

Rejoining hands is more difficult than abandoning a circle. It requires distraction. When the light was just a shade brighter, and all eyes were on it, Mac recaptured her seat and gently pulled the hands apart, sitting between Maud and a little old lady who surely *was* a little old lady. She gripped their hands in a terrified, arthritic shake. She hoped it would hide any fumble, cover up the trace of *two* hands momentarily holding their own.

Now, she could appreciate the artistry.

A light hidden in the curtains set itself ablaze in a bright orange-white, pure fire, that must have taxed the grid. *Someone's* lights would flicker. At the moment the light spread across the room, there was a dull thud from inside the celling.

Mac reconstructed the remainder.

She supposed the mother's "ghost" was hung on a platform with a spring-loaded hammer. The hammer was timed with the light. It must hit something inside the ghost—Mac fancied glass vials filled with water, sodium, and potassium salts—providing a satisfying bang. She had imagined a light had been shattered. But this explained the petroleum; something to make the rest of the special effects—the set dressing, as it were, the crinoline that the light cast itself through—would burn away.

"Peace! Peace! What message do you bring us, oh spirit?" Esmée's eyes snapped up into her head.

When she looked back at the table, she met their eyes one by one.

"It was a messenger spirit, tasked with a message to each of us." She locked eyes with the boxer. "To go forth. With our lives, without guilt. Our families wait beyond time and pain, whatever they endured."

The show concluded, Esmée escorted them to the vestibule.

Maud met Mac's gaze, behind the glasses, and for just the slightest moment Mac let the disguise fall away. Her own smile, as an assurance, and then the old lady brushed her off and caned and hobbled and hopped down the Brownstone stairs.

As she wobbled out the door, she leaned down on her cane and stared at the street-sweeper. "That's enough of that, sonny! You'll be out of a job!"

As he stared at her, that same half-memory look as from the gym, she set off for a taxi.

No sedan followed her.

She made her way through the park, telegram in hand, and stopped at a certain bench. A man looked up at her, peering over a newspaper.

"You came. Bess said you wouldn't—said I'd been too mysterious and up on my own hype, but I said bushwa.

29

Mystery'd get you here quicker than standing out in the open. Telegram from a 'Mysterious Patron'd' get you here in a flash. How'd I know about the business? Managers talk. You can only keep so many secrets on stage. Or canvas. And I heard about Myra, too."

He was certainly a tiny man. He barreled up to his feet, shaking her hand. He had the same spark of the showman—but none of the occult tiddlywinks or implication. He was nearly conventional, but *off* here, or *off* there, until he was unmistakably himself. His hair was parted, yes—but down the middle. His clothes were quality—but a little too loose. He had the look in his eyes—but it was a piercing gaze, the sort of hunting look William Gillette would never possess.

"Rose Mackenberg. I thought you'd be older. Old women aren't the easiest thing to pose as." He seemed to speak from experience.

"Harry Houdini. I thought you'd be shorter. Milk cans aren't the easiest thing to fit inside."

He grinned.

"If you're not too busy with matronhood, I have work you may well be interested in…"

Incredible Graft in the Sale of "Magic Charms, Amulets and Love Philtres" Is Revealed

Rose Mackenberg

If you browse through old tomes on Medieval witchcraft, you will find amazing records of human credulity in the purchase of charms amulets, voodoo bags, lucky jewels and mystic oils. All very laughable, you will say, and childishly superstitious.

But if you venture into certain sections of London—or for that matter, into certain sections of any town on the continent of North America—you can find those same superstitious practices being freely indulged in and taken very seriously.

Today we are inclined to regard as utter ridiculous the fifteenth century faith in the slaying of dragons to extract precious gems from the vitals; to sneer at the Black Stone of Mecca; to make fun of the belief that certain emeralds can cure the gout and goiters.

But I, myself, have, as Harry Houdini's assistant, penetrated to haunts and dives where, for "a certain price," I have procured charms "guaranteed" to perform the most miraculous feats, such as the restoring a missing husband—I am unmarried—warding off bats and vampires and insuring me against the ravages of old age.

Truly, in the midst of so-called civilization, the miracle-monger thrives just as lucratively as he did in the Middle Ages. Scientific progress has been able to little to cure our inherent gullibility.

Curative Geegaws

The curative properties attributed to these geegaws by the mediums who sold them to me surpass anything I have ever read in Elizabeth Villier's great treatise on the mascots, or any of the classic works on amulets, charms and spells, such as Montague Summer's "Geography of Witchcraft."

Yet these three small objects before me are, respectively, merely a flat rectangular stone, encased in a chamois skin; a twist of yellow cloth; and a small cameo! I paid five dollars apiece for them. If you were to multiply that sum by the number of people in the world who believe in the efficacy of amulets, you would see what the staggering business the vendors of these charms can do.

Callous moderns were recently shocked and disgusted by the "hex murder" of a man named Rehmeyer at York, Pennsylvania. Details of the crime, of which two youths and a boy of 14 were convicted, are too fresh in the public memory to need rehashing here, but the stir caused by the revelations about witchcraft incidental to the slaying shows how ignorant the average citizen is of the abuse to which the "powers of darkness"—so called—are put.

Monstrous Superstition

To the clearheaded, it is nothing short of monstrous that people of primitive mentalities should actually believe that cutting a lock of hair from a man's head will banish a "hant," or that a victim of fever will immediately recover if a glowing coal is carried three times around his bed.

But the point I want to make is that, nine times out of ten, the people who resort to "hexing" and gratefully consult "pow-wow" doctors are firmly convinced of the efficacy of such methods; I am not a spiritualist, heaven knows, but I think the faith that simpleminded persons put in the alleged "black arts" can do irreparable harm in the community.

Even as I am writing these lines comes the news that the authorities have started a fresh secret drive against witch-doctors in New York City. I wish the officials luck, but I doubt they will make much headway. The practitioners of the amuletic arts are firmly entrenched in the affections of their followers, and if a woman is fool enough to part with half the weekly salary for a phial of tinted water or a marked ball of yarn, who shall say that she hasn't a right to have her enjoyable folly?

Crafty Charm Sellers

I have personally investigated so many scores of cases that the mere recapitulation of them tersely would take up a page. Just to show you how craft some of these gentry are in the way of "stage settings" and "effects" I will briefly describe a visit I paid to one vendor. It is typical of hundreds of other such investigations, only he "put on a better show."

Houdini had tipped me off that this man was doing a bustling business in a small town, and had dispatched me to get the low-down on the racket. I proceeded by train to the village—which shall remain nameless—and found that to locate the "witch" it would be necessary to hire a driver to a remote suburb and then proceed on foot to his house, which was situated in the rocky basin of a ravine.

Never shall I forget the weird spectacle that met my eyes. As I clambered slippingly down to the rough and rocky path, the full moon rose and piercingly illuminated the patch of ground below. The house of the charm-and-philtre vendor was an unsightly cabin-like affair, in the doorway of which stood the bowed form of the aged "seer," beside that of his wife, who held aloft a lamp. The feeble rays from this flickered over the surrounding ground, revealing patches of white marble thickly scattered about.

The wily couple had established their "consulting room" in front of a graveyard! They had a genuine sense of "stage direction," of the effect produced upon impressionable minds by eerie, ghostly "props," and they didn't in the least mind living so near the reminder of this, so long as the customers continued to patronize them.

All Hocus-Pocus

Fortunately, I am not easily impressed by this sort of hocus pocus and I remained calm during the "consultation."

At the end of it I purchased two charms, assisted in the "blessing of handkerchiefs" and departed serenely for home. It was all most sublimely silly, but instructive in the foibles and fallacies of human nature. This man was later exposed and left his sensational-looking setting for parts unknown. I have no doubt he is today thriving under another name and doubtless working a different racket.

Inhabitants of large cities, however, need not preen themselves on the score that they are harder to fool than their rustic brothers. In the heart of Manhattan, "phrenology"—I do not refill to the genuine scientific attempt of that name—in a certain come-on for the gullible. Gypsies' palms are daily crossed with silver for transparent little "revelations," and nightly gaudily-robed astrologists promise everything from cures for warts to the recapture of an alienated sweetheart's love—if you have the money.

"Magic" Powders

The favorite charms—the manufacture of which would scarcely bankrupt a pauper—are neat rectangles of paper containing "magic" powder, usually simple coal dust, sifted, or pepper and salt. These charms sell for any sum, ranging from a quarter, in the slums to two dollars and a half in the better sections.

For getting a "spell" on an enemy—as in the case of the

hex slaying—the fee is, of course, perceptibly higher, but if anyone with the "evil eye" is bothering you surcease can be had, or at lease promised you, for the price of three packets of cigarettes.

The nomenclature applied by these soothsayers is quaint in the extreme, and indicative of the sources—many of them Medieval—of modern "black art." Half of block from Broadway you can buy samples of the Devil's Shoestring, Adam and Eve Root, John the Conqueror Root, French Love Drops (to ensure the return of a faithful suitor), Lucky Black Cat Wishing Bone, Spanish Drawing Lodestone Powder, Attractive and Quick Luck Oils and Anointing Oil and Mystic Dust.

Impudent Coolness
"Healer" salesman of these charms face serious opposition, every day of their lives, from the police, the public prosecutors, the city health department, the Attorney General, the medical societies, the spiritualists baiters, like Houdini, as well as former dupes who have revolted against such practices. Yet their impudent coolness remains unshaken.

One reason, of course, why this is so, is that the making and vending of charms is, comparatively, a cheap and easy matter. Where a regular "consulting medium," in order to mop up the dollars, has to establish herself in a residence with a séance room and other cumbersome and costly trappings, and leave herself open to raids, the amulet and philtre "experts" can conceal their wares in their pockets, and, too, can do business in a jiffy on a street corner, in the subway, or even in bright daylight.

A survey of any city's "charm belt" would show—and I can prove this by quoting from my personal notebooks—that its range extends from the lowest sections to the highest. All are prolific sources of such manifestations. Superstitious Negroes offer the quickest "turn-over," but there are countless "spiritualists" and "witch doctors" who disdain any clientele except what is known in the theatrical problems as "carriage-trade"; this is people wealthy enough to afford automobiles.

WILEY AND FURTIVE

In the fashionable, aristocratic and exclusive sections, the more fashionable brand of charm-dispenser and soothsayer can sometimes be unearth—but not often. He is a wily and furtive creature and the cruder methods of come-on razzle-dazzle find no favor with him in his dealings.

His usual procedure is to rent a comfortable but not ostentatious little apartment, taking good care that the address is a "nice" one. This he outfits with painstaking taste. He never runs the dangerous risk of advertising, trusting, instead to an invaluable, human tendency to do his advertising for him by word-of-mouth.

This negative policy usually bears juicy financial fruit: for it is a common desire to seek out and consult "esoteric" people who seem to be denying themselves to the general public.

This type of "mystic" you will generally find coy in making appointments, so that your appetite for his mysteries is automatically whetted. I have personally investigated eight of these cases, but only in one instance was able to get the goods on the soothsayer.

They are wary birds and to fight them takes both time and money. For besides their shrewdness they are generally in possession of ample funds, due to the exorbitance of their charges and the fact that most of their patrons are men and woman of independent means.

A grotesque, but fully documented instance of the

gullibility of the rich and influential came to light recently when it was disclosed that two United States Supreme Court judges, an enormously wealthy widow, and a learned professor of Greek had been clients of one of these "hideaway mediums."

This particular specimen announced himself not only as a "mystic," but also as a "healer." He could have "cured" any form of malady, he told me, including "peevishness" and the smoking of tobacco. His treatment may have eliminated the first-named "disease" from my system, but I'm afraid I still like my cigarette.

CANNOT BELIEVE ANYTHING

The "professor" did not rely entirely upon his otherworldly powers, his amulets and philtres. He had also invented a most pleasing little machine composed simply of two electrodes. By grasping these firmly, the patient was cured of any malady—mental, physical, or spiritual—after fifteen minutes. Truly bless are the feeble in brain, for they can believe anything!

But it is, perhaps, in certain parts of Brooklyn where the charm mania runs most happily rampant. A cozy coterie all of "spiritualists," recently disbanded of their own accord—things were getting a little too hot for them—did a land office business in charms. Strung beads and brightly colored bags containing ground-up roots were among their most valued offerings to distressed humans.

I went to one of the séances—the most amusing experience—and was surprised to find that attendance at the sitting only cost two dollars. The ante was swiftly raised, however, to five when an especially "difficult case" demanded praying over the consultant.

I was reminded, by some of their incantations, of the

historical "Stones of Healing" that were employed in the olden days by people who believed, or who said they believed, that the touch of a ruby or coral would "remove discord" between husbands and wives.

There was scarcely, then, a single precious or semi-precious stone, from the diamond to the sydonyx, that was not believed to have magical curative powers. The modern practitioners of the "black arts" have carefully nurtured this superstition and kept it alive, although my little playmates were content to use jade and even colored pebbles.

High-Priced Specialist

I knew—but "not socially"—one voodooist who could be accounted a really classy vendor of charms. His prices were high—$1000 for a Black Cat's Wishbone: a bottle of cat's ankle dust, $50: New Moon powder, $25, and King Solomon's Marrow, $1500. He also specialized in the common forms of cure for "hants," such as Guffer Dust, rabbit's feet, silver-plated bullets—he had evidently read "The Emperor Jones"—carved elephants and incisor teeth from dog's jaws.

So pretentious did this individual grow—I believe his income was estimated at $7000 a year—that eventually he came to regard himself as a real power in twentieth century society, and he bull-dozed and bamboozled his clients with such effrontery that, eventually, he dug his own financial grave. Some of them complained to the police, and a speedy conviction followed, to the astonishment of the crestfallen "mystic."

Not all of the voodooists are black and some of them are sincere but they have to be cautious and many of them list themselves as "Doctor So-and-So." They are too foxy to fall into the trap of calling themselves M.D.s, which would bring them into the dreaded limelight of the law.

My next chapter, I shall devote to Harry Houdini, the greatest master of natural magic who ever lived as a personality, with little personal touches of characterization that only one who had worked with him for years could provide. I shall tell about his disguises and escapes—and finally I shall tell you about the only spiritualist phenomenon for which Houdini could never find an adequate explanation.

All That Jazz
M.H. Norris

"After the fourth round of murders…gosh that musta been about twenty years ago, the neighborhood around Jefferson Street was getting a little shy, y ou see. Sure, there was crime around here…but nothin like this.

"People didn't know what to think, people turnin up dead like that, jazz music playing, kids couldn't play on the street, people didn't want to leave their homes.

"We were all wonder who was next? Was there even going to be a next?

"Dark times those were. Shoulda been celebrating the Feast of the Magi and Mardi Gras wasn't far away, just like now. People shoulda been celebrating, not hiding in their homes afraid of their own shadow.

"A message went out, no one could find out from who. Oh you wouldn't believe the scene that made. People even came from Washington to investigate it. But no one could find out who sent it. Some said the ghost of an old singer, some said whoever it was killed themselves, some say it was from some group. All the message said was that houses that played Jazz would be safe.

"And that's why this area is called Jazz Street, little missy. That's why there's jazz playing all over the neighborhood.

"Cause the killings stopped. Some said the ghost decided it could rest in peace. Others said the killer got his way. I don't know what I think…I'm just glad it stopped.

"We've moved passed it for the most part. Nothing keeps New Orleans down for long.

"But I'll tell you one thing. It will be a long, long time before you stop hearing jazz on Jazz Street."

"The legend of the Grunch has been around almost as long as New Orleans itself." Margaret McConnell looked out at the attendees of the symposium. "People use them as a reason for why children shouldn't wander off. Thus far, no solid evidence to prove their existence has been submitted."

The opportunity to talk about folkloric creatures had come to her shortly after the holidays and Margaret couldn't say no to a chance to lecture in New Orleans.

"People say they originated as some of the original settlers of this area. But interbreeding, as well as their isolated way of life, caused them to eventually turn into the creatures now known as the Grunch. They were isolated because legend states they were albino and that was a time in our history where anything different from what was considered normal was considered the work of the devil."

Margaret had been pleasantly surprised to find her lecture hall mostly full and stepped away from the lectern to engage them more, though she did lower her volume. "There are people today who still think that."

That earned her a chuckle and the rest of her lecture passed smoothly All she could think about was getting back to her inn.

As tempting as finding a speakeasy to get a drink before bed was…after giving several lectures on several topics in one day she thought a cup of tea would have to do.

Stepping outside, she pulled her jacket around her, noting that it could be worse. She could have agreed to do a symposium in New York City. Snow had fallen the day before. Maybe birds were on to something, flying south for the winter…

Jazz seemed to flow from every house, creating a mélange of style. It only seemed to happen here. Other places, homes were already settling down into the quiet of the night. Here, it seemed as if Mardi Gras was starting a few weeks early.

Walking down the street, she saw the Jazz Inn—this neighborhood really liked its jazz—and made her way there. Out of the corner of her eye, something moved, and she turned to see a dark figure flee down an alley, footsteps echoing. He was male, three or four inches taller than her. There was a lump almost lost in the shade of nearby buildings.

Margaret carefully made her way to this shape. Despite the jazz faintly all around her, the road was still. Once she was beside the lump, she could make out what it was—and wished she hadn't.

A red pool spread under the form. A deep, bleeding cut ran up all four limbs, terminating at a gaping hole where the victims heart should have been. Red hair sprawled out. The girl's eyes were thankfully closed.

Who would do this to a person?

Why would they do this to a person?

Margaret held back bile. The smell of iron, perhaps imagined, seemed to overwhelm her.

But she needed to get out of here. She needed to get away—as far away as possible from the smell and the sight of the body...

Away from the jazz music that was so desperately out of place in the middle of a scene like this.

So she ran out of the alleyway, pausing bending over so her hands rested on her knees.

TWO WEEKS LATER

There had been three other murders before this, and two since the one she discovered.

Six murders—six in an area that was already linked to

murders almost twenty years ago. The legend that people seemed to lend credence to, the one anyone she bothered asking would tell her. Margaret had to have talked to at least a dozen people from librarians to men in bars and every single one of them had a different version of the story—of the neighborhood known as Jazz Street, and why it had earned its name. She had the time to ask them everything. The police had asked her to stay in the city.

The reporters from outside of New Orleans, who had come for Mardi Gras, were latching on to it. Murder sells papers.

Why were people so fascinated with murder? If they'd seen what she'd seen, they'd run as far away as fast as they could.

Like she wished she could.

Instead, she was left wandering New Orleans, the same questions circling through her head.

Why now?

Why this neighborhood?

Was it the same killer?

Margaret had already dismissed the "ghost" theory. There was no such thing—even as a folklorist she didn't believe in them. The neighborhood psychics were making money off of the idea that they could talk to ghosts, that it was a ghost that was killing this people.

Why would a ghost kill anyone?

No one seemed to be asking that question.

No connections between the deceased. No clues as to who the murderer would go after next.

With a sigh, she sat down the papers she'd been compiling, grabbed her coat, and left the inn. Now was as good a time as any to clear her head.

Maybe she needed to. Get her mind off the case and stop

pretending that she was a detective. She was a folklorist. She lived in the land of legends, not in the land of crime.

Even with a murderer on the loose, Jefferson Street was bustling with afternoon shoppers as Margaret made her way into a department store.

Mardi Gras decorations lined the main sales floor and Margaret wondered if she would be free to leave the city before celebrations started. But it didn't hurt to look. It was one of her favorite things about her travels, seeing how fashion changed region to region.

Off to one side there was a certain woman. Wire rimmed glasses were perched on her nose as she surveyed the options. It took Margaret a second to finally realize that she knew her. Walking up, she pretended to look at clothes on the rack beside her.

"You mean to tell me your boss is adding to the madness that is Mardi Gras in New Orleans?"

The woman turned to her with practiced ease, not showing a trace of surprise (if she was surprised at all). "Margaret McConnell, aren't you a sight for sore eyes!"

Margaret hugged her friend. "Rose Mackenberg! Still on the job?"

"Of course. I assume you're here tracing another one of your monsters?"

"Came for a symposium, ended up being a witness to a murder and now I'm stuck here for the latter."

Mac pulled out a dress. "What do you think?"

"Grab the coat off that mannequin and you're set. And don't wear the glasses, dear. Not here."

Mac sighed. "Being able to see comes before fashion, I've found. Have you crossed paths with anything particularly interesting?"

"I've decided to play detective with all my spare time and you'd be amazed at what a renowned folklorist can dig up at City Hall. I'll tell you over coffee. There's a great cafe down the street. Where are you staying?"

"I've yet to decide."

"I'm down at the Jazz Inn."

"This neighborhood is jazz-obsessed, isn't it?"

"Old story." Margaret led her friend to the cashier. "I'll tell you *that* over coffee too."

As they made their way to a cafe, Margaret enjoyed the company of a friend she hadn't seen in a while. With all their traveling, it didn't make it easy to pop over to the other's for tea.

That would require one or both of them actually knowing where to pop by. Also something that didn't happen very often.

She hoped the diversion would help clear her head. It didn't hurt that she was helping Mac and by extension, her boss. She was an amateur, they were the masters.

Coffee in hand, Mac hummed. "I was thinking, the last few days. Who would benefit from murders like this? It throws the neighborhood into a state of fear. I'm assuming they refused your help when you took this to them?"

Margaret shrugged. "Not unexpected. After all, what help could a folklorist be in a murder investigation? We both know I'm not a detective but this killer is hiding in the 20-year-old story that surrounds this neighborhood. Now folklore, that's something I know a thing or two about."

"And what does your folklore tell you?"

"Jazz is the crux of the folklore. Supposedly, it prevents the murders—though that doesn't seem to be the case.

Folklore built up around a core of truth—i.e., the murders. Nothing new there. With the reemergence of the murders, it has seemed to drive the jazz frenzy up a notch. Quite frankly, I have had quite enough of the genre." She paused. "I'm not sure I'll ever hear it and not tie it up with the sight of that girl's body. How can I help you?"

Mac gave her an encouraging smile. "There's a neighborhood psychic parlor. It's run by a brother-sister duo, and I've wanted to take a look at."

"Why so?"

"They thrive on exclusivity. They're not the Doctor So-and-So that turns to vapor as soon as light is shined their way. They're long-established, and cater to the higher classes. The La Croix siblings. Isabella and Nicholas. She does the front-end work. He mainly handles the paperwork, it seems.

"They deserve investigation, but…even Harry Houdini's secret police sometimes meet a wall. References are required for even a meeting, let alone a séance."

"Well, I may be more helpful with your investigation than my own. I have an appointment this morning, made it through a conference connection—a friend of a friend trying to convince me my folklore isn't lore. She especially adores Isabella. 'The best in the city,' she says. A pillar of the community, like her mother before her. She had the gift too."

Mac pulled a pad out of her satchel, and wrote. "What about Nicholas?"

"They're a second generation act. Their parents did it but died about the time Nicholas came of age. Isabella is younger, about thirty. Both never married, both keep to themselves—except when Isabella takes clients.

"They would have been thirteen in 1906 when the first series of murders occurred. Paperwork states that his parents were diagnosed with some illness, the paper trail becomes scattered at that point, about two years later. Both died in 1911."

"With a background such as that, they may be true believers."

The pair finished their cups of coffee before vacating the table and making their way out onto Jazz Street. Already, street bands were set up in their traditional places, lending their sounds to the atmosphere that made up this area.

La Croix Parlor was located a few blocks from the coffee shop and Margaret could see how Mac fooled so many with her disguises. She blended right into Jazz Street with an ease that Margaret would never achieve.

Isabella was out front, watering the plants in the windowsills. Nicholas was beside her, about three inches taller than Margaret.

"Isabella, I hope it's not too much of a hassle but my darling friend Mackenzie surprised me by coming into town. I figured that she knew my father so well and would love to hear from him as well. It's not a problem is it?"

Isabella turned, a smile on her face that Margaret easily saw through. "Of course not. Welcome, Mackenzie, was it?"

"Yes." Mac smiled, holding out her hand. "Margaret told me all about you. Thank you for being willing to help us."

"It's my pleasure, darling. If I can use my gift to help others, I'm truly grateful for the chance."

Isabella led them inside, and into the parlor.

"Have you had this gift all your life, Isabella?"

The woman nodded. "My mother has been training me since we discovered it. I wish it could be in person, though."

They settled down at a table with Isabella taking her place at the head, Mac across from her and Margaret in-between. "Shall we begin?"

The lights dimmed in the parlor, and Margaret glanced at Mac to see her studying something that wasn't quite in Margaret's field of vision.

"We are here to call upon the spirit of Margaret's deceased father." Isabella paused, looking to Margaret.

"Richard Michael McConnell."

"Richard. It may take some time to reach him as the spirits are beyond life—"

A lantern floated down the wall, the fire inside gleaming as it passed, disappearing as quickly as it came.

"And death."

A knife flew by her head. She caught a quick glimpse of it and shuddered—it was caked in dried blood.

The faint smell of iron in the air forced her to take a deep breath. Surely she imagined it…

"Richard, we ask you to come to this place and speak with your daughter. Richard, if you can hear us, please let us know."

Silence filled the room until she heard a record player crackle, and a woman single in a language she'd never heard. Isabella's face lit up when she heard the voice though. "Mama! Mama, welcome to this session. We are trying to reach Margaret's father, Richard. Is he nearby?"

The next half hour seemed to want to never end but finally Margaret and Mac stepped outside and after waving goodbye to Isabella, made their way down the street.

"That knife…" Margaret wobbled, and fell against her.

Back at the coffee shop, they continued their conversation. Margaret seemed nearly back together, thanks to the darkest roast on offer.

"What about the knife?" Mac asked as gently as possible.

Margaret turned and saw that Isabella had already made her way back inside. "That knife looks like it could have done what I saw. I mean, who could have done something like that to multiple people?"

"The knife was on fishing wire. You're saying it could be the murder weapon?"

"Yes…but…what's the murder weapon doing in the house of a psychic?"

"Who would look for a bloody murder weapon among the tricks of the spiritualist's trade? Skeptics think it's all stage trickery—the blood would be paint. Believers imagine the effects are incorporeal. Whoever you ask, it wouldn't be the real knife, crusted with the real victim's blood." Mac held up her hand. "The La Croix were thirteen when the last series of murders occurred. Thirteen is old enough to commit acts such as those. If he's connected to the initial spate at all, of course."

"If perhaps their parents began showing signs of an illness after those murders even if they were not diagnosed for two more years…"

"That could have been motivation to stop for a couple of years. Purely circumstantial, however."

Margaret shrugged. 'It's more than the police have. It's been a few days since the sixth body was found…" She stared, distant.

"We possess speculation. Impressive speculation, but speculation none the less." Mac laid out a map of the city on the table, taking a pen and circling the neighborhood. "In my initial reconnaissance of the area, I found over a dozen psychics each with their own specialization. What makes the La Croix siblings stand out from them? Let's assume the knife is genuine."

Margaret reached for Mac's pad, and pushed it toward her. "Write out the psychics."

Giving Mac a minute to write them down on a separate sheet of paper, she took the list and crossed off over half the names. "These came in after the initial set of murders. There was a shift in the population according to records at City Hall. People left because of fear. Others replaced them."

"But why just focus on psychics? Surely there are other people who stayed here after the murders."

"These all stayed. But it comes down to motive. Who has the most to gain, this time around."

"As opposed to the previous time this happened?"

"Part of the legend talks about how the killer talked through a note. Now the neighborhood psychics say that the killer is talking through them."

"Including the La Croix siblings?"

"Actually, they are the only ones who aren't. They are being unusually quiet. Isabella doesn't often talk to the public, after all. You have to make those through Nicholas. Otherwise, she mostly stays to herself."

"So, further suspicion is based on their silence?" Mac hummed. "People have gone to the police with less."

Margaret needed a drink.

Prohibition was highly overrated.

Gone was the unassuming disguise. In its place: a determined woman who stood out. People around them moved to let her through.

They stepped into the police station. Mac surveyed the various desks before taking a step forward. "Who's in charge?"

The officer at the desk by the door stood up. "What can I do for you ladies? Miss McConnell, we told you we'd ring for you if we needed information from you."

"I am Rose Mackenburg. We have evidence regarding the case where Miss McConnell is the key witness."

"As we told Miss McConnell, we have this investigation well under control."

"We believe we have evidence as to where the murder weapon is hidden."

"And where is that?"

"The parlor of the La Croix home."

"Now what evidence do you have that this weapon, should it exist, is in their parlor?"

Margaret watched as the entire station seemed to freeze and, like her, watch this scene play out.

"Miss McConnell and I both saw it during one of my investigations."

"Are you a detective?"

"Of sorts. I investigate for private concerns."

Margaret had a feeling Chief Whisley was about to say something Mac would make him regret. "Well, why don't you let the real detectives handle this?"

Mac her satchel on the desk and pulled out an envelope, taking the letter out of it. "I've been summoned to speak before the Congress of the United States in May to give testimony. By giving me a summons to testify, that means the Congress of the United States of America believes my testimony is not only worthwhile and valid, but worth their time. Who are you, Chief Whisley, to question the Congress of the United States of America who make the laws you've sworn to uphold? If the United States Congress' track record makes you doubt them, I am also in the employ of Mr. Harry Houdini. Surely one of those names carries weight.

"I believe that establishes my bona fides. The knife which killed all six present victims—and quite possibly those from

51

twenty years ago—is the prop Isabella uses at the beginning of her séances. Nicholas committed these murders—he matches Margaret's description—and he hid it in plain sight. Surely all of this, taken together, is enough reason to investigate?"

Police raided the La Croix home late yesterday, in connection with the "Jazz Street" murders. The murder weapon was recovered there, having been used as part of the La Croix séances. Nicholas La Croix was arrested at that time, insisting he was solely responsible...

Mac folded the newspaper, placing it in her satchel.

"I'm glad you were here." Margaret turned to Mac. "I wouldn't have been able to find out how this legend ends if you hadn't been there to catch the fishing wire."

"I wouldn't have been able to have an appointment with Isabella if you hadn't already had one."

"Poor Isabella, wonder what's going to happen to her."

Mac shrugged. "I don't know. Where can one go? If she didn't know her brother was behind it, given how much she relied on him...then again, perhaps it will drive business. You can never tell. Where will *you* go?"

Margaret smiled. "Perhaps back north. Home by Easter. But there's stories everywhere Mac. So many beautiful, wonderful tales. I can't stop trying to write about as many as I can. And who knows? Maybe there are more cases where people hide such horrible acts behind my beloved stories. Perhaps I've learned something about how to help others."

If Margaret had thought New Orleans was bustling before, it was worse now with Mardi Gras in full swing. People lined the streets. Jazz music played faintly from the coffee shop behind them.

"Two series of murders two decades apart. I wonder if this

neighborhood will ever recover."

"If my line of work has taught me anything, Margaret, it's that people won't necessarily want it to recover. Fear is worth much more."

Moses Callahan's Last Chord
Brendan Foley

I don't like to think about it. I don't like to admit to things. Never have.

But things being as they are, I might as well tell you about Moses Callahan and his last concert.

I used to tend bar at this hotel in New York, place called The Griffin. It was the sort of spot that had been in some sort of state of rundown for close to half a century, but somehow the idea of trying to fix it up sounded like sacrilege to the folks who ran and frequented the place. They loved the smell, the rot, the groaning pipes, the water marks.

When I heard that they closed the place down about ten years back, I wasn't the least surprised.

It was an 'elegant' joint, that was the word that everyone used. Elegant. It's funny how eyes can be trained to see past stains. You stepped through the front door and were met with swirling staircases and glittering chandeliers, woodwork decorated with angels strumming harps while around them flowers came into bloom.

'Elegant' was the thought that went into the bar. They made us dress up, made us style our hair and shine our cufflinks til they had a mirror sheen. The bar itself was this great slab of oak, apparently all in one piece that had been hollowed out and fitted with every kind of booze imaginable. And on the floor of the dining area, someone had painted a system of stars, arranged in a spiral around a giant central sun. Time had lightened up the black space and chipped away at the brilliance of each of star, but something about that pattern always stayed with me.

Sometimes I lie awake in bed, feeling myself sinking into

the pattern and falling forever in the black nothing while infernos beyond comprehension glitter hatefully in the distance.

There would be times I would be pouring a drink or chatting with one of our few customers, and my eyes would drift to the strange constellation. The paint seemed somehow to wave and shimmer, its heat reaching my face, blistering my hands as I raised them up for protection.

Then someone would say something or tap my arm and I would be back in myself, trying to figure out why I was so damned foolish to be scared of an old painting.

Most customers would give me dirty looks. But Old Chet, he'd pat my arm and smile, asking me where I'd been.

I don't miss much about The Griffin. I don't miss the person I was when I worked there. But I miss Chet. Old Chet, as he insisted we call him. He'd been a busboy back in the old days, and he was as embedded into the building as the chandeliers or the little angels. The managers forbid us from ever taking so much as a single dime off the old man. It would've been sick to do that. Wrong. We all knew that.

Old Chet's skin had turned a dusky grey with age and sickness, his wrinkles stacked so high his eyes disappeared behind folds of disused skin. He had been a big man once. His clothes hung off his body, like a child trying on their daddy's suits.

Chet would come into the bar every day except Sunday, and always at the same time (1 PM). He would order his usual (gin on ice) and he would sit and he would talk. Sometimes people would be there to listen, sometimes not. But always he talked.

We were told that his wife had passed on, that he visited her grave every morning and sat with his back to her name and read a chapter of whatever book he was reading out loud to the wind. He liked to flirt with the girls, calling them "doll" or "dear" and telling them about the fine dinners and dancing he'd take them on, were this fifty or sixty years ago. They smiled and played along, except for Maggie H. Maggie H. didn't waste her smiles on anyone. I do not miss her.

I can't remember what it was that finally made me ask him about the painting. Maybe we were just especially slow that day (I can't remember if there was anyone else in the bar, but I think no) and I was looking to pass the time, or maybe I'd just had one of my hypnotism spells. But whatever the reason, it got to be One PM and Chet took his seat and got his drink and he commenced to talking.

When he paused to breathe, I said to him, "Old Chet, you were here when this placed opened in the twenties, right?"

"Re-opened," he said, his voice a wheeze. He'd had a deep voice when he was that other, bigger man, but an operation on his lungs had left his voice all squeaky. "The Griffin first opened its doors in 1865, but a fire put it out of commission for 'bout a decade. When I was just a little boy, we used to chase each other through the hallways, pretend we were racing through the guts of a whale, like Pinocchio. You ever read Pinocchio?"

"Think I saw the cartoon a million years ago."

"Oh yes, the Disney film. A fine picture. Not my favorite, no, no that'd still be Sleeping Beauty. I like the dragon. My wife, she always preferred—"

"What I was meaning to ask is, is if you know why the floor is painted the way it is? With the stars and all that."

"That? That was painted in 1925 by a German fella named Hugo Kerr. He never pronounced the H and dragged out the errrrrrrrr, just like that. Why, I even fetched him supplies when he ran low. So long as all the other customers had their needs seen to, Charlie Paddington, that was the manager and as class an act you could ever hope to meet, he would let me help Mr. Kerr."

"Do you know why he painted it this way?"

"Oh, sure. That was on account of the guests. We had this millionaire and his wife in residency here for a number of years. He was a Mr. Reginald Golly, made his money as a young man sifting for gold in San Francisco. Hit it big young, then had nothing to do with the balance of years except spend. She was Mrs. Mary Louise Golly, originally from Texas, where she did a kind of dance where you start out with a bunch of feathers covering your bits, and by the end of the dance there's no feathers and there's just your bits. She was thirty years his junior."

"'Course she was."

"But they were nice folks. They were…they were the picture of what a self-crowned king and his queen should look like. They lived in the top floor from 1921 through 1930."

"And then they left?"

"In a fashion."

"How do you mean?"

"Well, the markets went bust. Mr. Golly, it turned out he'd been living beyond his means for a few years already, and suddenly all the folks he'd been borrowing off of, they were in need of cash themselves. The pressure mounted and he, well, he reacted poorly."

"How poorly?"

"Quite. He hung himself from the penthouse balcony. He dangled for a couple hours, the birds picking at him. Nasty business. Mrs. Golly was in a state of distress, so they led her away. She came back a few days later, claiming she wanted to gather up some of her favorite baubles and trinkets. They don't know if she brought the razor blades in with her or if she found them in the bathroom. But anyway, it went how it went."

"Jesus."

"Don't blaspheme boy."

"Sorry, sorry. It's just…wow."

"A true tragedy. But they lived well while they could. Spent a lot of money in those nine years, kept a lot of good times rolling for quite a while. It just gets hard to see the bill coming due sometimes."

He gave me one of those looks. The kind of look where his eyes glittered in their deep sockets and you felt, you knew, that beneath the jokes and the infirmity, there was something within this man that was unbent and unbowed by the years.

"But why," I remember asking, wanting those eyes off me, "why did they want the floor to be painted with stars in this sort of pattern?"

"Oh," he said, stirring the ice, "well, I believe they thought it would help them in their occult ceremonies."

Now it was me staring at him.

Old Chet took a drink. I stared at him.

"At their *what*?"

"Occult ceremonies," he said. "Now *those* were some parties."

The thing you have to remember, *Old Chet told me*, is that these practices were in no way uncommon.

No sir, back in those days, the good days, the roaring days, there was nothing to fascinate the lively quite like death. Men with their hair slicked down to the skull and women with pancaked white faces and adorned in their bells and boas and feathers, one and all would dance all through the evening, drink towers of sparkling champagne, and finish off the party with a séance.

There was a couple out of New York City that would, with

the imbibing of a scotch-neat (him) and a Vodka martini (her) regale any and every audience with tales of exorcising spirits, sharing a chat with downed angels, or finding a back-alley with a lonely door ajar that led directly to the spirit world but could never be found twice.

"Watch yourself you're walking down the street and hear a young girl whispering about the chill in the air," the mister warned. "You might just follow that lullaby where you oughtn't."

Treasures from mummies' tombs made the rounds of each metropolitan, polite society trampling over one another to get just a little bit closer to the glass cages constructed around the glinting jewels and gems. And in their shimmering surfaces, was it possible to see the macabre presence of the rumored curses? The spectral forces that struck explorers down in their prime, that seemed to summon weather strikes and freak occurrences wherever they went?

Out west, there were tour groups for the great and terrible mansions of the gun and oil barons, every one of whom, almost to a man, met fates of despair and madness. Poor Mrs. Winchester, consumed with grief and led down paths of psychosis. Convinced that her husband's fortune in guns had damned the family and the only way to bind the demon that stole her children and sapped her mind was to construct an endless house. A house with stairways to nowhere, doors that opened into brick walls, dimensions consuming one another until there was no sense of place, of direction, no sense of sense. The wealthy came in their shining chrome cars, laughing with great cheer as they wandered the labyrinth, all the while the little old woman sat in a drawing home, consuming herself.

In New Orleans they had voodoo garden parties, the daughters and granddaughters of slaves fawned over like silver screen stars. Crisply laundered suits splattered with chicken blood, manicured hands rough with specks of bones and dirt. Evening gowns were cast aside so the women might walk bare in the midnight swamp, dark water lapping against their thighs, alone save the buzzing of fireflies and the low chanting of the witch women as they bid the dead reveal themselves.

And there were stories of those who went further. The stories always came from a friend of a friend of a cousin of an associate, never one-to-one and never direct. There were stories of bacchanals that went far stranger, far more wrong, stories of modern men descending into savagery that would turn the most explorative of lotharios pale. Stories of men and women by the dozen, bare together and enmeshed in flesh and blood, by their decadence attempting to will gods without name or face or age back from depths of lost madness that they might live again on this new earth.

Reginald and Mary Louise Golly weren't much for that scene. Mostly they just liked to have a good time. It was a gas, a gag, to have the gang over and swap spooky stories.

Every so often a friend would bring over a true believer and the party would play out whatever new ritual was brought before them. Mary Louise made a strange sort of priestess in her heels and her blonde curls. She lit the black candles with a grin on her crimson-colored lips, the lapsed Catholic schoolgirl delighting in the perversity of such a simple action.

There was a witch who claimed to remember seventeen past lives, each life culminating in murder at the hands of the same mysterious male figure.

"You'd think she would remember to get the old boy's face down pat after the first dozen goes," Archibald Lilly had muttered to Mary Louise on that occasion. Her laugh turned into a blush as his hand found her leg.

There was a gentleman in a turban whose name no one could pronounce. Elizabeth Stockwether disapproved of having that number of snakes in the ballroom, but the rest of the group agreed it was a fine show.

All except Mary Elizabeth Dunston. That night, her husband Frank came to her and she refused him.

"None of you heard," she said. "None of you paid attention." Attention to what, he asked. "They spoke with one voice," was all she said.

She was gone the next morning, back to Iowa and her original name.

Frank went a tiny bit mad after she left him, dropping all interest in his businesses and newspaper and going on a three month bender through the south.

He turned up in August with a different car than the one he'd left in, a limp in his left leg, and a bride by the name of Petunia who spoke five words of English. Those words were "mine," "more," and "on the rocks."

It was Dunston that told the others the story of Moses Callahan's last concert. He did it at what proved to be the final meeting of their informal supernatural society.

There was no special guest this time, so mostly the order of the day was trading stories.

Montgomery Braxton told the others of the bushman who remained a defiant warrior for his tribe even after his head was removed by cannon blast. Catherine Marigold shared a story given to her by the Irish nanny of her children, a tale about a castle haunted by the ghost of a bride slain on her wedding night by the groom, who absconded with the family's troves of pretty shiny things. Any married man who set foot in the castle met this girl. She would press up close and ask them if they were accompanied by a wife or lover. If the man spoke true, the girl would give them a gentle kiss and vanish with the sound of a gently tinkling bell.

If the man spoke false, she revealed her true face. None lasted more than a week after such revelation, and none fought to remain above the grave.

The party giggled and gasped at each new twist in the wretched bride's tale. Only Frank Dunston stayed silent.

"Frank!" Reginald Golly cried. "Give us a tale!"

"No no," he said, "that's quite alright. Someone else go."

"Nonsense!" cried Mr. Golly. An hour before the party, he had found an embossed lighter, not his own, on the floor underneath his wife's side of the bed. This was four hours before the party and the party was several hours deep, and Mr. Golly had drunk each of those hours down.

You've been absent of your duties, sirrah!" he said. "You can't be a member of the club and not perform the function of the club that a member is meant to do. See what I say? Come now, somewhere in your libertine wanderings you must have come across a spook or a specter worth mentioning?"

"I…I heard of one," Frank said. He had been a big man, before. Now, the man was a cowed, flinching thing. "I don't know if it's the kind of thing that we go in for. It's not within our frivolous brand of oddity."

"Come on, come," Reginald kept on, and now the rest of them were egging him on.

"I heard about this one fellow," Frank began. "A Negro bluesman. Things started out bad for him. Then things got better. Then they went as bad as things can get. His name was Moses Callahan. They say he played a mean guitar."

Moses Callahan came into the world in the year of 1900 and by the year of 1928 he was gone from it.

His grandfather had been a slave, whipped until the spine was exposed. He died feverish in his own sick, his own waste.

62

Moses would here the story of his grandfather and say, "Not me."

His father was a sharecropper. A good man, a hardworking man, a man who feared God and treated all his fellow men as brothers beneath His merciful gaze. He died covered head to toe in tar, dangling by his neck from an oak tree in front of the house. Moses would stay up at night, remembering his father swaying in the breeze. And he would say, "Not me."

There was one possession in the Callahan family, passed down from son to son, and that was a guitar of black wood, hand-carved by Moses' great-grandfather. The family kept it secret from the slavers, and the family kept it safe from the white men with their badges and their hoods as they tore through the house, bashed the windows, and pressed their bulks against the women-folk.

Moses taught himself to play from before he was four years old. The first song he learned to sing and play was the song of his granddad's death. The first song he ever wrote was the song of his dad's death.

He found steady work that way all through his childhood, with many black folks and even some white folks hiring him special for their weddings or their garden parties. His sister once asked him, who's better to play for, a white crowd or a black crowd? Moses had strummed the guitar and shrugged, said something like he didn't give a damn about any audience, he played for himself and no one else.

He got to be pretty famous in his little corner of the world, so much so that when he was seventeen a man from Tuscaloosa drove up one day and asked to listen to him play, saying that there may be a record contract in it, if Moses Callahan impressed enough.

So Moses Callahan brought the man from Tuscaloosa to the kitchen and sat him at their dinner table and he pulled up a chair and began to play. He poured his everything into that playing, his long-blistered fingers breaking open with the fury and speed of his picking. Sweat beaded down his forehead and down his back. He closed his eyes against the sting, the music forming clouds of ambient color behind his lids, puffing and swaying and swirling as he played for the man from Tuscaloosa.

It was the greatest performance he had ever given, there in his kitchen for only the one man.

That man listened intently to the song, face betraying nothing, and when it was over he took his glass of water, drained it, said, "You're good. But I got ten niggra boys every bit as good. My thanks for the drink," and left.

Moses Callahan sat silent in his chair for a full hour, feeling nothing.

There are other men with better ears, his sister said. Don't you worry Moses, don't you worry. You just have to bide your time and wait your turn, that's all.

Moses Callahan, seventeen years old, Moses Callahan broke his silence to say, "Not me" and he got up and walked out of the kitchen.

It was dusk when he left his house. The world sank around him as he walked, until the sky was painted with black pitch. Moses walked until the road gave way to dirt, and he kept walking until the crescent moon was high ahead and the crossroads lay at his feet.

There are languages that have nothing to do with words. You know them, down in your bones.

Moses spoke in such a tongue.

Batwings flurried and another black man stood beside him, the biggest black man that Moses had ever seen. He was dressed all in black silk, complete with a black cape with red trim that he folded in his arm as he approached.

"Do you know who I am?" the other man said.

Moses Callahan replied that he knew what the man was.

The man took a silver dollar from his pocket and begin to flip it, the coin whistling as it turned in the silent midnight air.

"But do you know *who* I am?"

Moses Callahan, he gulped and he said yes, yes he did.

"And what would a man of your kind want with one of mine?"

Moses Callahan, barely all of seventeen years old, he looked at the dirt and he said he wanted to be the best guitar player who ever lived, who ever would live.

"But my son, my lad, you already got as much talent as any other man so blessed by the Good Lord could hope to be," said the other. "Isn't it greed, most malicious greed, that would prompt you to desire even more yet?"

Then call it greed, was what Moses Callahan said. Call it greed, call it pride, call it whichever or whatever suited you. He was talented sure, but not more talented than anyone else.

The other man flipped the coin with his right hand, only to suddenly snatch it out of the air with his left. With a flick of the wrist, the coin was back in his right hand. With a snap, the coin twirled through the air and into Moses Callahan's hand.

"So long as you have that coin on your person, you will be the best guitar player that ever lived," the other man said. "But you mind me, Moses Callahan. That coin is yours for ten years, and on ten years to the night I will return to collect it. Do you understand?"

Moses said he did.

"You don't," said the other. "You are hardly yet a man, and if I had my senses about me I'd refuse to do such a deal with such a one as you. But we are all as God made us. I'll be seeing you, then."

The other man walked away, the flourish of red trim

hovering just a moment in the dark before it vanished.

The walk back home was shorter than the one away. But when Moses went to open the door, he found it locked.

His sister's voice from behind the door, "Momma knows where you been. What you did. She says not to let you in, never again."

He pounded on the door, demanded he be let in.

"She's getting the rifle, Moses, she's getting it down and loading it. Best you leave, go quick."

"I need my guitar."

The door opened a crack, just wide enough for him to see the grief and illness on his sister's face. She thrust the guitar into his arms and then closed the door once more.

"Get out of here," she said. "Go enjoy what you got. Oh Jesus, oh God, oh Lord, go enjoy it."

Moses Callahan quit that place.

His first stop was to the local watering hole, where Fats Brown held court. Brown was on stage, the crowd spellbound as he told them of the crimes of Stagger Lee, wielding his pistol against everyone from his neighbors to the law, all the way down to the devil his own mean self. Moses found himself a table right in the middle of the audience and sat himself down.

Moses Callahan saw Fats Brown see him. He ordered a drink and sipped it silently, pulling long faces of disgust at each strum of Fats Brown's fingers. The guitarist grinned through gritted teeth, but he couldn't make it through the rest of the song before he abruptly stopped and called:

"It seems we have a gent in our joint doesn't appreciate the hard work that we humble men put into entertaining you folks. What seems to be the problem, mister fella?"

"No problem, no problem," Moses Callahan said, the dance hall now silent. "I was just wondering if I should abandon this drink or order another four more. Which do you think will get me away from this jackass's braying?"

"Oh is that so?"

"Oh that's so. Came here to listen to some music, I did, not listen to alley cats caterwauling up in each other."

The crowd was into this now. They murmured with excitement, then shut up real quick as the steam rose from Fats Brown's head.

"And I suppose a punk like you supposes that you could do better?"

"Ain't no supposing about it. I tell you here, I tell you now, there ain't no man alive can play the guitar the way I can."

Grins on the faces in the hall, feet tapping in anticipation.

Fats Brown flashed a hungry shark smile and bid the young man up on stage.

"If you play half so big as you talk, you just may the best ever yet," he said. "Okay, boy, play us something."

Moses Callahan, seventeen years old, he took up his guitar and he began to play.

Things moved awful fast. He tried to cherish each minute of each hour of each day of each year but they slipped away, the ways things do. Every band wanted to play with him, every makeshift tavern and barn bar wanted to feature him. The man from Tuscaloosa came back with a piece of paper and a promise of money, and Moses Callahan had the distinct pleasure of showing him the still-wet ink on the contract signed for three times as much.

"Your offer is good," Moses said. "But I got ten white men making offers just as good."

The women were as plentiful as the money. After the shows, they would escort him back to whichever room he was crashing in for the engagement. He would sit up in bed, the

67

guitar across his naked lap, and pluck low strings and sing in whispers. Married women and single women, good girls and bad news, all swayed to the rhythm of his crooning, shedding their garments and joining in on his song.

The coin he left buried at the bottom of every bureau, collecting it only at the last moment before it was time to pack up and return to the road.

After nine years, he began to try and lose it. There was no conscious choice made to do so, but Moses Callahan began to leave the coin in rooms after he checked out. He left it in his pants pocket when he sent the items to be laundered. He would take the coin out and spin it on the bar and when it was time to go back on stage he would leave it where it lay.

The coin always returned to his pocket. He never could pinpoint the moment it returned. In one instant it would be gone, and in the next it would be safely cushioned in his pocket as though it had been there all the while.

Accounts dispute what Moses Callahan's disposition seemed to be on the night of his final concert. There are some folks who claim that he had a secret, furtive look to him as he tuned up. That elusive 'they' that drives all rumors and spread all gossip, 'they' claim that he was twitchy and on edge, looking over his shoulder and peering out the windows with red-rimmed eyes. 'They' will tell you that his skin had gone ash-gray and he was unkempt and unclean as he took the stage that final time.

The bartender of this particular evening, a man named Rudolph Stein (Rudolph Stein would tell any story to anybody, but he never would or did explain how a black man in Mississippi came to be named Rudolph Stein), would go to his dying day insisting that the man Moses Callahan had been composed and even-tempered all the while leading up to the show.

"He'd been at my bar a bit," Rudolph would tell those who asked. "So he was a might bit drowsy when the early evening came 'round, but I tell you true that he perked up when it was time to go on and get to playing."

Not even his band can be counted on for unity. Stan Bishop and Rizzo, the white guy they kept around to book the gigs at the upscale joints, both say that sure, Moses was a bit antsy leading up to the show, but they were sure it was on account of Moses' most recent late night singing partner being a married woman with a husband that stood a foot taller than Moses and carried an extra hundred pounds.

And still others in the band will say no, no, Moses Callahan was his cheerful and swaggering self right up until he stepped on the stage he would never leave.

But all sources agree to two things. What everyone agrees on, to a man, is that the concert Moses Callahan played that night was the best they had ever seen.

And they all agree on how it ended. A thing like that…you don't forget.

Moses Callahan sat down in his suit and his hat and he began to play that old guitar. When he sang, it was an old song at the edge of his lips, a song heard a hundred times over in the course of a life. But Moses Callahan hit the notes so clean, it was as if the song was born anew on that little wood stage.

He hadn't been playing for more than five minutes, and the crowd was already transfixed. They leaned in to the music, shut their eyes against the world so that the notes might become the world entire. Each harsh twang of the string was a jolt to the spine, each flow a wave that lifted the assembled out of the dingy confines of that place and rolled on into the larger sea.

No one noticed when the big black man in a black silk suit

ambled into the audience. He took up a seat by the bar. Rudolph Stein poured him a drunk, his mind so full of the music that he would never remember the big man's face, or what exactly it was that he poured.

The big man sipped his drink and swayed a little to the crooning.

The tempo got faster now.

Discordant chords in the larger flow snapped the audience out of their reverie. Eyes fluttered opened, hands mopped sweat away from brows.

Moses Callahan had his head down, eyes only for the instrument as his fingers worked with unnatural speed.

The tempo got faster now.

It was nauseating. The guitar was shrieking, sounds aligned in ways that ears were not meant to interpret. Some in the audience even went so far as to cover their ears against the screech.

Behind the squeal of the strings, there was a deeper noise. A low hum, or was it a buzz, coming from out of the air, from inside your ear, a thousand angry flies throwing a riot in your mind where you cannot swat them away.

Stan Bishop was riveted to his spot on the stage, eyes that he had no power to control staring into the pandemonium. Blood coursed in two thick streams from his ears

And the tempo got faster now.

And the guitarist was smoking now.

Smoke, yes, smoke was pouring off Moses Callahan's back. Black smoke, running out from under his pants legs, out his sleeves, out the front of his shirt between the buttons and up through his collar. Embers floated up from between hair follicles, joining the mounting cloud forming above him.

He began to sing, black smoke gushing from between his lips.

He sang the first song he ever learned, that of his grandfather. He sang the first song he ever wrote, that of his father. He sang a new verse, his own, screaming out the words as his clothes disintegrated from his body and tattoos of orange flame exposed themselves across his naked black flesh.

"Not me!" he cried. "Not me!"

He struck the strings ten times in half a second and raised his pick for one final chord.

"Not me!" he called one last time, and brought the pick down.

His fingers were flame. The chords snapped at this last touch, the guitar itself crumbling into wretched ash.

Moses Callahan exploded in a ball of fire, the heat ripping through the windows of the speakeasy and overturning every table. The glasses above the bar exploded, the liquid evaporating into fumes.

The final chord lay in the air, haunting the air of every terrified soul now lying bloody and damaged the torn.

The shock reigned for a moment, maybe two, and then the screams and confusion began to set in. In the commotion, no one noticed the big black man set his empty glass on the smoldering bar, gather up his coat, and sauntered up to the stage. He sifted in the ashes for a moment, collecting up a single scorched but still solid coin that shone from the ruins. Flicking the coin as he went, the big man whistled a jaunty tune as he strode out into the Mississippi night.

"Well, it's a fine story," Amador Puccini opined. "I've never had an affinity for Negro music myself, but it's a fine enough tale."

The rest of the party agreed that it was an amusing enough diversion, and began to make motions towards their own bar. It had been a lengthy telling and throats were parched.

"It all just sounds like nonsense to you, doesn't it?" Frank Dunston said. The look of defeat and loss that he had worn when he first walked in had curdled into something else. "Just like that nonsense with the snakes. Just a game, just a laugh, never mind who it hurts."

"None of that old boy, none of that," Mr. Golly said. He'd gotten his meanness out of the way and wanted the party back up and running. "We're all just here to have a good time."

"A good time?" Sweat running down Frank's face like he was front row to Moses Callahan's last chord. "Don't you understand that this…that all this *matters*? That there's consequences to every choice you choose?"

"You big silly," said Mary Louise Golly. "It's a party."

He turned to her, and the look on his face drew a gasp from Mrs. Golly's throat. It was so…empty. That face would linger with her for the few remaining years she had. When she lay bleeding out on the floor of the bathroom, the last thing she saw before the darkening vice sealed was that empty stare, regarding her without any knowledge of love.

"Sure," Dunston said. "Sure." He reached into his pocket. "Well, parties have a price."

He flipped the silver dollar in a lazy arc. It made a little metallic jingle as it danced on the bar before coming to a halt.

Frank Dunston quit that place.

None of the other partygoers said a word. One by one, they left and returned home.

Except for Mr. and Mrs. Golly. They were already home.

Reginald Golly left no traditional note before hanging himself. The closest any investigator ever got to understanding the man who hung himself from his own balcony was a scrap of torn paper in his left pocket.

On the paper, scribbled, were the words "Every party has a price."

Wrapped inside the paper was a scorched silver dollar.

I didn't last much very long at The Griffin after hearing Old Chet's story. I took his hint and a week later I was gone, out of the state.

Chet didn't last much longer. I found out later that almost a month to the day that he told me the story of Moses Callahan, Old Chet was found in his easy chair, carbon dioxide alarm screaming unheeded. No one knew whether it was intentional or an accident, and Chet had no family to kick up a fuss, demanding answers.

The first and only time I ever lied to my wife was when I went back to see his grave. I told her I was going to see my Mom. I promised the kids I would bring them back some of her famous brownies.

She's a good woman, my wife. Our kids are beautiful. Happy, healthy. My co-workers like me. They think I'm reliable. We'll go out to dinner and they'll act as if they know me. They'll laugh together and think that I belong among them.

I did see my mom that day, but that wasn't the reason I came back.

Brownies packed tight in the car, I went to Old Chet's grave and got down on my knees. I took the scorched coin from my pocket and I buried it in the ground by his stone. It was the only thing of his that I'd kept. Everything else I stole, by that point, I'd either spent or traded away.

"You knew, right?" I said. "You knew? That's why you told me the story?" The air was cold and it stung my wet eyes. "I'm not that person any more. A man can be forgiven. The past can be forgotten."

The breeze blew softly as it passed across the tombstones. I sat with my back to his name and whispered prayers on the wind.

"Please," I cried. "Please."

Chet had nothing to say to me. He'd played his tune, and all that's left is that last chord, an echo accompanying me even after all the world is silent.

DOUBLE D

Donald J. Bingle

It's tough to be a dame in Chicago.

Even tougher when you spend all your time in dive bars on Water Street, just waiting for some big hunk of a man to buy you a drink so you can chat him up and make all his dreams come true.

Why, yes, darling, I would like a drink. How'd you ever guess? I'll have a Southern Comfort Manhattan, bless your heart. Smooth, but powerful, just like you.

Light me up a cigarette, will you, big guy? Might as well add to the cloud hanging low off the ceiling like the morning haze over the steel mills near the Indiana border. Unfiltered if you got 'em. I like to taste the flecks of tobacco leaf, all sickly sweet and tangy, in between draws. Gives my tongue something to do, you know.

Nah, sugar, I'm sure you're right. The girls back in Tupelo, Mississippi, they ain't nothing like me—not that I wasn't all sweet and innocent and giggly once upon a time. Now, I'm sweet and tangy, just ready to taste.

Awww. Why'd you have to go and kill the mood, honey, by asking a question like that? You corporate types, you're always thinking business, business, business. ABCD. Am I right? Always Be Closing the Deal.

Well, jelly bean, you're right and wrong, all at the same time. Just like me. It so happens I am a working girl, just not the type you're thinking of.

How can I tell what you're thinking of? Honey, unless you swivel that stool so you're facing the bar a bit more, everyone here can tell what you're thinking of, if you get my meaning. Trust me, cherub, I love enthusiasm, but we have to strike a bargain, first. Right?

See, snookums, that's where you were on target. I am a working girl of sorts. Y'see, I'm a Double D.

And there it is. There's the eye drop, right on schedule, like you were watching an art dealer fumble a Ming vase or your Aunt Matilda let go of the baby. You just can't help but look down to witness the spectacle. Well, eyes back up here, fella. Not that they ain't nice and soft and…a bit of a spectacle, but I ain't talkin' about my headlights. I'm talkin' about my job. And, yeah, I was telling the truth when I said I could make all your dreams come true.

Y'see, I'm a Double D, but that stands for Dream Demon. And that means I can get you anything your heart desires, Toto. Anything at all.

Don't laugh so hard, sugarcakes, you'll suck in too much smoke and have a conniption. Don't believe me, right? This just ain't advertising, cowboy. This is the real deal. Anything you want, I can arrange.

I've seen that smirk of doubt before, big shot. Nobody thinks a dame can get them anything they want, unless…well, you know…all they want is the dame. I can do that, of course, if you want to sell yourself short. Yes sir, you can have all this…two girls if you want. Hell, you can have a guy or a midget or a Mexican donkey, if that's what floats your boat, but you don't need me for that. Just go to the front desk at any of the big hotels in the Loop and ask for the "Businessman's Special." They can hook you up with all the debauchery you can afford.

But, I'm much better than that. I can get you anything at all…your fondest dream come true…for a price. That's what Dream Demons do. We make deals and deliver dreams.

Still don't believe me, do you? Okay, I'll prove it to you. Yes, right here in the bar…and, no…I don't do dreams for free, not even little ones. Just look into my eyes and I'll prove I'm a Dream Demon. Up here, hot shot, at my eyes.

Jeez! You're the jumpy type, ain't you? Spilled your drink and let the lit cigarette fall out of your mouth. You gotta be more careful. You could start a fire that way—there's time enough for that later.

Any professional women you know can turn their eyes completely coal black? I didn't think so. Only demons do that. Look it up in the good book, if you want.

Well, hell's bells. You've got no reason to face the bar anymore. Must've scared you good with the old Eyes of the Abyss look. Not that you weren't scared before, but it was the excited kind of scared, with maybe a touch of worry about whether I was going to tell your wife or your secretary or maybe steal your wallet while you were in the bathroom. Now that you think you know who I am, it's more the is-she-going-to-turn-me-into-a-pillar-of-flame-and-rotisserie-my-firstborn kind of scared.

I like it. It suits you. And, to be truthful, I do deserve a certain amount of respect. All working girls do.

By the way, I'm nothing but truthful. With me, a deal is a deal and the terms are straightforward. You tell me your fondest desire and I deliver.

Say, Einstein, you are clever. Must be the up and coming kid at the company. Straight to the crux of the deal: duration of your dream life. My boss, he thinks long-term. So us Double Ds, we don't quibble about details of duration. Why fuss and argue about five years, ten years, twenty years, when they are all just drops in the bucket? You ask, you automatically get a lifetime guarantee.

Sure, now that you mention it, I do have a bit of discretion about how long the lifetime lasts. Generally, we just let things run their natural course. No sense meddling with cosmic events unnecessarily. Besides, satisfied customers can be a great source of future referrals. But I do confess to having an ability to act with discretionary authority to manipulate the lifetime part of the guarantee when someone is too big of a jerk or goes blabbing to the press or tries to weasel out of his end of the deal.

I don't take kindly to that kind of trouble, so I shut it down right quick.

Acts of God. Ha! If only they knew.

And I can and sometimes do interpret things a bit on the literal side for parties of the second part who rub me the wrong way. And, yeah, I mean that literally. Some cad gets handsy with me at the bar, I don't do him any favors in the negotiations. I may just be borrowing this body, but it's mine for the moment and I don't allow no trespassers on my property, even if I am an attractive nuisance. You want to mow the grass, you stay in your own yard. Understand?

Good. Now where was I? Ah, price. That's right. Just what you'd expect. You get your dream life, my boss nicks the soul out of your body as you exit this mortal coil. Yep, as you exit. You want to go through life soulless, go into advertising. With my deal, you get free, unfettered use of your soul during your lifetime. You just can't sell it to somebody else, 'cause we've got a prior claim—kind of like a first mortgage.

I know, I know. The whole eternal damnation to the pits of hell thing is making you hesitate. Am I right? Of course I'm right. Those nuns, they really pound that into you. Child cruelty, if you ask me. Hell's actually a pretty nice place. Streets might not be paved with gold, but they are paved with good intentions. And trust me, you've got a much better chance of meeting up again with your loved ones—friends, relatives, fraternity brothers, whatever—in hell than you will upstairs. Not exactly a well-attended party there. Besides, you can't even have a pleasant conversation up there about the meaning of life, even if you do find a friend to chat up. All those cherubims and seraphims singing "Holy, Holy, Holy" all the time make it really hard to communicate.

I can see the wheels turning, bucko. Take your time. The bar doesn't close 'til two AM, not that I'd recommend strolling back to your hotel at that time of night. Rolling drunks is a great Chicago tradition. St. Patrick's Day is like Christmas to the local thugs.

If you do stay late, though, you can walk back to the convention hotel through the Emerald City and you'll probably be alright.

You've never heard of the Emerald City? Most tourists haven't. That's what the locals call lower Wacker. Y'see, there's an entire street below Wacker Drive, used for deliveries and somesuch. They light it with green lights for some reason. In any case, tourists don't know it's there, so the muggers don't lurk in the green shadows. Follows the curve of the river, but you can access it right here near Michigan Avenue.

But enough of that. You got any dreams, mister?

You've decided already? Jeepers, you are a born executive, aren't you?

Wait a minute. Let me guess. A girl's gotta have some fun on the job, you know.

Hmmm. You don't seem the power-hungry type, so it's gotta be money or love. Am I right?

Money…money's always more complicated than people think it is. They think they can wish for a million bucks and they're set for life, no worries and no complications. But it just doesn't work that way and it's not because anybody on our end of the deal is messing with you. It's just because money is always complicated.

Say you wish for a big load of cash and I pay off on the deal, 'cause that's how things work with a Double D. Suddenly you got a big load of cash and everybody, they want to know where you got it. Who'd you rob? Where'd you find it? And even if you convince them that you ain't a crook, then the government wants to tax it. Or maybe somebody tries to steal it, whether with a gun or some clever investment portfolio, it doesn't make a difference, not in the end.

And, of course, everybody's got their hand out, 'cause you got the greenbacks and they don't. So your life is an endless line of sob stories and con men and women. You'll end up especially leery of the dames, since you won't ever be sure that they're making nice 'cause you're a swell fellow, rather than them just being heartless gold-diggers. With cash, you spend all your time on edge until it's all gone.

After that, you spend all your time regretting your choices—your choice of wish and every choice after that, too.

And, of course, some people get greedy. They wish for a million wishes, so that's what they get. A million wishes. Hell, you can do that without me, wish a million times— nothing in that wish says any of 'em will come true.

You're a sharp tack, so I figure you figured that all out already. You're the kind of stud who thinks about all the angles. You got that dreamy look that comes from sitting back and thinking about what really makes you happy, what makes your motor purr. But you don't just want your motor to purr, you want it to rev up whenever you want and keep running forever, like them big diesel train engines, that they start up and just never turn off for twenty, thirty years.

Maybe you're thinking about how to phrase the request. After all, you don't just want to love someone or just have someone love you, you want it to be mutual. And you're not looking just for spiritual love, you want the sweaty stuff, too.

Once, twice a day. And three times on Sunday.

That squinty-eyed look tells me that you're figuring all the angles, too. So let me be clear: you ask me to grant a dream that's romance related, I won't sell you out. The lifetime guarantee, that goes for the both of you. None of this tragic love that's cut short when your sweetie gets hit by a Mack truck the next morning when she runs out for eggs to make you breakfast. A deal's a deal.

Double Ds, we don't double deal.

But that goes both ways, lover. If I make a deal for my boss to take your soul when you die, he expects to collect. Don't go thinking that if you ask for true love, you somehow skate through a loophole because your soul is already given to your true love, or some claptrap romantic nonsense like that. I told you already, when we make a deal, your soul gets a first mortgage on it. When that debt comes due, the boss forecloses on your soul. My boss ain't a softer touch than the local bank manager, and you know what bastards those guys can be.

Last call? Jeez, it's later than I thought. Time to cut to the chase, lover. What's your temptation? Make your decision. Fulfill your fantasy. Tell me your dream and I make it come true for the price of your soul. No limits; no exceptions.

What's it gonna be, boy? What's it gonna be?

…

Damn you to hell for all eternity, buddy. I never expected that. Why'd you go and have to do that?

Still, a deal is a deal. You want all Dream Demons banished from earth forever, that's what you get, even if it means you're spoiling the party for everyone. I wouldn't have guessed you to be such a sanctimonious type, not from the way you stare at a gal.

Go ahead, take a good long look. I can dawdle for a few minutes, 'til closing time. After all, I'm not in a hurry to get to where I'm going, to where you've sent me.

Let your gaze wander all over my body. I don't mind. I'm the last Double D you'll ever see, that anybody will ever see.

Well, at least until you join us in hell. We both have that to look forward to. And if you think Double Ds are imaginative in making dreams come true, wait 'til you see what we can do with nightmares. After all, there's a whole army of us with nothing to do for eternity now, but think of ways to torture you.

You'd better settle up your tab with the barkeep now, hon. We'll settle up later.

Hoodoo Man

John Linwood Grant

The smooth tones of the saxophone; the taste of cigarette smoke under her tongue. Late Monday night at the Ivory Club, and she was almost ready to fall towards her bed. A last dancer sat on the edge of the stage, listening to the sax and trying to pick gum off the sole of one of her shoes. There were only ten or eleven patrons left.

"Anything here you can't handle, Marcel?" she asked the thin man at her side.

He shook his head. "Lieutenant Chase is crying into his martini again, that's about the worst of it."

"Have one of the girl find him a cab."

"Sure, Miss Garvey."

She glanced around, checking those shadowy corners of the club where deals were made and hearts broken. Under the peeling stucco of a fake arch, a large man sat protectively over a brandy bottle and a half-empty glass. She peered through the lingering smoke.

"Who's that guy?"

Her manager hesitated. "Some limey. Been here a few nights, on and off."

"Trouble?"

"Maybe if someone pokes him. Hettie tried it on with him, says he growled and gave her the hard eye."

"Hmm."

Hettie was a pure-gold package, a dancer with the face, body and voice for Broadway. No-one turned her away. Intrigued, she wandered over to the arch and perched on a chair at the man's table.

"Florence Garvey," she said softly. "The owner of the

Ivory Club."

His clothes were wrong—old-fashioned and not New York cut. He didn't look up.

"It's rude to ignore a lady, you know." She gestured to Marcel.

She would have one final drink for the night, she decided. The manager brought a shot-glass for her, and she poured herself a neat brandy from the bottle on the table. This was the good stuff, brought in through Canada via Quebec. She waved Marcel away.

The big man looked up, and Florence Garvey remembered what it was like to be a small, uncertain child.

"I apologise," he said.

His eyes were the colour of something long forgotten, a deep brown that drew you in, and he had a face which reminded her of her father, even though the skin was far paler. She rarely met a white guy with presence, but this was the real deal.

"In town on business, or for pleasure?" She swilled brandy over her gums.

"Neither." He settled back, glass in hand. "I came here to drink, Miss Garvey."

He'd obviously clear half a bottle of brandy, but he showed no sign of it.

"The Cotton Club has more to offer than my small joint."

"Corruption and prejudice?" His laugh was sharp. "I prefer the more honest inebriation and lack of attention here. They say that you pay fairly, and don't judge on colour."

"That matters to you, Mister...uh?"

"Dodgson. Henry Dodgson. It's not a fair world, Miss Garvey, but I hardly think we need to help it along that way, do you?"

She smiled and emptied her glass. He had an old-fashioned

84

way with his words as well.

"We're closing soon, need to clean up a touch. Will I see you here tomorrow night, Mister Henry Dodgson?"

"It's possible."

There was no smile there, but no frown either.

Florence slept the morning through, then dealt with paperwork for a while toying with a black coffee in her apartment over the club. Takings were up; trouble was down. Hers was the only black and tan for a few blocks, and perched on the edge of Harlem, she managed to get the right mix in the club most of the time. The rich white girls and their daddies, the Sicilians and the numbers bosses all went further in, seeking that 'negro' experience or doing their deals where the cops felt on edge. She wouldn't end up ritzy, but she'd never have to go back to dancing.

She ate light, and wandered into the club around seven. The after-work drinkers were in, and only the piano was playing. Black faces and white faces, a few Italian guys coming down from a day on construction. The Ivory Club opened its quiet side-door to anyone who drank, paid and left without a fuss. Even the cops drank here, before they raided a joint somewhere else that gave them real problems.

"He's in," said Marcel, tugging at his thin moustache in that fey way of his.

"Who's in?"

"The limey. Hettie says he's a major."

"A major what?"

He giggled, the only fault of an otherwise perfect club manager. That giggle always made her clench her teeth.

"As in the army, Miss Garvey. You know, they had a war a few years ago. Remember that?"

She sighed. "Yeah, yeah. Go nag the girls, Marcel."

The stage shows didn't start until ten. They'd never get Cab Calloway here, but Johnny Pane and the Harlem Boys did a good job, got feet tapping and a few on the floor. The girls did the rest. No touchy-touchy but plenty of eye contact and long legs.

Florence didn't come easy or cheap. And she didn't date customers. But still, she wondered…

An hour later she was in that cramped corner, watching for plaster that might fall into her highball.

"An army man, huh?" She poked at her twist of lime with a cocktail stick.

The man was hunched into a seat too small for him. His broad shoulders made him look like a bull that was considering whether or not to smash out of the corral.

"Some time ago."

"Did you have it bad?"

"People died. Most of them died terribly, achieving very little."

She felt stupid.

"Yeah. I knew a few who didn't come home so good, either."

The brown eyes were on her again. It wasn't that they looked into you—it was the fact that you didn't know what *you* were looking into. She clicked her fingers, and a waitress brought them more drinks. They knew to make hers mostly ginger ale.

"We don't see many British guys here."

He almost smiled. "I picked a dry hotel, it seems, so I looked for a quiet drinking spot. I don't know New York."

That seemed like an opening.

"Want to see more of Harlem? The real place."

"I'm not sure…"

His large hands were spread flat on the table. She saw

short, clean nails, and a raking scar across the back of his right hand, from the base of his little finger to the base of his thumb.

"That from action, Major Dodgson?"

She nodded to the scar.

"A different kind of war," he said, and reached for his drink.

They talked—about the news, the Ivory Club, anything but each other. She knew that she was attractive, but that seemed to have no effect on him. She didn't think it was a colour thing, either. He was seeing her words and the way she spoke, but not her face or her body.

There was no way she was letting this one go. After half an hour, with a fair amount of brandy down his wide neck, he reluctantly agreed to join her the next afternoon.

"It's a different world over here, Major. They're calling us 'the big apple,' the prize you just have to win. Pretend you're a stranger, never seen people before."

She didn't think that he'd find that difficult.

War, a woman, or something she couldn't imagine had hit this man hard.

They wandered through Central Park first, on a warm June morning. Florence wanted to ease this man in. An attractive well-dressed black woman, and the large frame of the Englishman, wearing clothes from before the war. People looked. She was interested, because it wasn't the usual type of look. They were watching him and wondering, just as she had done the first night at the Ivory Club.

"This speakeasy thing." His gaze was on the trees. "Damned silly. You'd never have it in England."

"It won't last," she said. "They'll need the taxes one day. All they're doing is putting money in the hands of hoodlums and moonshiners."

"You're an economist?"

"If you're in this game, you have to be."

"And what if you're a woman in 'this game'? I imagine that must be harder."

She laughed. "Most men compliment me on my hair, or my perfume. They want to talk dancing, or see if I'm easy."

He stopped.

"I can't do those things, I'm afraid, Miss Garvey. Should I escort you back to your club?"

"No, it's fine." She placed her fingertips lightly on his arm, as if she were daring herself. "It's nice to have a change. Let's see the sights."

He drank too much, she could see that. When they visited her cousins and bottles of rum were brought out, he sank two glasses of it while she had one cup of coffee. Then a trumpet emerged, guitars and an old banjo, and music bounced off the walls. She watched the big man as he stood in one corner, listening intently to an old black harmonic player—she couldn't remember his name—and felt pleased with herself.

That was until her cousin Moses turned up. She dragged him into the kitchen, hoping that Dodgson was safe to be left for a moment

"Marcie's gettin' worse, Flo." The skin around his eyes was puffy and tight. He was drumming the fingers of one hand on the cooker, though she didn't think he knew he was doing it.

"The hoodoo woman didn't help none?"

Moses scowled. "Helped herself to ten dollars."

She reached into her purse and tugged out a few notes.

"Look, Moses, I don't know what to do. Try the doctor again, maybe a different one. Hell, there's the minister at Lenox and 122nd—"

"He don't want nothing to do with us."

She hugged him.

"We'll think of something."

When she went back into the main room, Cousin Joe was asking if there were negroes in England, and somehow—maybe through the rum—they found out that he'd served in the army in South Africa, more than twenty years ago.

"So did you kill black folk out there, Major?"

Her half-sister, Eleanor, always marching with Du Bois's movement. Her eyes had narrowed as soon as Florence had brought a white man into the apartment.

"I killed people, Miss. A Lee-Enfield rifle doesn't worry about the colour of a man's skin." He down looked at his chipped glass of rum. "When its dusk on the veldt, all men are grey, God help us."

She whisked him out of there, thanking her relatives, before he became morose. She had a feeling that he could go that way quite easily.

"Sorry about Eleanor," she said as they walked back to the borderland between Harlem and Upper West Side where her club and his hotel awaited them. "She does a lot with the NAACP."

He raised his eyebrows, and she laughed softly.

"Oh, you wouldn't know, would you? National Association for the Advancement of Coloured People."

"A worthy cause, I imagine. Tell me, you went away for a few moments—the man who looked distressed."

"Moses. Yes, his daughter's not so good. Eleven years old, down with some sickness."

"I'm sorry to hear that. Is she in hospital?"

"We've had…specialists to her. No progress as yet."

Feeling she could say nothing more, they wandered the sultry Harlem night. The music on the streets seemed to interest him—he professed that he didn't understand jazz, but it had a certain freedom about it.

"Come to a house party this evening. I'll leave the club in Marcel's fluttery hands. There'll be music, good company—and a bottle or two."

"You like the idea of having tame Englishman?"

"A breath of local air for you, English air for them. Does it matter?"

"I suppose not. Very well. Thank you Miss Garvey, I'll come."

Despite his courtesy, he wouldn't call her Florence.

She saw that as a challenge for later.

The house party was a success. The biggest apartment on West 135th, turned over to a night of music and dancing where only chosen guests were allowed. No awkward cops, no high-hats looking down on them.

She introduced him around, "The Major," and maybe because he was English, he went down well. Johnny Pane showed him trumpet fingering, and a local poet argued with him about Ezra Pound and T S Eliot, neither of which Dodgson had read, it seemed. She saw that he'd sunk most of a bottle of rum, yet was standing solid, ready, as if he were always expecting something to happen.

They walked back close, but not arm in arm as she had hoped. When they reached the side-door of the Ivory Club, she asked him if he'd be joining her, upstairs.

It was a mistake.

He stiffened, as if listening to some far distant tune, and then he was striding away, a tall figure in the mists of the city.

Florence was relieved that her mistake hadn't been too great a one. Dodgson was back in the club two nights later. He accepted a brandy from her when she asked if she could sit at his table.

"Would you care to stroll with me again at some point, maybe?" she asked. "If I promise to act the lady?"

His expression was unreadable.

"Miss Garvey, you're a clever, interesting person—and you are a lady. But I cannot…there can be no romantic element to our knowing each other, only friendship. I'm sorry."

"Because I own a speakeasy? Or because of my colour?"

The small band on stage played Maple Leaf Rag, infused with touches of jazz on a seemingly random basis, and she felt a headache growing at each temple.

"Something mellow, boys," she shouted, and they shifted down a notch.

Dodgson sat looking at her, not drinking.

"It never occurred to me," he said slowly. "That either of those would matter."

And she knew that he was telling the truth.

"Maybe it's me who should apologise, then." She tried to sound light about it.

"Not at all. But I might still welcome a friendly guide. A pleasant companion, who knows where she's going."

"Then you'll have one. Henry."

They rode the El across the city, and she showed him what she knew of New York. The traffic alarmed him, and she learned that he disliked motor cars in general. He couldn't even drive, which surprised her.

On the third days of their excursions, they returned to the club to find her cousin, Moses, waiting for her outside the entrance. His long fingers played at his suit cuffs, and he was shaking slightly.

"It's bad, Flo." He paid no attention to Dodgson, standing behind her. "We're holdin' one of them sittings, same as they did for Aunt Evie. I paid the hoodoo woman again, jus' had to."

"What is she using?"

Florence and her cousin turned to stare at Dodgson.

"This ain't your concern, mister," said the tall black man.

Dodgson ignored him.

"Did you know, Miss Garvey? Did you know that I was here in your city to get away from such things?"

"Such things?"

"You said the girl was sick. You don't holding sittings for the sick, not that kind. You're talking about spiritualism, or whatever you call it over here."

She flinched at the coldness in his voice, and her own tone rose in response.

"Henry, what's gotten into you? You've never said why you came to America at all. I asked you, remember, and you said it was private, so I respected that. I don't know what you're on about, surely I don't."

"No. Perhaps you don't."

Those deep eyes seemed to darken.

"Mister…?"

"Moses Smith."

Dodgson gripped her cousin's left hand. They were much of a height, but she thought that the Englishman could have folded Moses up like a deckchair.

"Henry Dodgson. What does your hoodoo woman say she's using?"

Moses was still held by the big man's grip on his hand.

"The Books o' Moses. An' she's a root-worker, so she tells."

"But you've had her before, and I imagine that it did no good."

"Marcie been sickenin' for two week now. Doctors say there's nothin' wrong; the ministers say she's got the devil inside of her, too strong. Reckon she's marked to go down. We done prayers, gave her mojo bags, lit candles and had the

92

hoodoo woman…"

Florence tapped Dodgson's shoulder and looked pointedly at where he was almost crushing her cousin's hand. He let go, and she tried to smile at her cousin. It didn't come out well— she felt suddenly adrift.

"How do you know about hoodoo, Mr. English soldier?" she asked.

"That doesn't matter. It's none of my business, like Mr. Smith says."

Dodgson turned to walk away.

"My Marcie's fit to die." That was Florence's cousin, his voice cracking. "And, no, that woman ain't done nuthin' worth a damn."

The big man halted.

"I need a drink. If you want to tell me about it, I'll be in my usual place."

He went inside the Ivory Club, not waiting for any response.

Florence looked at Moses.

"He's different," she said. "I'm not sure how, but he's different"

"He knows a touch, maybe. But I ain't too happy to be beggin'. That's how it starts, ain't it, goin' to the white man for help? Ends up you owe more than you'll ever have."

"He's not like that. Let's talk to him, at least."

The dancers were rehearsing, tap and shimmy on the hardwood central floor, and it was too difficult to hear, so she took them into her private office. As she lived above, it was little more than a storage room—a table with old ledgers on, a couple of chairs and boxes of costumes from the various routines of the girls. She sat on the edge of the table.

"So…" She met Henry's dark gaze.

"I used to…help people. Years ago."

"You got the sight?" asked Moses, his back against the wall.

"Not in the sense you mean. I've learned a lot, seen a lot."

"So you could help Marcie?"

Dodgson sighed. "I can tell you what not to do, where your money will be wasted. I don't know if I can help."

Moses Smith tapped his fingers on the wall, looked at his cousin.

Florence shrugged. "Can't hurt. Could you bring Marcie to the club? It's private here, quiet." A dozen pairs of heels slammed down on the dancefloor outside. "My rooms above, I mean."

"Not tonight, Flo," said Moses, more agitate than ever. "The sitting is tonight. She's so much worse…"

"I'll attend, if you'll permit me, Mr. Smith," said Dodgson.

Moses gave a single, jerky nod.

They were not in the Harlem that Florence had shown him before. The Smiths lived in an over-crowded tenement further north—since Moses had lost his job at the printers, even some of the rent had come quietly out of Florence's purse.

"Said we was printin' 'seditious material,'" said Moses. "The boss is fightin' it, but you can't pay folk with court dates."

He invited them into the one bedroom apartment on the fourth floor.

"Moses' wife died of the influenza three years ago," Florence explained. "There's only him and Marcie."

She thought that he swore under his breath.

"You lost someone that way?"

"Yes."

It was a blunt, closing *Yes*, one which locked the subject away. They walked into one large room which held the stove, a sink, and a range of chairs which had been gathered up around an improvised table—two doors laid flat next to each other, propped on mismatched legs.

"Normal one ain't big enough," said Moses, looking uncomfortable.

Florence knew three of the other four people in the room, though she didn't like all of them. Jacob Jones was a trouble-maker, always leading Moses to the bottle since the job went, and his wife was a tattler, probably keen to tell more stories on the stairwells and steps around the block. Ma Cumber, blacker than polished coal, was good-hearted, but she heard spirits when the telephone wires sang, and had no sense in her.

And there was the hoodoo woman. A gangly figure in her late fifties or sixties with horse-teeth and a left eye which never quite followed you. They said her mother had been the same, that she was the spit of her. Or they were the same person, others said, which Florence doubted.

"Mamma Lucy." She nodded respectfully. "I brought a friend, Major Henry Dodgson. He's from England, and he knows things."

"Few enough like that around." The hoodoo woman's voice was hoarse and low. She fixed her right eye on Dodgson.

"I learned me to lay tricks from Aunt Caroline Dye. I been here, and I been there. You come to bring me grief about our ways?"

The big man seemed to be giving her the same scrutiny as she was giving him.

"That depends, madam. You're using the Sixth and Seventh Books of Moses?"

Her smile showed what Florence thought was an impossible number of large teeth.

"Not if you're here, I ain't." Unexpectedly, she winked at the two of them. Moses and the others were talking by the sink. "Suits the folk, but there ain't enough in them for this troubled child."

Dodgson tugged at the corner of his moustache.

"I haven't seen the girl yet. What would you say is the problem?"

"It's a haint, all right. I can read you, white boy. You got hurts aplenty, and more than a touch of hoodoo y'self. Old lady like me ain't going to fool you none."

He frowned. "A haint. That's a possession of some form, is it not?"

"Somethin' fell into that little girl, somethin' not from Heaven. Fifteen days it's been, and I done rootwork, gave her mojo hands, even been to a crossroads or two. It ain't shiftin', and she's getting' mighty close to givin' in."

The three of them turned as Moses coughed loudly.

"Gonna bring my Marcie in now."

He carried her into the living room on his own like she was no weight at all, a thin girl in a blanket. Florence drew in a breath—the girl had been as rich a brown as her father the month before. Now her skin was slate-coloured and beaded with sweat. The weight had dropped off her, and her exposed hands and feet moved with small tremors. He laid her on the surface, gently tucking the blanket under her chin, and Florence could have wept.

The old woman lit thick, waxy candles in the corners of the room, then came to the table.

"Take your seats, now, and think good thoughts o' this little girl." Mamma Lucy stood at the end by Marcie's head. "Florence Garvey, you should stand at her feet, stop the haint causin' trouble elsewhere. They don't like strong women, these things."

Moses Smith sat by his daughter's side, close to tears. The eleven year old hadn't opened her eyes. She twitched slightly, one hand clutching at nothing.

"This didn't do nothin' last time, Mamma Lucy," said her father, thick-tongued.

"Desperate times, son. Thought we might have had time before, but this lamb ain't goin' to last much longer, and we got ourselves a friend now. We gone beyond the easy roads." She looked directly at Henry, sitting opposite Moses. "You know it's got to come out, don't you?"

He nodded. "We used…other tools when I faced this sort of situation. Science, certain devices—a…"

"E-lec-tricity. I heard of that way. Rootwork's surer, but maybe it's too slow. We'll see." The hoodoo woman said a muttered prayer. "You all are God's witnesses, exceptin' this Mister Henry—he's maybe here to lend a hand, but he ain't so sure of God no more."

The big man set his jaw, but said nothing.

"Moses and the rest o' you, you set back and give this child love."

As she leaned over, Florence saw the hoodoo woman as a scraggy crow in a cheap print dress, her arched nose twitching. Claw-hands brought out small cloth bags from under the dress, placing them in various spots around the child.

"Time to be a-talkin'."

Mamma Lucy took a simple incense burner from a bag on the floor, lit a candle underneath, and began to shred a handful of dried herbs into the brass cup. The smoke which rose from the burner writhed in small drafts from windows and door, a grey trail written in the humid air of the apartment. Florence smelled bitterness, and something else she knew, perhaps sage.

"You use hyssop," said Dodgson, sounding as if he approved.

"I sure do. Now hush."

The street-light right outside the window shone in, setting

different shadows to the bulb hanging from the ceiling. The candles around the room added to that, until it seemed as if there were more shadows than a place this size could hold.

Florence shivered despite the heat. She looked at the two of them, Mamma Lucy and the Englishman. This wasn't a side-show. She'd thought that the hoodoo woman could be a fraud, or maybe well-meaning enough but no use. Now she was no longer sure. The big man, who had seemed so solid and practical, believed what was going on. Or believed, at least, that there was something there inside poor Marcie.

Mamma Lucy drew the smoke into wide nostrils, and bared her horse-teeth.

"Inside's got to come outside, outside's got to go where it should be. You in there, you speakin'?"

She slammed her hands down on the tabletop, making everyone except Dodgson take a start. The girl's mouth opened, saliva running from one corner.

"I got ways as will hurt you both—don't make me do this." The hoodoo woman clicked her tongue, and unwrapped a length of dried roots like shoelaces. She squeezed a few together, and threw them on the girl. "Got me white thread and whisky, and there's things I can do—"

Marcie jerked, one heel drumming against the table. Her father whimpered, and Florence knew that he wanted to scoop her up and run.

"Stay steady, Moses," she said, looking at him. He swallowed, and sat back.

"You don't like that?" Mamma Lucy lifted another handful of the roots. "Mebbe I should look deeper under these conjure-bags o' mine?"

She sounded confident, but Florence smelled something else on the air, a sort of sweet corruption, and Marcie looked worse than ever, her skin a greasy slate-grey which was sickening to see. The girl's eyelids parted, and people gasped as they saw the red-veined wrongness of those eyes, the pupils down to pinpricks. All but the Englishman edged back, and Mamma Lucy swore.

"This haint has her, Mister Henry. It'll see her dead, just for the fun o' it."

He looked to Florence.

"When you were showing me around, Miss Garvey—you said that Harlem had had a large Jewish population once?"

"They've been moving out, moving on, these last few years," she agreed. "But ten years ago, yeah, most of this area was Jewish families. Why, Henry?"

He stood up, his face suddenly lined.

"We may not be able to help. It's a dybbuk. You know of those, Mamma Lucy?"

The hoodoo woman nodded.

"Evil for evil's sake, set on wreckin' whoever it gets inside of. Mebbe been waitin' round since its own people went, lookin' for an easy touch. Ain't got no time for findin' a rabbi, though, even iffen one could do somethin'. This girl, she won't see dawn."

This time it was the old woman's left eye, milk and honey, which fixed Dodgson in its stare.

"'Lessen you stop your own hidin' and step up with me."

Florence read faces every day, judging which clients at the Ivory Club were trouble, which were trying to get something out of her. She knew men, and if this one was different, he was only a touch different. He was struggling with history and memory, with things that he'd left behind in England. Or had hoped to leave behind.

"It's Marcie's life, Henry," she said. "Maybe her soul."

And in saying that, she would have sworn on the Bible that there was another figure there in the room, a slim shadow behind the big man. Florence had a sense of long, dark hair, black silk and the scent of violet water, even though the herbs and candles burning around them.

"What would she have had you do?" she added, reaching wildly without really knowing what she meant.

He darkened, an angry glare.

"She..."

Florence drew in that scent of violets. She knew that she was no hoodoo woman, no conjure-wife, but she had one single word in her head right then, without her bidding it come.

"Abigail. You lost her, and now Moses is going to lose his little girl. No justice for anyone in that."

Mamma Lucy's look darted between her, Dodgson, and the prone girl, who was now shuddering and gasping. Her father had his face in his hands, sobbing, and the three witnesses had scraped their chairs back, too scared to speak, too scared to run.

The streetlight went out suddenly, leaving candles and the unshaded electric light to show a dying black girl, laid on a table in a cheap apartment.

The big man reached into his jacket. He drew out a simple black silk choker adorned with a cameo. To Florence it was blue, but not a blue she'd seen before, more an idea of what the pure colour might be. Azure and indigo, all at once.

The hoodoo woman sighed.

"Saaamaaa," she said, and took it from him. "No common haint goin' to wait around to feel that, if we does it right"

She tied a few of the shoelace roots around the silk, and spat on her hands.

"Want to lead the dance, Mister Henry?"

He shook his head.

"This is your place, Mamma Lucy. Your people."

The anger had gone, though Florence feared what he might say to her afterwards.

Mamma Lucy smiled at him. "A strong heart always has people round it. Can't help lovin' a strong heart."

She leaned over Marcie, and slipped the choker around the girl's thin neck. Marcie gave a choked cry, and her father threw his chair back, making to go to her.

"Hold him," Mamma Lucy snapped.

To Florence's surprise, it was fat old Ma Cumber who reached out, grabbing Moses' arm and tugging him back with all her strength.

"You won't talk, and you can't stay." The hoodoo woman took the little girl by the shoulders, gripping her with large, gnarled hands. "Aunt Caroline used to say, 'No haint can take the blue,' and I'm guessin' no dybbuk can, neither. Say the words with me, Henry Dodgson, and you're savin' a life tonight."

And they chanted. Florence could think of no other word for it. Two strangers, the gangling black woman in her print-dress and the big white man in his clothes from another age. The words they used made no sense, not to her, but candles flared, and for a moment that street-light outside shone again, as blue as a noon sky…

Marcie twisted, her shoulders still held by the hoodoo woman, and she screamed, a high wail that came from beyond an eleven year old's throat and set the light-bulb swinging.

"Out, by the Third Sign, the Fifth Sign, the Archangels themselves and the good Lord's grace!" Mamma Lucy shouted.

One jerk, like a small fit, and Marcie lay still.

"Dear Lord, no," whispered Moses, and Ma Cumber squeezed him like he was a child himself.

Then the girl opened her eyes. They were hazel-brown, and

clear.

"Daddy? Where've I been, daddy?"

Johnny Pane and his Harlem Boys played sweet music, whilst three girls shimmied in the middle of the dance floor. Lightweights, out for a drink and a dance but not going too deep. The crowd was mixed, just how Florence liked it. A few black writers and poets, on the hard stuff, cooking up anything from free-form verse to political pamphlets in the alcoves; Jimmy Toll, who ran an almost legit numbers game around here, and a gang of old musician, one of whom kept lifting his battered trumpet and matching Johnny's sax. Lieutenant Chase was in and sober—he had the hots for Hettie, but didn't know how to ask a black girl out.

"Wonder if they'll all be black and tans one day?" She sipped her highball, heavier on the bourbon tonight.

Dodgson smiled. "We could hope, Miss Garvey, though I doubt it. There's always a reason to hate someone, even if you have to make it up."

"Do you hate me? For last night, for what I said?"

"No."

But he didn't elaborate, and she knew that he was leaving soon. Leaving New York, when she wanted him to stay, to tell her more—or even let her in altogether.

"Who was she? Abigail?"

A high note shook the chandelier over the dance floor.

"My wife. She died when the influenza came to our part of London in 1920. She was so strong…yet it took her, all the same."

"That was her cameo, wasn't it? The one you passed to Mamma Lucy. Was she a hoodoo woman as well?"

He was expressionless again, just as he had been when she first saw him. Deep brown eyes in a tanned face, but if those eyes laughed or wept, she couldn't tell.

"In a way."

His right hand touched the pocket of his waistcoat, and she knew that the choker and cameo were back in their place.

"You and Mamma Lucy saved one life, maybe two. Don't know that Moses could have carried on if Marcie had died."

She leaned over and kissed him lightly on the cheek.

"I'll miss you, hoodoo man."

They listened to the music, drew in the sounds of a new age, and yet all that Florence could take in, over the saxophone, the cigarette smoke and the bourbon, was the old-fashioned scent of violets.

Gabriel's Trumpet
Jon Black

The Savoy Ballroom was jumping. Fess Williams led his Royal Flush Orchestra through a furious rendition of "Hot Town" as patrons Lindy hopped across the dancefloor. Others listened to the music or were content to see and be seen. Women wore fancy dresses. Men wore suits. The Savoy's dress code was stringent.

Even for Harlem's swankest nightclub, the evening was exceptional. Five thousand people crowded inside. Thousands more stood outside on Lennox Avenue, hoping to get in. All of them came to see a miracle.

Frank Marvin's husky tenor vocals gave way to a clarinet solo, which melted into a glorious crescendo of saxophones. As sax notes faded away, a slender young man with delicate features and mocha complexion took the spotlight. Raising a gleaming silver trumpet to his lips, the crowd waited expectantly. This was what they came for.

Long, sweet, and clear, his opening note rung like a church bell through the Savoy. The trumpeter began a sonorous melody of rapidly accelerating tempo. Playing notes at lightning speed, his fingers melted into a translucent blur. Shifting tempo up and down, always just before the audience expected it, he kept them hanging on every note.

At its most frenetic, the Savoy's dancers struggled to keep up. But his long, slow passages moved the crowd most. The trumpeter's sound was haunting and ethereal, sweetness and melancholy inseparable from one another. His music beckoned visions of dreamlike landscapes and conjured long-forgotten bittersweet memories. Even the Lindy hoppers stopped to watch.

At last, he took the silver trumpet from his lips.

"Ladies and Gentlemen," Fess Williams shouted from his bandleader's podium, "put your hands together for Gabriel 'Resurrection' Gibbs."

The crowd exploded in applause. It was a remarkable performance. Especially for a man who died two years ago.

Gibbs bowed, a tiny smile on his lips. Raising the trumpet, he played on.

In the crowd, Langston Hughes looked on thoughtfully, scribbling notes. Moe Gale, the Savoy's owner, nodded approvingly, hearing profit in the trumpeter's every note. Near Hughes, two men watched Gibbs and eyed each other suspiciously. They stood out. Not because they were white, the Savoy had always been proudly integrated, but because they were square. One, younger and tall, compulsively cleaning his glasses. The other was portly and pallid, as if recently escaping confinement.

Near the bandstand, another outsider lingered. Motionless and stony-faced, he stood, unmoved by the revelry surrounding him. Bald and sturdily framed, the man knocked at the door of middle age. His suit epitomized the conservative style of another era, in contrast with Savoy regulars who self-consciously embraced the cutting edge of Harlem fashion.

As much as the squares, this man was an outsider. Packed as the Savoy was, patrons remained at arm's length, heeding warnings their conscious minds were unaware of. Unobserved amidst the crowd, the interloper produced a revolver and fired, empting the cylinder toward the bandstand.

Crying out in pain, "Jelly" James dropped his trombone and grasped his shoulder. But all eyes focused on "Resurrection" Gibbs. Blood plastering his white tuxedo shirt, the trumpeter swooned before collapsing into the drums.

BOSTON; AUGUST 31ST, 1929

"You can judge a man by his library," Marcus thought, pacing along the well-apportioned bookshelves of a Beacon Hill mansion.

All the titles marking an educated, patrician man were present. So, too, were some curious outliers: bound editions of Madam Blavatsky's correspondence, Capron's *Modern Spiritualism*, Frazer's *Golden Bough,* even an unpublished autobiography of Franz Mesmer. What was absent were the Moderns: no Anderson, Fitzgerald, Hemmingway, or Joyce.

He heard the double doors opening behind him. "Dr. Roads, thank you for coming."

Marcus turned to face Dr. Walter Franklin Prince. The research director of the Boston Society of Psychical Research was old, Marcus acknowledged, but the curiosity and determination in his face made that difficult to remember. Prince was, in fact, the society's driving force.

"As I've said, call me Marcus."

"Very well, Marcus, please be seated."

Reposing in a high-backed leather chair, Marcus cleaned his glasses, a nervous habit since childhood. Prince's secretive phone call unnerved him. Why did he want to meet away from the society's headquarters? And why was he tightlipped about his purpose?

"Do you remember our discussion of Gabriel Gibbs last month?"

"The trumpeter. Down in New York, correct?"

Prince nodded.

Marcus recalled something of it. The musician, rumors said, died somewhere down south, but was resurrected with his musicianship much advanced. Now in Harlem, Gibbs was quite the cause célèbre.

There had been discussion of the BSPR investigating the case. Discussion mixed with laughter. The story was preposterous. Séances were one thing, resurrection quite another. Anyway, how would one investigate such claims? The idea was quickly shelved. It intrigued Marcus that Prince referenced it again.

"The ASPR is investigating Gibbs," Prince said, lips curling into a grimace. "I have no choice but to open an investigation as well. If those New Yorkers go off half-cocked again, we've have to be able to counter it."

Marcus nodded. Based in New York, the ASPR, American Society of Psychical Research, was the BSPR's rival. Both societies conducted the rivalry with all the bitterness of the civil war it was. The two groups had once been one. Then came a medium named Margery…

In 1925, the ASPR issued a report championing her authenticity. The society's leadership actively defended Margery against allegations of fraud. Many of its members, however, felt compelling evidence existed to question Margery's bona fides. That segment departed the organization, establishing the Boston Society.

"Even so," Prince continued, "many of our members would be unhappy about treating this case seriously. That's why I asked to meet at my home. This investigation is unofficial, unless we need to go against the ASPR report."

"That's reasonable," Marcus acknowledged, "what do you want from me?"

"Why, dear boy," Prince smiled drolly, "You're heading the investigation."

Marcus hoped the choking noise he made was only in his head. "You're not serious. Why me? Why not Rhine? He's more experienced. Or Lydia Allison? She's better with people."

"You're every bit as good as them. Besides, Rhine's down at Duke now," Prince scolded. "More importantly, you're a physician. If anyone is qualified to determine whether a man has returned from the dead, it's you."

His argument made sense. And it would be an opportunity to break the tedium of recent investigations. That brought its own difficulties. "This isn't like checking out a séance. It's different from anything I've done," Marcus explained. "I can't just look for wires and cheesecloth. I'm not a Pinkerton. I don't know how to go about this."

"You'll figure it out," Prince smiled. "If in doubt, start at the beginning."

"I accept." Marcus grinned. "Do you know who the ASPR has put on the case?"

"Theodore Fenno," Prince replied.

"Oh." This time, it was Marcus who grimaced.

Mississippi Delta; September 5th, 1929

Marcus had never spent so long on trains: Boston, New York, Chattanooga, an overnight in Memphis. This morning he caught the Jackson Bell, traveling south along the river, bound for someplace called Pilate's Point.

Marcus caught up on back issues of the *Journal of the American Medical Association*. His work as a physician had led him to the society. He'd seen things. Possible occurrences of astral projection or clairvoyance by unconscious patients. The ubiquitous "bright light at the end of a tunnel." Were these hints of a life, and afterlife, of wonders? Or were they prosaically explainable artifacts of mundane organic processes? Marcus wanted to know.

The Gibbs case was unlike any he had undertaken. Marcus had investigated séances and haunted houses along the East

Coast. He examined a poltergeist in Key West, a serpent-handling faith healer in Appalachia, an automatic writer from Ohio farm country, and even a New England doomsday cult. He had found cheesecloth ectoplasm, rigged tables, vivid imaginations, cranks, cons, and hysterics. He had not found evidence of the spirit world or other phenomena the society studied.

After his medical journals, Marcus reviewed materials on Gibbs. An article from the *New York Sentinel,* one of many papers energizing what was being called the Harlem Renaissance, collated most of the information. Gibbs came from Gates County, Mississippi, born in the grandiosely-named Venice and raised near Pilate's Point. Marcus noted the curious spelling, P-I-L-A-T-E, as in Pontius, not P-I-L-O-T, like a steamboat navigator. Gibbs was musically talented from a young age. Furthering his career, he moved to New Orleans, frequenting its infamous Storyville district. Gibbs was murdered there, the case unsolved, a death certificate allegedly filed. He was buried back in Mississippi in the Gates County Cemetery. Afterward, sightings of Gibbs were reported in New Orleans. He later turned up in New York, where Harlem was emerging as America's musical capital.

Marcus yearned to go straight to New York and confront the trumpeter. The scientist in him knew visiting Mississippi and New Orleans to get a baseline for Gibbs was the best way to determine if the man in Harlem was the same person and, allowing the indulgence, whether he had returned from the dead.

Miles clicked away over the rails. Small towns and clusters of shacks passed by. In the wide spaces between were fields brimming with cotton and irregular patches of woodland and wilds. The Delta. Marcus saw England and France as part of his finishing after school. Had he been a little younger, he would have seen them from the trenches. Yet, in their way, London and Paris felt less exotic, less "other" than this place.

Marcus knew Pilate's Point the moment he glimpsed it. Sitting on a high bluff over the Mississippi, buildings stretched from its peak down to the base, spilling onto the surrounding flatland. Near the peak, the mansions and churches proclaimed opulence. The buildings further down, less so.

The train station sat on flatland away from the bluff. Stepping off the Jackson Bell, even after Memphis, Marcus was overwhelmed by heat and humidity. Walking into town sounded singularly unappealing.

"Afternoon," he said to the driver of a passing wagon. "Would you be willing to take a passenger into town?"

Marcus agreed to his price.

The driver smiled. "Well, Figaro likes your money," he indicated his horse. "And I like your manners. Climb in."

On the way, they talked. Bartholomew Jenkins delivered goods throughout Gates County. He had learned quite a bit about the area, sharing local lore with Marcus. In turn, Marcus circumspectly explained his errand.

"I know the Gibbs family," Bartholomew responded. "They're good people. Their spread is a couple miles northeast of Pilate's Point along old Lula Pike."

They drove high up the bluff to Marcus's hotel, in part of town Bartholomew called, "The Point."

Marcus thanked him for the ride.

"Welcome. If you need to get about while you're here, find me in Underbluff."

Drained by heat and travel, Marcus was indifferent to the Mississippian Hotel's commanding view over the river. He napped in his room until hunger woke him at twilight.

Entering the dining room, he heard an unwelcome voice.

"Hello, fishmonger."

Even before the schism between ASPR and BSPR, Theodore Fenno had no love for Marcus. Never mind Marcus's hometown of Marblehead had become a respectable suburb for Boston's elite. Never mind he was a physician with honors from Harvard Medical School. At some distant point, Marcus's people had been Cornish fisherfolk. That was enough to earn scorn from the portly Knickerbocker, whose family name was prominent on New York's social register.

"So, Boston finally decided to pay attention to the Gibbs case?"

"If the ASPR is doing so well, why are you still here?" Marcus retorted.

"No matter. Our investigation is almost complete."

Marcus wondered if it was true or if the New Yorker bluffed.

"Even with a head start, your minds would be too closed to appreciate this case," Fenno continued.

"Glad to see you're not rushing to conclusions."

Their exchange typified dialogue between the ASPR and BSPR. To the Boston Society, their New York counterparts grew dangerously credulous. From the ASPR's perspective, the Bostonians were ossified and reactionary. Each waged a constant war of words to dominate debate over supernatural phenomena. Both societies wanted to believe. In Marcus's opinion, the ASPR wanted it too much.

"Forget communicating with spirits," Fenno elaborated, "We're talking about actual bodily resurrection. No longer losing loved ones. Death abolished forever. Contemplate that. If you can." With that parting shot, his rival departed.

Marcus restrained himself. He always did with Fenno, at least since hearing gossip around headquarters.

The man's venom would not ruin his meal.

Seeking Bartholomew next morning, Marcus learned the geography of Pilate's Point. Below the patrician Point, Midtown played host to commerce and regular people. Sloping down to the river was Bartholomew's Underbluff. There, riffraff and ne'er-do-wells congregated in brothels, hovels, and speakeasies.

The driver smiled at Marcus's reappearance. They journeyed out of Pilate's Point along a rural lane to a cluster of houses too few to be called a village. Bartholomew stopped at a two-story wood-frame house.

The home was small but tidy. Flower beds accented the front yard. Two young girls played, half-heartedly tending the flowers. A vegetable garden dominated the backyard, where a woman hung washing. On the porch, an elderly woman sewed in a rocking chair.

"Can I help you, friend?"

A robust man about Marcus's age emerged from the fields. Many people might be wary finding a stranger in their yard. The man's smile said he meant the "friend."

"I'm Marcus Roads. I'm looking for the Gibbs place."

"You've found it. I'm Sampson Gibbs. Sam."

Sam and Bartholomew exchanged nods.

"I'd like to talk to you about Gabriel," Marcus asked. "Your…brother?" he ventured a guess.

The man nodded affirmatively. "Gabe? He's quite popular these days."

Sam's next remark confirmed Marcus's suspicion that Fenno had come calling, "I don't have answers for what you really want to know. But I'm happy to talk."

He invited Marcus onto the porch, adding, "Ma and pa are in town shopping." He introduced the Gibbs family. Two young men coming in from the fields were his younger brothers, Ezekiel and Enoch. Their younger sister, Hannah, was baking inside. The old woman on the rocker was Aunt Mancie, Sam's maternal great aunt. His wife, Henrietta, was the woman hanging laundry. The two girls in front were their children, Mary and Myrna.

"So, that's the family?" Marcus smiled.

"Yep," Sam's face grew solemn. "Well, except for Gabe, of course. You know about him. And my sister, Rebekah. She's not really with us anymore, either."

Wanting to keep conversation light at first, Marcus switched topics, "You've got a beautiful place."

"We've done alright," Sam replied as Henrietta served iced tea. "Dad always plants the right crops at the right time. Some folks whisper it's not quite natural. Truth is, he reads three things every day: the Bible, the almanac, and the crop futures. Not necessarily in that order."

"Before I forget," Marcus interjected, "do you have a photo of Gabriel?"

Sam nodded, handing him a family photo. The Gibbs were distinctive. Ma Gibbs and her children had delicate features and expressive eyes.

"That's Gabe," Sam said, indicating a slender youth. The smallest of the Gibbs sons, Gabe's eyes possessed a distant, dreamy quality.

"Thank you," Marcus said, returning the photo.

"Keep it. We've got a couple."

Marcus slid the photo into his jacket. "Tell me about Gabriel?"

Looking reflective, Sam began the story of his brother's life, "All us kids were born in Venice. My folks were sharecroppers then. With pa's skill and ma managing money, they put by enough to buy this place.

"Gabe was four when we moved here. He was an odd kid. Got lost in his own thoughts. He was easygoing, except when he got a notion. Then he was a mule. His music was like that. Gabriel always loved music. He'd seek it anywhere he could. Mostly, that was church.

"Being a Northern man, you don't really understand about church. You think you do, but you don't. Down here, church isn't just someplace you go on Sunday. It's the center of your life. And the Ascending Glory Tabernacle had a stronger pull than most.

"Actually, the pull was its Pastor. Jericho Cullen was larger than life: broad shouldered, balding, filled with boundless energy and enthusiasm. Always exhorting his flock to walk the righteous path. He had lots of opinions about what that meant. And the tabernacle had music. Only holy music, of course. Choir. Call and response between pastor and flock. Pastor Cullen had a fine baritone voice and was a trumpeter.

"My brother heard the pastor playing trumpet and his eyes lit up. He started demanding one of his own. For his birthday, ma and pa bought him a brass trumpet from the catalogue store.

"The moment he got his hands on that thing, Gabe was obsessed. Every evening, he'd play it in the parlor, Rebekah watching. Those two were inseparable, always together fishing, playing tag, or pinching a bit sugar cane from the field. Of us all, I think she loved him most. When he died, she died too. At least on the inside.

"Gabe got good fast. He loved showing off, holding those long, perfect notes for a minute at a time. One day, making the rounds, Pastor Cullen heard Gabe working through a piece the pastor played at church. His hard face softened. He showed my brother how to play it. They stood in the dining room playing a duet.

"After that, Pastor took Gabe under his wing. Called him 'My Little Lamb.' He had my brother perform in church every chance he got. When he did, Pastor Cullen got that warm glow he never had otherwise. During services, they'd play duets of old spirituals.

"The pastor started talking to my parents about sending Gabe to seminary when he got old enough. I think it was even in his mind to hand the tabernacle over to Gabe one day.

"Everything was unfolding like part of some bigger plan. Then pa brought home that Crosley radio…"

Sam looked up. A smartly-dressed couple walked toward them, arms laden with parcels. Ma and Pa Gibbs had returned. Spotting Marcus on the porch, Ma Gibbs's eyes went wide. "Oh no you don't! I won't have someone else spreading lies about my baby."

Yes, Theodore Fenno had been here.

Flustered, Marcus explained he was different from Fenno. He just wanted to learn about Gabriel. She would have none of it. Pa Gibbs' eyes were apologetic. They were also unyielding. "Son, I think you better leave."

As Marcus and Bartholomew returned to Pilate's Point, Marcus touched his jacket. He felt the photo, glad he asked for it at the beginning.

Next morning, information from the Gibbs family cut off, Marcus cast a broader net for informants. Engaging Bartholomew, Marcus talked with residents along Old Lula Pike. He found plenty of people who knew Gabriel. Most did not want to talk.

Some could only be persuaded with quarters or half-dollars. Marcus heard wild tales about deals with the Devil. Others said witchcraft worked through that silver trumpet, and that Gabriel robbed a grave to get it. What grave? Nobody seemed sure. Whenever he dug deeper, Marcus was disappointed. Informants credited stories to "a friend of a friend" or "everybody knows." Opinions split on whether Gibbs returned from the dead. But most found something nefarious about him, in life if not death.

One piece of intriguing information came from the rumormongers. They recalled Gabriel as a very good musician. Not a great one. How could Marcus square that with the man in Harlem?

For hard facts, Marcus needed to mend fences with the Gibbs. Fortunately, he caught a break. The next day, he found Sam Gibbs in the hotel lobby.

"Can we talk?" Sam asked. "After you left, we had a serious talk. There are lots of things we don't know about Gabe, especially after he left. We'd like to know. You seem in a position to find out. Pa said, unlike that other man, you seemed like a stand-up fellow. Ma didn't say, but I think she agrees. We'll help you on two conditions."

"Name them."

"Share anything you learn with us. And, if the person in Harlem really is Gabe, tell him to come home. Between him and Rebekah, we've lost two family members. She's in the hands of God, and the doctors, but maybe you can bring Gabe back to us.

Marcus agreed. He would ride with Bartholomew to the Gibbs place, so Sam wouldn't have to drive him back to Pilate's Point afterward.

Marcus arrived at the Gibbs' home bearing a glazed ham and a bouquet of coneflowers and black-eyed-Susans, tokens of sincerity about making peace. The family, in turn, invited him off the porch and into the parlor. If Marcus understood the complicated southern etiquette correctly, that signified their acceptance.

Sam resumed his story where he left off, "Pa brought home that Crossley," indicating the rosewood radio in one corner. "He said it was for weather and crop reports. I think he just wanted to listen to baseball. But Gabriel got the most from it. He discovered worldly music and it changed his life."

Marcus's face announced his incomprehension.

"There's a big gulf between church music and worldly music down here. Church folks call worldly music 'Devil's music' and they're not joking.

"Gabe loved it all: ballads, polkas, dance reels, blues, sometimes even the Opry out of Nashville. Especially jazz. The boy was jazz mad. Broadcasts from big Harlem nightclubs were his favorite.

"One night, we listened to Louis Armstrong playing at the Cotton Club. Fingering his trumpet along with Satchmo, Gabe turned to Rebekah and me, saying, 'I swear, someday I'll headline one of those fancy New York clubs. No matter what.'

"Pastor was a firebrand about worldly music. Even more than most. Maybe being a church musician, secular music especially appalled him. Maybe, in his heart, he was tempted. Either way, he banned secular music for his flock. We weren't supposed to listen to it at home. We sure weren't supposed to play it. Lots of families flouted that commandment outside the pastor's sight, not just us. But Gabe got careless.

"At the tabernacle, Pastor Cullen overheard Gabe playing 'Squeeze Me,' that old Fats Waller tune. It looked like the pastor was being called Home right there. He dragged Gabriel by the ear to the cane field behind the tabernacle. Pastor took a cane stalk and gave my brother the worst whupping I've ever seen. He kept repeating, 'Music cannot serve both God and Satan.' Pastor told Gabe not to return 'til he decided who

117

he served.

"Gabe hardly spoke for a week. Most folks figured it for embarrassment. I knew better. He was thinking things over. That Sunday, Gabe went to the tabernacle one last time. Interrupting the service, he shouted he was a better trumpeter than the pastor and would keep getting better, no matter who it served. To prove it, he pulled out his trumpet and played 'Squeeze Me.'

"When Gabe did that in front of the congregation, Pastor Cullen's eyes rolled back in his head and he yelled, 'Get behind me Satan, I cast thee out.' Like he was Jesus himself casting out Legion. Pastor chased Gabe from the church.

"We were pariahs at the tabernacle for a while. Ma took it hard, especially the whispering behind our backs. Eventually, we were let back. Nobody mentioned Gabe. But the whispers continued.

"Gabe threw himself into music. He'd practice by day and play country dances, Underbluff speakeasies, or Colonel Scobie's fancy parties for money at night. But there was more than that. He took to wandering. Folks spotted him at odd hours all over the county. About that time, the silver trumpet showed up, too.

"We knew what folks were saying. Whenever we asked Gabe, he kept his lips shut. He knew what they said, too. He told us he hadn't gone to the crossroads, but that's all we got. Where he went, what he did, and where that trumpet came from, we hadn't a clue.

"Everything came to a head when King Oliver came to town. To promote his new recordings, Gennett Records sent him all over the country judging jazz trumpet contests. The prize was $10. Each local contest winner played against the King for $100. Of course, nobody won that prize. Well, almost nobody...

"Gabe showed up. He wasn't alone. Every trumpet blower in Gates County came. One contestant took everyone's breath away just by being there. Pastor Cullen, after everything he'd said about worldly music. I figure his pride couldn't abide it if Gabriel was named Gates County's best trumpeter. That, I guess, meant more to the pastor than anything else.

"From the first, the real contest was between Gabe and the pastor. They played like men possessed, like their lives depended on it. In a way, maybe they did. Both were magnificent. But Gabe knew jazz better. Maybe he wanted it more, too. When the last note faded, King Oliver declared my brother the winner.

"Pastor Cullen staked everything and lost. He knew it. His flock knew it too. He tried to keep the tabernacle going. But folks drifted away. With a year gone by, the tabernacle's doors shut. Pastor Cullen became a recluse and eventually disappeared. Rumor says he's preaching somewhere else now: Clarksdale, Panther Burn, Tutwiler, maybe down in Jackson.

"Squaring off against King Oliver, Gabe did something risky, playing nothing but the King's own tunes. In most ways, he just matched King Oliver. But everyone thrilled at his long, bold notes. Gabe held them longer and stronger than the King could. Red Allen, King Oliver's junior trumpeter, judged the contest. He had to acknowledge his own bandleader was beaten by Gabe.

"Gabe took that $100 and made his way to New Orleans. 'The bigtime,' as he said."

A knock at the door interrupted Sam's tale.

"Sorry to disturb you folks," Bartholomew apologized, "but I've got deliveries that need making."

Returning to Pilate's Point, Marcus turned to the driver, "Do you think Gabriel went to the crossroads?"

"I don't rightly know," Bartholomew answered, "Does it

really matter?"

"What do you mean?"

"It seems like bargains folks make with themselves mean as much to them as ones they make with God or Ol' Scratch."

Marcus asked another question, "People say 'the' crossroads, not 'a' crossroads. Is it a specific place or can it be any crossroads?"

"I reckon any crossroads might do," Bartholomew paused, "but there's one on Old Terraplane Highway. You'd know it if you saw it. But it's not a place for decent folk to linger."

They lapsed into silence until back in town.

"Bartholomew, do you work every day?"

"Every day except Sunday."

"That's tomorrow."

"Yep."

"I'd like to relax, see a few sights. Can I hire Figaro and the wagon for the day? I'll get him back to you Monday morning."

Seeing the driver hesitate, Marcus flashed a $20 gold piece.

"That would be just fine."

Marcus felt badly for deceiving the man about his intentions.

Picking up horse and wagon the following morning, Marcus discovered a hitch in his plans. Stores in Pilate's Point closed on Sunday. Nevertheless, Marcus required certain items for the day's activities. Instead, he "liberated" what was needed: canvas tarp, crowbar, hooded lantern, pick, and shovel. *In the name of science*, he told himself. Hanging the lantern from the wagon, he loaded the tools in the bed alongside items Bartholomew was scheduled to deliver tomorrow. Not wanting awkward question, Marcus covered his acquisitions with canvas.

No expert driver, Marcus could still manage a wagon along Gates County's sleepy byways. As Pilate's Point faded into the distance, he followed directions from Sam.

The Ascending Glory Tabernacle was a long, narrow box. A covered porch protected double doors at one end. An obelisk-like steeple jutted heavenward at the other. Whitewash peeled from weathered boards. Weeds, brambles, and sickly sunflowers grew on its grounds. Only the churchyard remained well-tended.

Leaving the tabernacle, Marcus guided Figaro along the dusty rural path called Old Terraplane Highway to where a rutted dirt track intersected the road. Though he had passed several such crossroads, a twisted oak set this one apart. As Marcus approached, other differences appeared. Opposite the tree were low mounds with faded wooden crosses. Graves, Marcus realized. In traditions that, clearly, had not fully died out here, those considered unworthy of hallowed ground were often interred at crossroads.

Various objects adorned the tree, primarily candles and liquor bottles, especially rum. A few other items stood out. A heart-shaped locket dangled from a branch. A knife protruded from the earth at the oak's roots. A ragdoll moldered nearby.

Past the crossroad, Old Terraplane Highway rejoined the main road. Marcus traveled eastward to Venice, Gabriel's birthplace. He arrived late in the afternoon. Nobody among that sad collection of tarpaper shacks recalled much about the Gibbs. Marcus turned the wagon around. Darkness descending, he lit the lantern.

Homeward bound, Marcus passed the crossroad again. By night, the gnarled oak assumed a sinister shape. Wind teased grass atop unhallowed graves and caused the oak's branches to reach for him. The Delta had a power, one Marcus also encountered in pockets of New England, rendering the mundane damnably suggestive. Little wonder the region was so steeped in folklore. It didn't make his final task, the real reason for his solo excursion, any more appealing.

His pocket watch showed it was after midnight when the wagon stopped along the faded wooden sign proclaiming "Gates County Cemetery, Est. 1898." He hooded the lantern so it cast only a thin beam. After cleaning his glasses several times, Marcus removed the tarp, revealing the crowbar, shovel, and pick in the wagon's bed.

To determine if a man documented as dead had returned to the living, Marcus resigned himself, it was useful to know what his grave contained. Not allowing himself time to think, he set about his repellent task.

Carrying tools from the wagon, noises behind Marcus brought him to a halt. Horrified, he watched a figure emerge from the bushes. Of all the people he might expect to encounter here, Aunt Mancie was not among them. In the lamplight, the matriarch appeared far more vigorous than on the Gibbs' porch.

"Aunt Mancie, what are you doing here?"

"I reckoned you'd turn up here sooner or later."

"How?"

"If I wanted to see if someone was alive or dead, I'd look here. And, if you're opening my grandnephew's grave, it seems a family member should bear witness."

"You didn't tell the others?"

"They might have stopped you."

"You're not going to?"

"I'm curious, too."

Digging up a grave was among the hardest, dirtiest things Marcus had done. Hours later, he bent over the exposed coffin of Gabriel Gibbs, holding his crowbar. Standing over the hole,

Mancie cradled the pick as if on guard. On guard against what? Marcus didn't ask. He was pretty sure he didn't want to know.

The coffin's lid opened smoothly, it had been forced before. The coffin was unoccupied, its upholstered interior unsoiled. A body had not lain here, or not lain long enough for decay to leave its mark.

Examining the interior revealed dark hairs and a small fingernail ripped from its owner during some epic endeavor. Breaking out? Breaking in? That was the question. But someone had been here. If not Gabriel, who? And to what purpose? Marcus pocketed the samples, hoping his companion would not notice.

"Can I offer you a ride?" he asked Mancie after covering evidence of their deed.

"I hoped you were that much of gentleman."

Marcus enjoyed the ride. Mancie had a lively intellect and great curiosity. She questioned Marcus about Boston and his career as a physician. She inquired into his work with the society, appreciating his answers better than most people. In return, she regaled him with local folklore: giant snakes, Hill Folk, Ol' Bloody Bones, Rougaroux, the Singing River, Skunk Apes, Two-Toed Tom, and variations of the ubiquitous ghosts, vampires, and witches.

"Do you believe in those things?"

"Anything's possible. What's likely is another matter," pausing, she added, "But I have a few opinions that might surprise you."

As conversation drifted toward Gabriel, Mancie supplied the remaining Gates County part of the tale.

"When Gabriel reached New Orleans, he wrote us that he was playing someplace called L'Original. He didn't say so, but we knew it was just some Storyville bawdyhouse. Not much came after that. One day, we got the telegram saying he died. Was murdered. Rebekah went to down to bring him home.

"When she got back, there was an awful fuss. Pastor Cullen had gone and the tabernacle shut, but a lot of people didn't want Gabriel in the churchyard. They still told those stories about him. We had to bury him in that county cemetery.

"Poor Rebekah was never right again. Just slipped into her own world. She chatted with Gabriel like he was there beside her. Like her brother, she took to wandering. Soon after, she disappeared. We got a letter from the State Hospital telling us Rebekah had been found, senseless, over in Panola County and been committed. Every so often we get a letter from her. Every so often we write. But she's not what you'd call lucid.

"A year gone by, we started hearing rumors. Someone spotted Gabriel in New Orleans. Or Jackson. Then New York. Gabriel, or whoever, was playing that silver trumpet and telling folks he'd 'come back.' We didn't know what to make of it. None of us have seen him. But a lot of folks have their notions and know exactly what they make of it."

Three sets of headlights blinded Figaro and his passengers. In the glare, Marcus made out three Model T automobiles and a dozen men. There were words for a group like this, a " mob."

"Look a damn Yankee," one shouted, pronouncing the last two words as one. Their comments about Mancie were less savory. The mob closed towards the wagon.

Mancie looked at Marcus. "How good are you at driving a wagon?"

When Marcus hesitated, Mancie grabbed the reins, swinging the wagon around in a single motion. With a stern "Get!" she sent Figaro pulling them down the road at backbreaking speed.

Rushing to their automobiles, the men gave chase.

"Climb into the bed and see if anything there will do us any good!"

Doing so, he examined Bartholomew's goods. Along with the tools he brought, Marcus found loose lumber and two barrels. One contained clout nails, likely part of the same load as the lumber. The second was full of flour. Marcus grinned.

He tilted the second barrel against backboard, tipping out 300 lbs. of flour. A cloud of flour dust now hung over the road. Marcus could not see his pursuers. Hopefully, the reverse was also true. He dumped the other barrel as well. About a fourth of the short-shafted, broad-headed nails landed point upward.

The cars roared out from the dust cloud and over the nails. Staccato sequences of hollow pops proclaimed the death of tires. The first automobile came to a hard stop in a ditch. The second spun out of control, landing on its side. Men scrambled from the wreck. Witnessing the fate of its fellows, the third Model T swerved into the fields, avoiding the hazard, before returning to the road.

Fortunately, Gates County's rutted dirt roads were as hard on automobiles as horses. Driving Figaro as fiercely as she could, Mancie maintained their lead. Unfortunately, horses tired. Automobiles didn't.

As the road passed through woods, Mancie shouted to Marcus, "Follow my lead!" Standing on the buckboard, reins in one hand, she hiked up her skirt with the other. With a wild yell, she leapt onto Figaro's back.

Moving to the buckboard, Marcus hesitated. The five foot jump looked impossibly distant.

"Let me suggest that this is an excellent time to grow a pair!"

Marcus jumped. Landing hard on the animal's back, Marcus concluded no, it was distinctly not a good a time to grow a pair.

Unhitching Figaro from the wagon, Mancie grabbed Marcus's arm and put it around her waist. She drove the horse off into the trees. Behind them, Marcus heard the Model T screech to a halt, its occupants cursing.

Mancie guided Figaro through woods and fields on an oblique route to town. Safely in Underbluff, as Marcus hitched Figaro outside of Bartholomew's, he observed Mancie studying him.

"Everything fine?" he asked.

He couldn't quite make out her response, spoken to herself more than Marcus. He thought she said, "Just wondering if you're old enough for me."

Mancie spent the night with a family friend in Midtown. Marcus dragged himself back to the Mississippian. At first light, he checked on her. Sore, but otherwise unharmed, the pair strolled and discussed the previous evening's events. As they walked, Marcus spied a familiar face. It was the limp that drew his attention. A limp acquired, no doubt, when his Model T overturned the night before.

The man didn't notice him until Marcus put a hand on his shoulder and spun him around. The leg gave out and the man collapsed to the ground. Deducing the leg must be bad indeed, Marcus had an idea.

"I don't believe we've been introduced," Marcus grinned as he put his full weight on the limb. "We met last night."

Wincing with pain, the man nodded.

"You know I'm a doctor?"

He shook his head.

"The way you're reacting, I'd wager that leg has a bad

fracture. There's a good chance you'll lose it unless you have doctor set it. Do you have money for a doctor?"

Again, the man shook his head.

"I'll set that bone for you, if you tell me about last night. Do we have an understanding?"

He nodded warily.

Marcus rigged a splint from handy materials and the contents of his black bag. As Marcus worked, the man spilled his guts. He and his companions were paid to scare Marcus, maybe rough him up a bit, but not do any real harm.

"Who paid you?" Marcus demanded.

"Some other Damn Yankee." Again, the last two words were pronounced as one.

"Oh," Marcus replied, his voice venomous. The man held up his end of the bargain. Marcus turned him loose.

"That took nerve, threatening a man with losing his leg," Mancie said approvingly.

"It would, if it was true," Marcus answered. "That's not how you treat a fracture. He has nothing but a bad sprain. Not that he needed to know that."

Mancie laughed. "Marcus Roads, I believe you may do alright out in the world."

Marcus stormed into the Mississippian. Time had come for a reckoning with his colleague from New York. Unfortunately, Theodore Fenno had departed.

"Checked out two days ago," the manager said, adding "I have a telegram for you."

TF in New Orleans. Wrap up Mississippi and follow. WFP.

Marcus didn't wonder how Walter Franklin Prince knew Fenno was in New Orleans. Prince had a mole at American Society for Psychical Research headquarters. Of course,

Marcus assumed the ASPR had a mole in Boston as well.

Marcus reflected on the situation. There were plenty of things about Gibbs' life in Gates County he didn't understand. But nothing suggested the puzzle's crucial pieces would be found here. It was time to follow Prince's telegram, and Gabriel's footsteps, to New Orleans.

New Orleans; September 10th, 1929

From Pilate's Point, Marcus took the Jackson Bell south. He considered stopping at the train's namesake. The Mississippi State Hospital was in Whitfield, near Jackson. Visiting Rebekah Gibbs might prove insightful. But without knowing anything about her condition, and with the telegram from Prince urging him to New Orleans, Marcus remained onboard.

Hours later, he pulled into New Orleans, one of the country's most distinctive cities. Nowhere else did America's peoples, languages, histories, and even architectures mix so freely, if not always peaceably. As a physician, Marcus knew New Orleans for other reasons. Of America's major cities, none was less salubrious. Yellow fever, cholera, smallpox, typhus, even plague, all paid occasional calls here.

Less than a mile separated the station from the stately Hotel Roosevelt. Even at twilight, the heat and humidity made Pilate's Point feel mild. Despite Prince's exhortations, Marcus was unable to begin investigating that evening. After a long soak in the ample bathtub, he slept as he hadn't since Boston.

Marcus's investigation began at the Orleans Parish Medical Examiner's office. As a doctor, Marcus had little trouble obtaining Gabriel's death certificate. The body of Gabriel Gibbs, male, 21, was discovered in St. Louis Cemetery Number One, the morning of February fourth, 1928. Cause of death was a gunshot wound to the head. Estimated time of death was sometime the previous day. A person named Rose Metairie had identified the body.

The certificate was helpful, especially if he could find Ms. Metairie, but hardly decisive. Marcus hoped talking with the coroner would jog the man's memory. The medical examiner was a harried man with thick spectacles. Underneath his white coat, stained with substances Marcus could identify but preferred not to, he donned a fashionable suit.

Marcus summarized the death certificate and asked if he remembered anything else.

Squinting, the coroner scrutinized the document. "If that's what I wrote," he replied, "that's what it was."

"Anything else you recall?"

"Can't say I do. Otherwise, I would have put it there."

"Surely…"

"Welcome to the murder capital of America, Dr. Roads," the coroner said ruefully. "I've worked hundreds of homicides, and thousands of autopsies, since this one. I'm sorry, but I've no memory of the case."

Marcus couldn't fault the coroner.

"I really am sorry. Perhaps you'd have better luck with the police." His tone suggested it was equally likely to snow today.

The police were Marcus's next stop anyway. Their official report added little new information. Cemetery groundskeepers discovered the body. It noted Gibbs' involvement, according to locals, with criminal and/or occult elements in Storyville. Though the case remained open, the file's most recent notes dated from just days after the murder.

Marcus located a lieutenant and sergeant who worked the case. "If it's the one I'm thinking of," the sergeant replied, "the body was between two tombs."

"Anything else?"

129

The lieutenant repeated the coroner's words about New Orleans being America's murder capital.

"Lots of folks get killed in St. Louis Number One. I guess folks want to save them the trip." While the sergeant chuckled at his own joke, the lieutenant had the grace to look embarrassed. Perhaps only to get Marcus to go away, the sergeant unexpectedly made himself useful. "If it's the one I'm thinking of, that photographer fellow was there. Bellocq. Talk to him."

"Bellocq?" Marcus inquired.

"E.J. Bellocq. Storyville's unofficial photographer. He's got a studio on North Robertson."

Commercial photography and traditional portraiture lined the walls of Ernest Joseph Bellocq's studio. After Marcus explained the nature of his inquiry, different photos came out. The silver-haired French Creole's private collection contained pictures of Storyville brothels and portraits of its working girls. Marcus admired his technique. Treating subjects polite society didn't acknowledge existed, Bellocq's photos were both candid and humanizing.

The man was another matter. Despite his urbane French Louisianan accent and foppish attire, Marcus found something off about the photographer. He laughed in the wrong places. He maintained eye contact too long or too briefly. And there was the private collection within his private collection. Bellocq photographed more than a few murders and seemed especially proud of his photos of the infamous New Orleans Axeman's victims. His memory, however, was acute. When Marcus said "Gabriel Gibbs," Bellocq quickly produced the photo.

A body lay in grass between two opulent mausoleums. Marcus had spent a lot of time looking at the photo acquired from Sam Gibbs. He had no doubt Bellocq's photo showed Gabriel Gibbs. The man had died. One question answered. As to whether he came back…

His physician's eye caught something else. When the heart stopped beating, gravity pulled blood downward. As a result, body parts closest to the ground appeared flushed and darkened. But Gabriel's upper parts were flushed. That meant he was killed elsewhere and put in the cemetery after.

"Can I purchase this from you?" Marcus inquired.

"Have it. If I want pictures of bodies in St. Louis Number One, I won't need to wait long." He laughed. "If you want one of my Axeman photos, we can talk price."

Thinking one photo of a body was more than enough, Marcus excused himself.

Passing the St. James Hotel on his way to the Roosevelt, a bad penny turned up.

"The fishmonger." Theodore Fenno smirked, exiting the St. James. Of course Fenno was staying in the one hotel more prestigious than the Roosevelt.

"You son of a bitch," Marcus hissed. "That stunt in Mississippi could have killed me."

"Quit being melodramatic. I gave strict instructions not to hurt you. This is a serious game, if you can't play dirty, maybe you should go home."

"Fenno," Marcus said, walking away, "you sure you want to play dirty with a dirty fishmonger?"

The New Yorker had the sense to look worried.

Marcus knew he should pity the man. Fenno's son, Edward, was the only thing Theodore ever truly loved. Edward went to France with the Aviation Section during the Great War. His life ended in some farmer's field. Edward's death destroyed Theodore. It also brought him to the ASPR.

131

Spiritualism offered a link with Edward. Fenno needed spiritualism to be real.

Yes, the world should pity Theodore Fenno. But the man made that well neigh impossible.

That night, Marcus braved America's most notorious neighborhood. Storyville was a collection of brothels, speakeasies, and music halls serving the high and low alike. It was a hotbed for jazz, a pilgrimage location for those seeking America's modern music. Many of Storyville's establishments occupied mansions and townhouses that, like their current occupants, had fallen from respectability. Revelers packed the streets. Conversations, shouts, and music merged into a Dionysian roar, punctuated by the occasional unsettling scream.

The area also smelt faintly of urine.

Originally known as "The District," it became "Storyville" in dubious tribute to Alderman Sidney Story, the area's political protector and benefactor. In 1917, the city made prostitution illegal. Rumors said the brothels, like the bars three years later, merely went underground.

L'Original, the establishment where Gabriel wrote his family he played, occupied a nineteenth century townhouse. Flanking its crenelated doorframe, two gaslights glowed through panes of red glass. No, the oldest profession hadn't gone far underground at all.

Warmly but dimly lit, leather couches and scarlet drapes filled the establishment. House girls, attired to display their assets, fraternized with patrons to entice them upstairs, where "business" was transacted. A jazz quartet played on a small stage and a formidable bar lined one wall.

Marcus questioned L'Original's working girls, bartenders, bouncers, and regular patrons for what he might glean of

Gabriel Gibbs. They recalled a great trumpet player who improved steadily. He was described as polite and kind. If he got a little wild sometimes, that was nothing exceptional by Storyville's forgiving benchmarks. But his focus was always music. In addition to L'Original, he played anywhere people paid him. This included "revels" in bayous south of the city. These seemed to be part bacchanal and part occult ritual, though their vague descriptions left Marcus surmising such events were more widely known than attended.

The topic led to discussion of two love affairs involving Gabriel. When Gabriel started playing the revels, he got involved with Queen Lola, a "Gris-Gris Queen" in the swamps who held revels every Friday. His informants intimated that Queen Lola had a temper and might already have "disappeared" a beau or two. Of course, they hinted, she could do worse things than killing a man, provided she allowed him the privilege of staying dead.

That got Marcus's attention but, attempting to learn more, his informants turned cagey. A few suggested something similar but contrary, that Queen Lola could have brought her lover back to achieve his musical ambitions.

Nobody seemed to know how to contact Queen Lola.

As an outsider, they warned, it was dangerous to try.

Later, Gabriel became involved with a house girl and occasional singer at L'Original. Marcus knew her name. Rose Metairie, who had identified Gabriel's body. She was also linked romantically with someone named Luc de Amant, a major figure in Storyville's business community or underworld. If there was a difference. At one time, de Amant owned the property occupied by L'Original.

Rose, the staff told him, was now a singer at the Moulin. Perhaps she remained a demimondaine or adventuress, but she was no longer just a house girl.

Informants considered Gabriel's death tragic. Beyond that, Marcus found little agreement. Some thought he got too involved with the occult. Others said it was related to endless turf wars waged by Storyville's gangs. Some observed, "These things happen in the District."

After Gabriel's death, his silver trumpet turned up in a Storyville pawnshop. That the instrument disappeared following a burglary during which the pawnshop's owner was murdered seemed a little too convenient. But what did it mean?

A final piece of information came from the staff. Gabriel never played L'Original after his mysterious reappearance. To their recollection, he never set foot inside the establishment. When they heard him play elsewhere, "Resurrection" Gibbs was distant with his former associates. But his music cased to be merely great. It was the best trumpet playing they ever heard.

Leaving L'Original, the night was young, at least by Storyville's clock. There might be time to catch Rose Metairie. Larger and fancier than L'Original, an enormous windmill graced the Moulin's roof. The establishment served as a house of assignation, where patrons and prostitutes met to arrange meetings, but in the main, it was a speakeasy and nightclub, not a brothel.

Rose was performing when Marcus entered. A striking octoroon woman with perceptive, almond-shaped eyes and curves reminding him of a Mesopotamian fertility figurine, Marcus understood Gabriel's interest. He listened to her sultry alto renditions of jazz numbers, including "Ain't Misbehavin'," "Honeysuckle Rose," "Sweet Lorraine," and "The Ballad of Mack the Knife."

After her set, Marcus bought the singer a drink and inquired about Gibbs. Rose acknowledged she and Gabriel knew each other from L'Original and had courted a few times. But it was nothing serious, she said, adding they were never close.

Accounts from L'Original's staff flatly contradicted that. Rose's guarded demeanor, stiff body language, and reluctance to make eye contact all also suggested deception. But he possessed no real authority or way to compel truthfulness. Marcus elected to call it a night.

Conversation at L'Original made it clear that untangling the strands of Gabriel's life in New Orleans necessitated a better understanding of Voodoo. He had read a little of Louisiana's syncretic faith. While not a primary concern for either BSPR or ASPR, pertinent articles circulated occasionally in their journals. He knew better than to trust them. He needed someone local.

The Roosevelt's concierge directed Marcus to a shop on Decatur Street. The proprietress, a woman with wild hair, red dress, and countless bangles, greeted him enthusiastically. Before Marcus could explain his errand, she began proffering love charms, brick dust, "authentic" graveyard dirt, fortunes told, and charms and curses for a thousand purposes. Marcus recognized patter when he heard it, doubting he'd find the needed answers here.

Leaving the shop, he heard a voice say "You're looking for something."

Scanning the crowd, Marcus beheld a diminutive man whose age might be anywhere from thirty to seventy. "You're looking for something and didn't find it there," the man repeated, puffing on a pipe. It was a statement, not a question. "I will help you," he added, his enigmatic smile revealing crooked teeth.

Marcus was willing, but grew nervous as the man led him

through a maze of backstreets and alleyways. Only pride's refusal to admit the small man intimidated him, and acknowledgement he was completely lost, prevented Marcus from backing out. They ended in a back alley bodega. Jars of herbs and powders lined rickety shelves. Colored candles piled in crates. A handful of nondescript cloth dolls hung from pegs. An elegant wooden alter that could have come from some venerable Latin American church stood in total contrast.

"What's with the altar? I thought voodoo worshiped…" he fished for the correct term, "loa."

"Not exactly," the man began. "Loa are not gods, not the way you mean. Voodoo is monotheistic. Our god is benevolent but distant. Loa are intercessors, like Saints. That's why, when my people were forced to the Americas, they easily combined loa and saints. All people tell the same stories, with the same actors, whatever masks they wear."

Marcus had read Jung. Hearing the Swiss scholar succinctly paraphrased by the little man surprised him.

Setting down the pipe, his informant produced a bottle of rum, two glasses, and cigars.

"I don't smoke, thank you." Admittedly a quirk, Marcus had the notion smoking was not healthy.

"If we discuss loa, we honor them with rum and cigars." When the man insisted, Marcus complied.

In an ancient book, the man pointed to evocative woodcuts scattered amongst the archaic French print as he described major loa to Marcus: Damballah, the all-knowing sky serpent; Maitresse Erzulie, loa of love, beauty, fertility; Marinette, wise, powerful, and terrible in her wrath; Ogou, the brave warrior; the dread Baron Samedi, loa of death and the dead; and others. He finished with Papa Legba, humanity's great intercessor and opener of ways.

"Legba likes you," the man laughed unevenly, "a solver of

puzzles, you, too, are an opener of ways."

Cigar smoke must have made Marcus heady. He could not remember telling the man about himself, what he did, or of his errand in New Orleans.

"I don't mean to offend, but many people think voodoo is evil."

"No, but it is different from the religion you know. Loa are not so tight-fisted with the spirit world's power. That power can be used. It can also be misused. And some people call anything in Louisiana they don't understand 'Voodoo.' Many things are here beside Voodoo. Most are benign, others less so."

"Would putting a fingernail in a coffin have any significance in Voodoo?"

The man frowned. "No. It wouldn't."

Marcus asked another question bearing on his investigation. "Can voodoo bring people back from the dead?"

"A few have that power, after a fashion. But it revives only the body, not the mind. Such a creature could not do what you ask."

Marcus knew he said nothing about Gabriel or his abilities. Had Theodore been here? Could this man be another of his agents?

"How do you know so much about me?" Marcus demanded, trying to stand. His legs buckled and head swam. Clearly, the man had slipped him a mickey. Struggling to remain conscious, Marcus dimly noticed crashing to the floor.

Marcus awoke on his bed at the Roosevelt. His head hurt. Rolling over to get out of bed, his side burned. Removing his shirt, Marcus discovered a tattoo across his left pectoral. The unfamiliar symbol resembled a Greek cross surrounded by four smaller crosses in circles bordered with other flourishes.

Marcus sought the concierge, inquiring how he returned to the Roosevelt. "You were unconscious behind the hotel. Two porters carried you to your room," he explained in tones suggesting that Marcus was not the caliber of guest the Roosevelt aspired to.

"Do you know what this is?" Marcus asked, showing him the tattoo.

"I'm sure I don't," his demeanor grew more disdainful.

Suspecting he knew who would, Marcus returned to the first Voodoo shop. It proprietress brightened at his reappearance, resuming her pitch. Revealing the tattoo, Marcus asked if she recognized it.

"It is the veve, the symbol, of Legba," she responded warily.

From viewing Marcus as a mark, she now plainly wanted him to leave.

Marcus visited the Canal Street offices of the *Times-Picayune*. Talking his way into the morgue, the newspaper's repository of issues back to 1837, Marcus sought information on the pawnshop robbery. He found it in the March ninth, 1928 issue, a month after Gabriel's death. Marcus expected an earlier date. On the night of March seventh, a person or persons forced entry into Storyville's Trois-Balles pawnshop and killed its owner, Luc de Amant. Marcus recognized the name of L'Original's former landlord and Rose's other paramour. Police surmised the intruders may have been surprised to find de Amant still at the shop and the murder may not have been premeditated.

"Only a few items were stolen," the story noted, leading police to believe the robbers sought something specific.

Marcus read ahead a few issues until he found de Amant's

obituary. The man was no simple pawnshop owner. At one point, his family owned much of what became Storyville, including the properties occupied by both Moulin and L'Original. De Amant sold most of that property, retaining only the pawnshop and the family's Basin Street mansion. The obituary noted he was a generous supporter of temperance organizations as well as groups that pushed through the criminalization of prostitution. That struck Marcus. In his experience, it was unusual for individuals to act against their material interests.

Leaving the *Times-Picayune,* Marcus wandered to the address given for the Trois-Balles pawnshop. He found the establishment still in business. Display cases of appliances, jewelry, and musical instruments filled the shop. Marcus attempted to engage the clerk in conversation, steering discussion toward the burglary and de Amant's murder. When it became clear the man regarded Marcus as, at best, a kook and, at worst, shady, Marcus departed.

He spent the following day visiting Gabriel's former bandmates and residences. The task took Marcus to areas making Storyville feel like Beacon Hill. Individuals who knew Gabriel before his death remembered the kind, gregarious man recalled at L'Original. The musician seemed different "after." He kept to himself, seldom staying long in one place. "Resurrection" Gibbs was a very private man.

As he departed a fleabag flophouse, darkness already falling, six large men surrounded Marcus. They showcased the diversity of New Orleans' population, the only admirable thing which could be said of the brutes. Marcus froze as one pressed a gun against his back. As his unwanted companions swept him into a rusting Nash Ajax, Marcus quietly maligned Theodore Fenno's entire lineage. The car rattled and belched smoke as it roared through crowded streets.

The Ajax pulled between two derelict riverfront warehouses. A white Morris Oxford idled nearby. The fancy British import contrasted starkly with the decaying industrial neighborhood around it. The brutes rushed Marcus out of Ajax, toward the Mississippi. A man resembling an elegantly-dressed bulldog stepped from the Morris. From the photo in the *Times-Picayune* obituary, he reminded Marcus of a younger version of the late Luc de Amant.

"You've been asking questions about Uncle Luc," the bulldog said. "Messing with things that are none of your business. I've got to stop it. Permanently."

Fenno wasn't to blame. Marcus cursed his own recklessness. Even if nothing else tipped this man off, visiting the pawnshop was a fool's errand. Hoping to play for time, Marcus played a hunch. "Gabriel discovered what you two were up to, didn't he? You killed him for it."

"If that bitch has been running her mouth…not the first time Uncle Luc's soft spot for skirts has made trouble. She'll get hers later." Returning to the Morris, he turned to his goons. "Take care of this for me."

So much for playing for time.

"Put him in St. Louis Number One when we're done, boss?" asked the thugs' leader, a gold-toothed ogre whose thin brogue argued that his parents had seen Eire.

"No. People might ask questions about this one. Strip him and dump him in the river." With that the nephew departed.

As gold-tooth held his gun on Marcus, the others roughly removed his clothes. One halted, eyes widening as he regarded Marcus's chest. The tattoo, Marcus realized. "Oh no. Oh no!" the man repeated. The others followed his gaze.

"I'm not messing with no Gris-Gris shit!"

"Come on, boys. We're not getting paid enough for this,"

gold-tooth concluded. They disappeared, leaving Marcus alone on the riverbank.

He suspected Rose Metairie, Gabriel's love interest turned songbird, was the "bitch" the nephew mentioned. Unless he moved quickly, the singer faced mortal danger. As he burst into the Moulin, Rose appeared surprised, and irritated, by Marcus's reappearance. Before she reacted further, he grabbed her wrist.

"De Amant's nephew is on his way. He thinks you've talked about what happened to Gabriel. We've got to get you someplace safe!"

Her expression gravely serious, Rose nodded. Marcus hailed a cab to the Garden District. Leaving Storyville behind, he turned to Rose. "Now will you'll tell me what really happened?"

"Luc had some scheme to get rich off land speculating in the District, something he'd been nursing for years," Rose began, trying to remain calm. "Getting rid of Alderman Story was part of it. Gabriel overheard Luc and his boys planning the hit. There's a regular at L'Original who's a city hall man. Marcus got him to warn the alderman. Must have worked, 'cause Story's still walking on God's green earth."

Face in hands, Rose started crying. "When Gabriel left that night, I went to Luc and told him someone warned Story. I thought doing him a good turn, he might do me one. And he did. He got me out of that working house and turned me into a proper singer. I never mentioned Gabriel. But he must have worked it out and Gabriel died." She sobbed. "I killed him. I killed Gabriel. When he came back, I couldn't face him. I thought he'd have it in for me."

"You did not kill him." Marcus awkwardly put his arm around the woman. "De Amant chose to try to kill Story. And he chose to kill Gabriel. You're not guilty of anything other than wanting a better life," Marcus said. That wasn't entirely true, she had been dangerously naïve. Saying so wouldn't have helped either of them.

In his notebook, Marcus had an address in the Garden District for a local sympathetic to the BSPR. A retired police inspector Prince met at a conference in St. Louis years earlier, John Legrasse. He struck Marcus as a straight shooter. Certainly, the man showed aplomb when a well-dressed Yankee and Storyville singer banged on his door after dark. Pouring out his tale, Marcus had the impression it wasn't strangest thing Legrasse had heard.

"That'd be 'Big Jim' Kessler," Legrasse said after Marcus described the man who'd casually ordered his death. "Yeah, he's de Amant's nephew. He's well-known to police, but too rich and too well-bred to take down."

Marcus and the investigator put their heads together. Luc de Amant sold his family's Storyville properties when prices were sky high. He must have had a pile of cash. New Orleans' guardians of public morality, not content with outlawing prostitution and alcohol, wanted Storyville razed to the ground. If that happened, land values would plummet and de Amant could snap up most of the District with his cash. When the area was redeveloped, he'd make his money back ten times over.

One thing stood in his way. Sidney Story embodied that uniquely Louisiana breed of politician: a smooth, probably even crooked, operator genuinely beloved by his constituents. As long as Story lived, Storyville was safe. De Amant, they surmised, aimed to remove him from the equation.

After piecing the man's machinations together, they turned to immediate matters. Tomorrow, the inspector would take Rose to the police to tell her story.

"She'll be safe," the inspector concluded. "If anything

happened to her afterward, it would be too high profile, too easy to tie to Big Jim." Beyond that, he was not optimistic. "This is New Orleans. I'd bet everything I have on Big Jim walking or getting slapped on the wrist. If years in law enforcement taught me anything, it's take your wins where you find them."

Marcus wanted another win before leaving town. Other than seeking Queen Lola, which Legrasse agreed was a risky proposition, he'd run out of leads. The investigation would shift to New York, where Theodore Fenno had the advantage. Marcus wanted to neutralize that. Besides, he owed the man payback.

In the morning, Marcus entered the Orleans Parish Commission for Public Health and Hygiene. "I'm Dr. Marcus Roads," he introduced himself to a clerk, "a physician licensed to practice by the Commonwealth of Massachusetts. Yesterday, at the St. James, I encountered a man displaying symptoms of yellow fever. I recommend quarantine until his condition is determined. His name is Theodore Fenno."

NEW YORK CITY, SEPTEMBER 21ST, 1929

Reversing his route over the rails that brought him to New Orleans, Marcus arrived in New York. After rural Mississippi and far-flung but low-lying New Orleans, the city's manmade canyons of iron, stone, and glass required readjustment.

Stepping out of the Martinique Hotel, Marcus discovered the southern weather followed him. The city sweltered and the papers were filled by the deaths of the very old and very young. Dangers other than heat, his cabbie informed him, stalked Harlem. A fiend dubbed "The Broadway Butcher" had killed a dozen young men in the neighborhood. His depredations were not confined to Broadway. But reporters, fond of sensationalist alliteration, found the moniker irresistible.

Marcus tracked down the names of a few places Gabriel had stayed and clubs where he played. There, Marcus got more names, leading to still more names. Like post-resurrection Gabriel in New Orleans, the musician took single rooms and seldom stayed anywhere more than a week. Gabriel even turned down rent-free living arrangements with other musicians. Whatever his secret, he clearly valued privacy.

Praise for the man's musicianship, however, was uniformly superlative.

Everyone here knew the story of Gabriel returning from the dead. They either didn't care or treated him as a local celebrity for it. Perhaps not knowing Gibbs before he came back made a difference but, in contrast with New Orleans, people here seemed content to take Gabriel's money or perform with him, alive or dead.

From the musicians, Marcus acquired information shedding light on Gabriel's Gates County exploits. In jazz circles, it was an open secret King Oliver suffered from advanced gum disease. No longer able to hold a firm embouchure, his playing suffered. Most of the King's radio and record solos were, in fact, performed by Red Allen. While no mean feat, Gabriel's besting King Oliver was not as miraculous as it sounded.

Marcus also learned he was not the only party actively inquiring about Gabriel. As least two others also trailed the trumpeter, one black, one white. Cursing, Marcus concluded Theodore Fenno had escaped his New Orleans quarantine. Of the black man, Marcus had no notion, especially as descriptions differed wildly. Perhaps Gabriel's itchy feet had more to do with avoiding someone than wanting secrecy.

Outside a boardinghouse catering to musicians, Marcus spied a white man waving his arms bombastically while talking with lodgers. From a distance, Marcus overheard the word "Gibbs." Thanking the lodgers for their time, the man departed. Resembling a thinner William Howard Taft, whom Marcus once heard speak in Boston, he was clearly not Fenno. Passing Marcus, the man nodded affably.

"Do we know each other?" Marcus asked.

"I don't believe so," he replied, "I presume you're the other white inquiring about Gibbs. Charles Fort," the man introduced himself.

"So, you're Fort. I'm Marcus Roads." The men shook hands. Marcus knew of Fort. In the intellectual war over the supernatural, Charles Fort occupied neutral ground. He scrutinized centuries of newspapers and journals from across the globe, identifying and collating reports of anomalous phenomena. He rarely took positions on his findings. For Fort, the reports' existence was the important thing.

For his effort, Fort was scorned by believers and skeptics alike. Believers maligned him for not pushing interpretations, specifically their interpretations. For skeptics, Fort's efforts implicitly encouraged belief in the supernatural, and that was enough.

The pair talked about their respective investigations. Discussing the Gibbs case with Fort was relieving. While Fort understood its importance, Marcus could trust him not to blab to the ASPR. Or BSPR, for that matter.

Though Fort lived in New York, encountering him surprised Marcus. From what Marcus understood, the man was more Mycroft than Sherlock. His proclivities ran toward armchair research, not investigation. Politely, he put that point to Fort.

"Disappearance and reappearance cases are favorites of mine. The best ones come from nineteenth century Britain. Sadly, you don't get them much anymore. With one happening in my city, I couldn't just stay home. Of course," Fort added, "you have the advantage over me."

When Marcus didn't understand what he meant, Fort clarified. "Reading as many accounts as I have, you see patterns. Everything which disappears reappears somewhere else. Everything that appears, presumably, came from somewhere. Most people are content seeing only their side of that equation, not the whole picture. You've been where Gibbs is from. You're where he is now. You're seeing both sides. Figure out what matches, and what doesn't, and you'll crack the riddle." Fort paused. "I think you've missed one thing already."

"What?"

"Inside the coffin, did you find marks from clawing?" When Marcus's eyes widened, Fort saw Marcus took his meaning. "That's right. Victorian England saw many premature burial cases. New England's had a few recently. Each time, the interred person clawed the blazes out of the inside trying to get out."

"I'm dealing with someone getting in," Marcus realized. Fort departed with an affable nod.

Afterward, Marcus was thoughtful. He was no longer a believer, if he ever had been. But he had no love for dogmatic skepticism. Perhaps his position matched Fort's closer than he had realized.

Days passed. Marcus continued interviewing Gabriel's universally distant acquaintances. On another matter, his thoughts evolved. Serving as expert witness in several trials, Marcus knew eyewitness testimony could be unreliable. But, either eyewitnesses had gotten worse, or two black men were on Gabriel's trail. One was polite, well-spoken, and a bit of dandy. The other was intimidating and incoherent.

His investigation detoured when a sinister possibility struck Marcus. Two informants, referring to separate Broadway Butcher victims, told him the same thing: *I thought it was Gabriel until I saw him at a gig later*. Testing a theory, Marcus visited the police.

Of the NYPD's 32nd Precinct, it could be politely said that most of its policemen did not appear to come from the neighborhood they policed. They, too, showed surprise finding Marcus at their station. Surprise, and if the ruddy-faced desk sergeant was anything to judge by, more than a little suspicion.

"I wondered if I could examine photos of the Broadway Butcher's victims?" Marcus asked.

"You some kind of sicko? Clear off, I've got work to do," the sergeant replied curtly.

"Please, I want to check something. If I'm right, it would benefit the police."

"For all I know, you are the Butcher. Move along, pal."

"I'm not the Butcher. I'm a physician."

The sergeant eyed him uncharitably. "Don't they say Jack the Ripper was a doctor?"

Marcus determined it was time to leave.

He gathered his thoughts following the setback. The only other group with a finger on the city's pulse matching policemen were journalists. Actually, if the 32nd Precinct was any indication, journalists might know more. Marcus found the offices of the *New York Sentinel*, the publication whose piece on Gibbs he read on the train to Mississippi.

Like any good paper, the *Sentinel's* newsroom was a study in chaos. Nobody cared about Marcus's presence. He located the reporter responsible for the Gibbs piece. Abbot Stevens was a young woman with a newly-minted journalism degree from Howard University.

Introducing himself, Marcus praised her story about Gibbs. Like every reporter Marcus had met, she basked in knowing someone valued her work. Despite her appreciation, she remained focused. "What can I do for you?" she asked, "I doubt you came from Boston to compliment my writing."

No flies on her, Marcus thought.

"I hope you'll help me check something out. If I'm correct, it's a scoop for you."

"I'm game," Abbot replied. "What do you need?"

"Do you have photos of the Butcher's victims?"

She pulled the relevant stories from the *Sentinel's* morgue, spreading them on her desk. Looking at the photos, Abbot whistled. "They could all be cousins." It was true. Some were an inch taller or shorter. A little fleshier or thinner, though none very fleshy. A shade darker or lighter. But none more different than that.

"This was worth my time." She smiled.

Marcus thanked her and left. What he didn't mention, and what Abbot didn't notice, was that Gabriel Gibbs would fit into that collection seamlessly. Either a murderer with coincidently specific tastes stalked Harlem or someone was trying to kill, or rekill, Gabriel Gibbs and doing a very poor job of it.

That revelation did not itself suggest a course of action. Marcus resumed tracking down the web of names and address of clubs and lodgings connected with Gabriel. At one, he learned of another close call for the musician. A boardinghouse where he stayed had burned to the ground, killing most of its lodgers. Gabriel, serendipitously, was at a gig when the fire occurred.

148

Morbidly curious, Marcus visited the site. All that remained of the St. Ignatius Street Boardinghouse was a hole in the ground filled with charred timber. At its rim, a makeshift memorial had grown: flowers, candles, and handwritten signs proclaiming "We Miss You" or "Now at Peace."

Nearby, a figure skulked in shadows. The imposing man wore the remnants of a once fine suit. His face was drawn, almost skeletal. He resembled the woodcut of Baron Samedi, loa of death and the dead, Marcus saw in New Orleans. Even without that association, the man triggered something primordial. Marcus fled.

The following day, departing Club Hot-Cha, where someone named Clarence said Gabriel was the best trumpeter he'd heard but didn't know anything else about him, Marcus noted a fashionably-dressed young man leaning against a wall while writing in his notebook. Priding himself on modern tastes, Marcus could not fail to recognize one of America's greatest poets.

"Mr. Hughes? I'm Marcus Roads. I'm a huge admirer."

Langston Hughes turned toward him. The poet's expression was warm but stopped Marcus in his tracks. Though it held no malice, Hughes' intelligent, perceptive gaze pieced Marcus like a knife. Nervous and star-struck, Marcus cleaned his glasses, thinking of nothing cleverer to say than "What are you working on?"

"A sketch." Marcus saw that words filled the man's pad. "A rhetorical sketch. Perhaps it will become a poem. Perhaps it will be one of those contrivances cluttering our desks forever."

Sudden inspiration struck Marcus. The poet was known for his curiosity. "You're looking into Gabriel Gibbs too, aren't you?"

"I am." He nodded. "You're the other one, then?"

"You've run into Fort?"

"Indeed." Hughes chuckled. "quite the character."

"I guess we're all looking for the same thing."

"We are looking for the same man," Hughes said pointedly. "Not, I think, the same thing."

"What do you mean?"

"You look at Gabriel Gibbs as a puzzle. Something to be solved, labeled, and cataloged. I give you credit for being ahead of Fort. For all his enthusiasm, I think the man sees only a datum for his collection. If you'll accept the observation, my perspective is greater. Resurrected or not, Gibbs' story is about renewal. For a society. For a people. For a community. One could say he's the living embodiment of the Harlem Renaissance." Hughes grinned. "Or, perhaps I'm grandstanding and wanting to justify a poem about him."

Marcus felt dressed down by the poet. Whether it was justified was something he'd contemplate later. "I just wish I could figure out where the man is going to be next."

"In that, we are correspondent." Hughes laughed. He stopped suddenly, gazing upward. A playbill hung from the lamppost:

Gabriel "Resurrection" Gibbs
Saturday, September 27
The Savoy Ballroom

NEW YORK CITY, SEPTEMBER 27TH, 1929

Screams filled the Savoy. When it became clear that shooting had ceased, the crowd moved to subdue the gunmen. Sturdy though he was, he could not match Jack La Rue, the Savoy's chief of security, aided by Frankie Manning and several other dancers.

Carrying the wounded Gabriel, Marcus led a procession into the green room. Carefully, he laid the musician on a table. Marcus began removing Gabriel's bloody tuxedo shirt to examine the wound. The physician looked at the others in the room.

"This man must be operated on immediately. Everybody out."

Everyone complied. Almost. Langston Hughes leaned against one wall. Theodore Fenno, still steaming about his recently escaped quarantine, sat stubbornly at a table. Marcus was disappointed by Fenno's reappearance. The ASPR's investigator grumpily dragged himself into the Savoy just before the show.

Having experienced Hughes' gaze, Marcus had no illusions about winning the necessary battle of wills to make him leave. Fenno, he could overawe. To Marcus's surprise, he didn't want to. The man was a rival. But, he, too, had made the journey. It felt wrong to deprive him of its conclusion.

Marcus stared at the musician's small breasts, carefully wrapped to further minimize them. This was the key. Sex was a difficult secret to keep, explaining "Resurrection" Gibbs' obsession with privacy and frequent relocation. Of the women who could have impersonated Gabriel Gibbs, only one was not well accounted for. "You're Rebekah, aren't you?"

Wincing, his patient nodded.

"You're not in danger. I made your injury sound severe to get everyone to leave. But the bullet is lodged in tissue over your hip and needs to come out. I can do that right here."

Reaching into his bag, Marcus dabbed chloroform onto a cloth. "Take a little nap now. We can talk afterward." He doubted she remained conscious long enough to hear him.

The operation was as textbook as he told her. The bullet extracted, he sewed her up. Marcus knew he did excellent stitch work. Still, Rebekah would always carry a scar to remind her of the evening.

Waiting for Rebekah to regain consciousness, there was a knock at door. Marcus draped his jacket over the musician's bare torso. Jack La Rue informed him the police had collected the assailant. They hadn't departed before beginning their interrogation, either. The Savoy's chief of security wagged his tongue about what he overheard.

Marcus already connected the gunman with the menacing figure in shadows near the ruins of the St. Ignatius Street boardinghouse. But he hadn't known he beheld the monstrous remains of a human being who had once been Pastor Jericho Cullen. Having lost everything else, the man couldn't let go of his pride, jealousy, and hate. They drove the pastor to seek revenge on Gabriel while burning everything human out of himself. The remaining shell wasn't much different from the walking dead Marcus learned about in New Orleans, but animated by rage rather than sorcery.

As La Rue left, he informed Marcus the police wanted to speak with Gibbs. The physician replied it would be several hours before "he" had recovered enough to talk. Shortly afterward, Rebekah Gibbs coughed and stirred.

"Seems like you've had quite an adventure…"

"You don't owe us anything," Hughes assured her, before admitting, "but we'd really like to hear."

"It's okay, I'd like to tell," she said weakly. "Some water, though?"

Rebekah spoke halting at first, rapidly gaining vigor, "As long as I've been aware…I've been aware Gabriel was different. Most folks are built from a little good, a little bad, and a lot of regular. My brother wasn't like that. He was larger than life. And he was a child, too. Not much strung the two together. Gabriel awed me. And I pitted him. Sometimes I felt like I was his big sister, not his little one. That's a strange thing. But it made me love him even more.

"I especially loved his passion for music and never tired of hearing him play. When he blew trumpet, he seemed more real, more alive, than most folks. One day, Gabriel vowed he'd headline a big show in Harlem. I believed him, too. And I knew I'd do whatever I could to get him there. Turns out, that took a lot more than I expected.

"Pa got the telegram about Gabriel's murder while he was in Pilate's Point buying supplies. He came home and just told us. No lead in. No cushion. Nothing," Rebekah paused, reliving that moment. "Time stopped. I thought the world would end. Turned out, that wasn't the worst of it.

"After all we'd been through with Pastor Cullen and Gabriel's reputation, Ma thought it would be easier to bury him in New Orleans. I love her. But I don't think I'll ever forgive her for that. Pa wouldn't say anything against her. Sam wanted to, I think, but didn't. Aunt Mancie was the only one who had my back."

Marcus could not suppress a smile.

"I said they could try and stop me," Rebekah continued, "but I was going to New Orleans and get my brother come hell or high water. He would get buried in Gates County if I had to dig the hole with my hands.

"On the train back home, my forehead pressed against that cheap pine box they'd given him down there, I kept thinking about that vow he made. It broke my heart he'd never see that Harlem spotlight. Then I made a vow of my own. I'd make Gabriel's dream come true. I don't know if you've ever grieved, really grieved, for someone. There's a time when you've cried every tear a body can make. Then you've got to figure out what to do. How to go on."

As Rebekah sipped water and took a deep breath, Marcus thought Fenno stirred uncomfortably in his seat.

"I decided my brother would headline that Harlem club after all. He'd get a standing ovation for it, too. How? I'd become Gabriel. Maybe folks would think reports of his death were greatly exaggerated. If not, Gabriel already had that supernatural reputation. It would make my job easier. I almost wanted to thank Pastor Cullen for it.

"Having that goal dulled my grief. I threw myself into planning how to take my wild notion and make it real.

"When I got back home, my folks told me we couldn't bury Gabriel at the tabernacle. I saw red. Even though Pastor was gone and disgraced, his former flock wouldn't let us bury my brother where he'd gone to church. I couldn't believe it. After apiece, I realized, for what needed doing, it was a blessing. The tabernacle was close to farms and homesteads. The county cemetery wasn't near anything.

"First new moon after the funeral, I dug up my brother. It's the worst thing I've ever done. I'm not just talking about digging up my flesh and blood. It's terrible work all on its own. But it needed doing. To convince folks Gabriel was back, that pine box had to be empty. Someone might be crazy enough to check.

Marcus meet Rebekah's glance with difficulty. "You ripped off a fingernail in the process, didn't you?"

Rebekah nodded, eyeing him carefully, "Uh-huh. The crowbar slipped when I opened the coffin.

"I dragged Gabriel's body to Able Creek and dumped it. He must have floated downstream and into the Mississippi. The week next, a body washed up in Issaquena County. It was in bad shape. Even if it wasn't, it didn't matter. Nobody looks for a man already buried.

"I knew I'd have to disappear to make my plan work. After Gabriel's funeral, to lay the groundwork, I started acting out of sorts. That wasn't hard. I was still in a bad place.

"When I vanished, I went back to New Orleans. I needed Gabriel's silver trumpet to pull this off. Folks wouldn't believe it was really Gabriel without it. More than that, the trumpet was like the ruse in a two-bit medicine show charlatan's trick. You've seen that trumpet. You can't take your eyes off it. If folks were looking at the trumpet, they weren't looking at my face and maybe thinking, 'Does Gabriel look a little different?'

"In New Orleans, I didn't say I was Gabriel's sister. I just asked after the trumpet. It was in some Storyville pawnshop. When I tried to buy the trumpet, the clerk told me to go away, it wasn't for sale. Seemed like something about me made him awfully nervous.

"That night, I broke in. A man was doing the books inside. Not the one from earlier, an older fellow. He surprised me. I surprised him. We scuffled. In the course of things, he fell and hit his head. He didn't get up again.

"I feel bad. But I don't feel as bad as I likely should."

"Remove any guilt from your conscience," Marcus interrupted. "That man was responsible for your brother's death."

She nodded thoughtfully, "Can't say I'm surprised. Something in his eyes. More like a mad dog's than a person's." Rebekah paused, "Anyway, I grabbed that trumpet and went!"

"From New Orleans, I went to Whitfield. I started working a laundry job at the State Hospital. It was grueling but gave me

155

a little money to live off. But I picked that job for another reason. They didn't mind if employees used the mailroom. I sent a letter to my family saying I'd got committed. It was postmarked from the hospital. Why wouldn't they believe it? A fellow working in the mailroom got sweet on me. If anything came for me, he'd set it aside. And, of course, if anyone telephoned, there was a Rebekah Gibbs 'at the hospital.' Just not as a patient. As long as their question wasn't too specific, I'd be safe.

"I worked every day. Each night, I went home and woodshedded with the trumpet until dawn. I'd get a few hours sleep and do it all over. Flourishes, licks, runs, riffs, I learned them all. I'd listened to Gabriel so many times, it felt like I had a record player in my head. The hardest part was playing those long, strong notes of his. But they were his signature, so I had to be able to do them. Finally, I got the trick of it. Something called circular breathing, it turns out. And I got pretty good with that trumpet. Not to be prideful, but maybe better than Gabriel."

From informants Marcus spoke with, there was no "maybe" about it. Post-resurrection Gabriel, or rather Rebekah, was the superior musician.

"After a year," she continued, "I started going into Jackson on weekends and playing on Farish Street, building my chops. I wasn't claiming to be Gabriel. Not yet. But I was learning to pass as a man. Dress like one. Walk like one. Talk like one. I didn't get it right all at once. There are some funny stories…well, that's for another time. Before long, I was playing in the clubs for cash, rather than on the street for coins. When folks cheered for me, I understood a bit about why my brother loved playing.

"Like I said, I didn't plan to be Gabriel yet. But, when I played the Brown Circle, there was someone in the crowd

156

who had gigged with my brother in Storyville. After the show, he came up to me and called me 'Gabriel.' I bolted through the back door fast as I could. But he saw me, heard me play, and took me for Gabriel. I'd passed the test. He told folks about seeing 'Gabriel,' alive and playing. That's when 'Resurrection' Gibbs was born.

"With the cat out of the bag, I might as well be in New Orleans. Even after leaving Mississippi, I kept the ruse of being in the State Hospital through my friend in the mailroom.

"New Orleans meant the end of being Rebekah by day and Gabriel by night. I was Gabriel all the time. Eventually, I mostly forgot I wasn't. In Storyville, I started making a name for myself. But I had problems. Too many people knew Gabriel there. I was always dodging somebody who'd known my brother or faking my way through conversations I knew nothing about. Coming back from the dead, Gabriel got plenty of attention from the occult folks. Plus, some lug named Jim Kessler had it in for me. One night, leaving a gig at Mahogany Hall, somebody shot at me. I had put by some money and figured it was time to make Gabriel's dream come true. I caught the next train to New York.

"Harlem had so much going on. Music. Theatre. Society. All this energy everywhere. New ideas floating around. I'd never seen anything like it. But I kept focused and threw myself into the music. I got big fast. No one cared if I was resurrected. Some of them, I think, got a kick out of it.

"After New Orleans, I figured staying on the move was the safest thing."

"Did you know so many people were looking for you?" Marcus asked.

Rebekah shook her head. "I just didn't want people seeing

too much or asking too many questions. It's hard keeping some secrets in close quarters."

"That probably saved your life," Marcus commented, explaining the near misses she'd had with the Broadway Butcher, who, he realized, was likely Pastor Cullen. "It's possible he also set the St. Ignatius Street boardinghouse fire. You were fortunate to have a concert that night."

"That's not how it happened," Rebekah protested, "I didn't have that gig, not originally. Heading back to St. Ignatius that night, an old woman got in my face. She warned me away, telling me to find someplace, anyplace, else to be. I didn't exactly believe her, but she gave me the nerves so badly that I went out found that gig just to calm down. When I got back, the boardinghouse was gone."

"You've no idea who she was?" Marcus inquired.

"No. I just carried on with my music. I've led a charmed life here, always getting bigger and better gigs: Tille's, Connie's Inn, the Log Cabin, Small's Paradise, the Radium Club, Lafayette Theatre. When Moe Gale told me I'd got the Savoy spot, it was the happiest moment of my life. That gig would fulfill Gabriel's wish.

"Has fulfilled his wish," she corrected herself. "Unless you gentlemen, and I hope you are gentlemen, tell anyone differently, history's going to say Gabriel Gibbs headlined the Savoy Ballroom and brought the damn roof down. Now, I have the choice to get my old life back.

"I never thought Pastor Cullen would show up here, too. He and I might be a little alike. Neither of us could let Gabriel go, even after he died. Except, maybe, I'm ready to now."

"You want to go back to being Rebekah?" Marcus asked.

"I love my brother and always will," Rebekah's smile was bittersweet, "but I swapped two years of my life for two years of his. I don't want to miss any more."

"Then, perhaps 'Gabriel Gibbs' dies tonight of his wound?" Marcus suggested.

"With no body? How are you going to pull that off?"

"I am a physician," he replied, "Mister Hughes and Mister Fenno are well-regarded locals. With their collusion, I suspect we can manage something."

At that, Rebekah Gibbs' bittersweet smile lost its bitter.

The three men helped Rebekah out the Savoy's rear door. "You'll be okay. Keep the stitches clean and don't do any running or heavy lifting," Marcus advised her before adding, "There's a family in Gates County that would be very glad to see you. You can't bring back Gabriel this time, but you can bring back yourself."

They watched her walk down the alley and out of sight.

"Time for me to depart as well," Fenno announced. Ambling the opposite direction, he tipped his hat. "Mr. Hughes. Fishmonger." It was Fenno's usual slight but, Marcus thought, absent its usual malice.

Returning to the greenroom, Marcus opened up about the case in a way he hadn't previously, not even with Fort. Hughes offered his thoughts and insights. They talked long into the night about the case and what it meant.

When the pair finally exited through the main doors onto Lennox Avenue, dawn's rays greeted them.

"I don't believe I shall compose anything about Gibbs, either of them," Hughes concluded. "I cannot tell the real story and anything else would be but a pale shadow of the truth." Shaking hands, the two men parted. As Marcus walked, it seemed the city's heatwave had passed. The morning was crisp, almost cool. The first whiff of autumn traveled on the breeze.

Over his shoulder, Hughes called after him. "I won't tell

159

you what to put in your report. But, whatever it is, be truthful with yourself about who it really serves."

The case of Gabriel Gibbs, Marcus reflected, was extraordinary but, in the main, prosaic. Gibbs had died in New Orleans. He had not come back from the dead. It was Rebekah Gibbs, with ingenuity, audacity, and talent, who successfully posed as her late brother to achieve his dream. Part of Marcus lamented that he again failed to find evidence of a life, and afterlife, of wonders. Or had he? Mysteries remained. What were the origins of the silver trumpet figuring so prominently in the tale? Marcus wished he had examined it before Rebekah departed. Perhaps the instrument possessed unusual properties. Who was the man Marcus met in New Orleans that, presumably, gave him the tattoo which saved his life? Who was the woman Rebekah encountered in Harlem, warning her away the night of the deadly boardinghouse fire?

To Marcus's knowledge, the ASPR never issued a report on Gabriel Gibbs. Perhaps Fenno's account was too wild and confused even for them. Or, just maybe, he learned something about grieving for a lost loved one.

These ideas and others swirled in Marcus's head as he pondered the report he must soon write. He found that Hughes' parting words loomed large in his thoughts.

BOSTON; OCTOBER 11TH, 1929

"I'm disappointed. I expected better from you, Dr. Roads."

It didn't seem like the appropriate time to remind Dr. Prince he could call him Marcus.

Glancing around Prince's library, Marcus thought it unlikely he would see its inside again. "I'm unhappy with the report as well," he admitted. He could do no better, he explained to Prince. But he couldn't tell the man why.

The report he handed the BSPR's research director was a chimera of half-truths, obfuscations, and deliberate falsehoods. To Marcus's mind, only its opening sentence told the unmitigated truth, "The Gabriel Gibbs shot at the Savoy is the same Gabriel Gibbs born in Mississippi and killed in New Orleans…in every way that matters."

The Uninvited Guest
Josh Reynolds

"Well, this is dashed nuisance, what?" Charles St. Cyprian said. The cramped garret room smelled of incense, cigarette smoke, and something else. Something sweetly rancid, like spoiled meat or rotting flowers. He waved a hand in front of his face, trying to dispel the odour. "One has better things to do on a night like this."

"Does one?" Ebe Gallowglass said, as she set the heavy Gladstone bag down on the table. She pushed up the brim of her flat cap and studied the room's silent occupants warily. They sat around the hardwood table in silence, hands linked, eyes locked on sights other than the face of the person across from them. Two men and three women, all dressed to the nines, for a night out in the West End. On the table was a bolt of purple cloth (likely pinched from an inobservant vicar), a scattering of vaguely occult bric-a-brac, and a skull.

"One most certainly does, apprentice-mine." At the back of the room, Guido Gialdini whistled "The Sheik of Araby" through the flaring horn of an old gramophone, which was perched precariously on a small stand. St. Cyprian went to it and lifted the needle, silencing Guido in mid-trill. He turned back to the table.

St. Cyprian studied the skull, careful not to touch it. It was old. Brown and cracked, with teeth missing from its jaw. There was a puckered hole in the centre of its cranium. Freshly dug up, to judge by the soil collected in the crevices. Someone had scratched various nonsensical alchemical symbols into the flaking bone, probably to make it look more impressive.

"Assistant, innit?" Gallowglass said, opening the Gladstone. Inside, the tools of their trade—vials of dust scraped from the stones of lost pyramids, the finger-bones of forgotten saints, and other, more esoteric items.

"What?"

"I'm your assistant."

"So you keep reminding me," St. Cyprian said. "Has it ever occurred to you that they are, in fact, the same thing?" He studied the table and the silent forms occupying it. They were still alive, thankfully. Death had a tendency to complicate these matters.

Gallowglass paused, as if considering this. "Says you."

"I assure you, they are."

"Bollocks."

"Quite." St. Cyprian frowned and reached into his jacket for his cigarette case. The sickly sweet smell was growing worse, or else he was simply becoming more aware of it. It was not a natural odour. Too pervasive for that. It was the smell of the abnatural. The stench of the Outside, seeping in. It was an aroma that he, as the current occupant of the offices of the Royal Occultist, was all too familiar with.

Founded during the reign of Elizabeth the First, the office of Royal Occultist was charged with the investigation, organization, and occasional suppression of the eldritch, infernal, and unnatural, by order of the Crown. Beginning with the diligent amateur, Dr. John Dee, the office had passed through a succession of hands in its long, unwieldy history. Here and now, in the year of our Lord, 1923, those responsibilities rested with him.

Well, with him and his apprentice. By tradition, every Royal Occultist was required to take one, and Gallowglass was his, for better or worse. In time, his responsibilities would pass to Gallowglass, though neither of them were in any particular hurry to discuss the inevitable. There was still time yet, and even if there wasn't, he wasn't certain he wished to know about it. Irresponsible perhaps, but there it was.

He glanced at Gallowglass as he lit a cigarette. The two of them were a study in contrasts. He was tall, with an olive cast to his features and hair just a touch too long to be properly fashionable. His linen suit was well-tailored, straight from Gieves and Hawkes, in Savile Row. Everything about him screamed 'swell.'

Gallowglass, on the other hand, was dark and slightly feral looking, with black hair cut in a razor-edged bob and a battered flat cap resting high on her head. She wore a man's clothes, hemmed for a woman of her small stature. He knew this, because they were his clothes, stolen from his closet, and altered with money stolen from his secret biscuit tin. Gallowglass was not a believer in the concept of private property.

Given what she'd been wearing when they met, he didn't begrudge her the clothes. Charity began at home, and all that.

They'd been called to the garret by an inspector of his acquaintance, who felt that the business was outside of Scotland Yard's remit. With all due respect to the inspector, he was right. Certain things man was not meant to know, not if he wanted to sleep soundly at night. That went for plods as well as spiritualists.

"That stink is familiar," Gallowglass said. She scanned the room, eyes narrowed.

"It should be; you've smelled it often enough." He circled the table slowly, pausing once or twice to knock on the hard wood. "That, my dear Miss Gallowglass, is the smell of a bad decision." He paused beside the woman he supposed was the medium, given her suitably exotic attire, and studied her. Her countenance was hollow and wasted, her skin waxy and cool—not cold though, not yet. From a casual inspection, the others were much the same, to a greater or lesser degree. They didn't have much time.

Most of the time, séances were harmless enough. Emotionally manipulative, perhaps, but generally lacking in actual danger to the participants. But sometimes…things went wrong. Given what he saw here, this seemed to be one of those times.

The spirit world was akin to a wide, dark sea, and the waking world, a reef. Leave the reef, you risked attracting the attentions of predators. Even in the reef, you sometimes risked provoking something hungry. "Before we go any further, I need to see what we're dealing with."

"That a good idea, then?" Gallowglass said, her tone making it clear that she thought it wasn't. "You could get caught up in whatever it is."

"Yes, you're right. Let's just burn the place down, shall we?"

She shrugged. "Worked that time on Shaftsbury Avenue, remember? The slug-house? With all of the slugs?"

He grimaced. "Yes, all too well." He shook his head. "But this isn't Shaftsbury Avenue, and I don't think that this is the spectre of a primordial gastropod." He hesitated. "At least, I hope not." He waved the thought aside. "Never mind. Back in a tick."

He closed his eyes, concentrating. He reached out and traced the sacred shape of the Voorish Sign in the air as his inner eye flickered open. Some adepts called it the spirit-eye, though his acquaintances in the Society for Psychical Research insisted that it was merely a very focused form of extrasensory perception.

Whatever it was, it had taken him years to learn how to employ it safely. Humans were, by and large, as sensitive to the paranormal as animals were to earthquakes. They simply couldn't process it as well. Humans needed reasons for things which animals took on instinct. The inability of the average mind to understand all of its observations was also one of its best defences. But sometimes, you were forced to shuck the blinders first thing, otherwise you risked being snapped up unawares. As the unfortunates at the table—and Asbury—had discovered. The smell grew worse as he let his senses expand.

The room went soft, and thin, like a piece of cloth frayed to the edge of dissolution. Colors without description pulsed at the edge of his vision, and everything took on a stretched, impressionistic quality. He could make out the Ka-glow of the people seated at the table, faint and flickering, like candles in the wind. The air was thick with icy smog and the faint echoes of Gialdini's whistling had become a train-whistle shriek.

From above the table, something turned its head to look at him.

He froze, wondering if it knew that he could see it. Then, he realized that it didn't matter. It knew he was there. And it was hungry.

It didn't have a proper shape. It was like…clay, stretched and shapeless. A splash of ectenic extrusion, rising from the skull like smoke from a chimney. The skull was the focus, then. He'd expected as much. Something inside it had been waiting for the right moment to blossom and grow, like some corrupt seed.

Feathery fronds twitched in the air, as if tasting his scent. It pulsed and shifted, forming apertures that might have been mouths and bulges that might have been eyes. It was—or had been—singing along with Gialdini, humming, vibrating its strands. Several of those fleshy barbs were wrapped about the forms of those seated at the table. The thickest was attached to the medium, which made sense—if she had awakened the

166

spirit, it would have latched onto her first. Then the others in the circle, before any of them realized something was amiss.

Contrary to popular belief, ghosts came in all shapes and sizes. Some were less lonely spirits than they were self-aware cancers, leeching sustenance from people or places, or both. This appeared to be one such. A Saiitii manifestation, or the seed of such. A spiritual malignancy or fungus, growing stronger and more real as it battened on the Ka of its victims.

St. Cyprian frowned. "You are an ugly thing, aren't you?" His stomach roiled as the smell seemed to grow stronger and stronger, inundating him. There was no telling who it had been, if it had ever been anyone at all. Sometimes these things were just…dirt, caught between two layers of the universe.

The mass stiffened. Blister-like eyes rolled in his direction. An unattached strand undulated languidly towards him. He took his cigarette from his mouth and jabbed the lamprey like protuberance, causing it to retreat. The cigarettes were hand-rolled by an acquaintance in Limehouse—a special Moro blend, offensive to certain spirits. He stepped back and allowed his spirit-eye to shut, restoring the world to reassuring solidity.

"That you?" Gallowglass asked warily. Her fingers inched into her coat, towards the shoulder holster holding the Webley-Fosbery revolver she habitually kept close to hand. Sometimes things tried to hitch a ride back, if you stayed in the dark for too long.

"'s me, innit?" he said, mimicking her. He took a long drag and blew a plume of smoke in her direction. The cigarette helped to calm him. The ol' nerves got a bit jangly, on occasion, after seeing the horrors that lay beneath.

"Go chase yourself." Then, "What'd you see?"

"Nothing pleasant." He stepped back from the table. "We'll need to break the connection, first and foremost. See if we can jolt whatever it is into retreating. And maybe get some answers as to what this was all about in the process." Pulling the participants apart was usually the simplest way, and the best. He gestured towards one of the men. A big chap, full soup and fish, with a Clark Gable moustache on a bulldog face. "We'll start with him. He looks fairly doughty, in an unfashionable sort of way. It probably hasn't been feeding on him as long."

"We don't even know what *it* is yet," Gallowglass said.

He rubbed his hands together. "Thrill of discovery, Miss Gallowglass. Now, help me yank him out of his chair."

"Sure that's smart?"

"Only one way to find out. Grab his shoulder."

Luckily, the grips of the other participants on their chosen test-subject were loose. He came free of the circle with a wet thump. St. Cyprian looked down and then up, at Gallowglass. "I thought you were going to catch him."

"Your idea, innit?"

The man groaned. St. Cyprian pulled a vial of smelling salts out of his pocket and sank to his haunches. He waved the salts under the man's nose and helped him to sit up. "Up we go, there's a good chap."

"W—what?"

"Trade the ol' horizontal for the vertical, what?" The smell had changed, subtly, and for the worse. He looked at Gallowglass, who nodded, her eyes narrowed. She could feel it as well, whatever it was. A definite worsening of the general atmosphere. Their trick had only agitated it, rather than forcing a retreat, as he'd hoped.

The man stared at him, blinking. "What?"

"Exactly. Who are you, then?"

"A—Asbury. Paul Asbury. Of the Sussex Asburys." Asbury looked around. He shivered, and clutched at himself, as if he were cold. "What's going on? Who are you? What happened?"

"Rather hoping you could answer that, old man," St. Cyprian said, as he helped Asbury to stand. Asbury shoved him aside brusquely.

"I don't need help," he growled, despite the obvious weakness of his limbs.

"Pull the other one," Gallowglass said. Asbury glared at her.

"Who are you people?"

"A better question is, what was this all about?" St. Cyprian said. He peered at Asbury. There was a distinct familial resemblance among the participants at the table. All of them were of a similar age. Siblings then, or cousins. He decided to risk the latter. "Why were you and your…cousins partaking in this excursion to the demimonde?"

"I don't see where it's any of your business, whoever you are," Asbury said. His hands knotted into fists. He had the look of a man who didn't like being asked questions.

"Oh, there you are quite mistaken," St. Cyprian said. He reached into his coat for his cigarette case. His hand froze as Guido Gialdini began to whistle again. St. Cyprian glanced at the gramophone, and then at Gallowglass, who shrugged. Asbury made to speak, but St. Cyprian silenced him with a gesture. "I think we woke it up," he said.

"Woke what up?" Asbury said. "What the devil is going on?"

"Quiet," St. Cyprian said. The air felt wet and close. It was getting hard to breathe.

He reached into his coat pocket, feeling through the various amulets and charms which he carried with him at all times. One never knew when one might need an Assyrian

169

demon-whistle, or a silver coin blessed by Prester John. Neither of those was what he was looking for, however.

He extracted a tiny copper vial, engraved with Arabic characters, stoppered with wax. He flicked his thumbnail across the wax and opened the vial, releasing a small amount of powder into his palm. He flung the powder out about him, and the air took on a shimmery haze reminiscent of the open desert at midday. A looping, lamprey tendril bled into view, as the powder did its work.

"Bleedin' Nora," Gallowglass cursed, reaching for her pistol.

St. Cyprian waved her back. "Chalk," he said. "And quickly. You know what to do." He puffed on his cigarette, filling the immediate area with smoke. The tendril retreated. He knew he'd only bought them a few moments, at most.

Gallowglass rummaged in the Gladstone and found the chalk. It had been made from the powdered bones of saints. Which ones, he wasn't exactly sure, but it seemed to do the trick. Swiftly, she bent and began to draw a wide pentacle on the wooden floor. As she worked, St. Cyprian retrieved something else from the bag—a tightly wrapped bundle, held shut by brass buckles.

'What—what is that thing?" Asbury said, staring in stupefaction at the twisting, eel-like extrusion. It had come no closer, but St. Cyprian knew it was only a matter of time before it gained the strength to do so. Soon, it would suck its captives dry, and seek out new prey. It would go after Asbury first, and then he and Gallowglass, with all the desperate hunger of a famine victim. He began to unbuckle the bundle.

"A ghost."

"A ghost?"

The way Asbury said it caused St. Cyprian to pause. "Yes. It's feeding off of your cousins, and the medium. As it was feeding off of you, until we pulled you loose."

"My cousins, are they—" Asbury began. He seemed enthused by the prospect.

"Not quite. Not yet. It's a bit like…a spider's web. They're all wrapped up in ectenic discharge, until it—he—finishes the meal."

"He?"

"Well, it's a man's skull." St. Cyprian peered at him. "Out of curiosity, why were you holding a séance around a man's skull? And don't tell me it's none of my concern, because I think you've grasped by now that it jolly well is. Speak, and swiftly."

Asbury hesitated. St. Cyprian snapped his fingers impatiently.

"Treasure," Asbury said, flatly, still watching the squirming tendril. "An ancestor of ours—Lord bloody Gideon bloody Asbury—was supposed to have hidden his wealth somewhere before the Parliamentarians got to him and stretched his neck."

"And you needed the money."

Asbury frowned. "An inheritance divided four ways is no sort of inheritance. The treasure would compensate for things, somewhat." His frown deepened. "Some of us had debts, if you must know."

"By which you mean you," St. Cyprian said.

Asbury grimaced. "A man has a right to enjoy himself." He cast a glare at the medium. "That witch said she could find it for a fair price. I got the others to agree, on the condition that we split it. All she had to do was ask his spirit."

"Which she needed his skull for," St. Cyprian said. "And you procured it for her, I gather?" Something billowed in a far

171

corner. Like smoke, only…not. Smoke didn't move like that. It spread like a thing aware.

"I—yes, I did," Asbury said, sourly.

"Hanged, you said?" More not-smoke, spilling upwards from between the floorboards. It stretched, rising to almost human height. Awake, now and aware, the ghost—the entity—was beginning to influence its surroundings. Testing its boundaries.

"He was. I don't see how that matters…"

"It matters, because there's a bullet hole in that fellow's cranium."

Asbury shrugged. "Maybe the legend was wrong."

"Or maybe you got the wrong skull," St. Cyprian said. But even as he said it, he wondered if Asbury had. He wouldn't have been the first man to try and use sorcery to procure ill-gotten gains. Before he could press the point, Guido's trilling began to repeat and skip, as if something had nudged the needle. He was tempted to scatter more powder, but had little desire to see any more than he already had, until it was absolutely necessary.

"That skull has been in the family vault for decades!" Asbury blustered.

"Then someone else got the wrong skull. Either way, we are left with something of a conundrum. Because your uninvited guest isn't going to drift back off to sleep any time soon." His hackles prickled, and he looked around. The air had gone cold. His breath plumed, uncoiled and spread, joining with that of Asbury and Gallowglass. No more time for mysteries, then. "Finished with that circle yet, Miss Gallowglass?"

"Do you want to do this?" she said, still on the floor.

"No, no, but haste would be appreciated." He studied the vague, thin, shapes as they drifted. There were more of them

172

now, and the smell from before was almost unbearable. They weren't quite human shaped, nor did they resemble the formless tendrils he'd seen. He glanced at the skull, wondering who it had been, and where Asbury had really found it. Saiitii manifestations didn't form spontaneously. They required mental and spiritual trauma of the most diabolical sort to inculcate the focus. "Give it some welly, if you would."

Gallowglass responded with a vulgar euphemism, eliciting a startled cough from Asbury. St. Cyprian chuckled and finished unbuckling the bundle. He cast the cloth aside to reveal a long dagger of unique design. It was a heavy thing, with a wedge shaped blade, and a thin hilt squeezed between an ornate crosspiece and a heavy pommel. The blade was etched with strange sigils, and devilish faces, with wicked tusks and protruding tongues, had been carved upon the crosspiece.

"What the deuced sort of heathen pokery is that?" Asbury asked, staring at it in disgust. "I've never seen the like."

"I expect not." St. Cyprian extended the blade and sighted down the length. The indistinct shapes were almost visible in the frost-tinged air. More lamprey-tendrils, perhaps, but visible now, as the manifestation stirred to full wakefulness. The séance had woken it, and his observations had caught its attention. He could feel the full weight of its malignant awareness, pressing down on him from all directions. A quaquaversal imposition, fumbling at his senses. He slashed out, and felt a quiver on the air.

"This blade was crafted before Hyperborea was buried in ice, and forged by a puissant sorcerer of that time, who made the hilt from the fang of an immense worm," he said. "The sigils are Lemurian, the iron, Atlantean, and the scabbard, Elizabethan." He slashed again, around the edges of the circle.

"The latter was made from dried and cured skin stripped from the back of a Basque magician who tried to wreak a terrible working on Queen Elizabeth." A third time, and a third quiver on the air. A vibration, as if of sudden retreat. "The fire that was used in its forging was kindled by a salamander, and dead men worked the bellows."

"None of that actually answers my question, dash it!"

"It's a knife, formerly belonging to one John Subtle, an alchemist of uncertain disposition," St. Cyprian said, with a sigh. No one appreciated a good pedigree anymore. "It cuts through spirit-matter as if it were flesh."

"A bloody knife isn't going to do any good against— against *that*," Asbury snarled, pointing at the indistinct shapes now gathering about them. "We need to run…"

"And leave your siblings behind?"

"Well I'm certainly not carrying them out." Asbury started for the door.

"I wouldn't," St. Cyprian said. "The ghost…"

Asbury gestured sharply and crudely. St. Cyprian blinked. Gallowglass laughed. "Guess he told you. Circle's finished, by the way."

St. Cyprian tightened his grip on the knife. "Asbury— come back to the circle. *Now.*"

Asbury had almost made it to the door when the shapes stiffened. Abruptly, St. Cyprian realized his mistake. They weren't figures, or even tendrils. They were *fingers*. Fingers that snapped shut about Asbury's bulky form with inhuman quickness. Asbury screamed as the pale things closed about him with sudden, bone-crunching force. St. Cyprian cursed and lunged. The ghost-knife sang out and passed through a pale knuckle. The fingers sprang open, and a sound like thunder shook the garret room. Asbury collapsed against St. Cyprian, wheezing.

"Oi, watch it," Gallowglass called out. He turned, saw more fingers descending from the ceiling. Like a man reaching into a matchbox. He slashed out with the knife, and the fingers retreated, wriggling. He half-dragged the shuddering Asbury into the circle and dropped him to the floor. The man fell with a groan. He likely had a few broken bones, but that was better than the alternative.

"Oh Lord, it's bloody killed me," he groaned.

"You're not dead yet," St. Cyprian said. "Though, now might be a good time to unburden the old conscience, what?"

"What do you mean?"

"The skull—it's not the one you were sent for, was it?"

Asbury's eyes widened, and St. Cyprian knew his guess had been correct.

"Whose skull did you bring, Asbury?"

"I don't know, damn you," Asbury said, clutching at his chest. "The medium—that witch—she swore she could find the treasure, but I—I…"

"Didn't want to share it," Gallowglass said, matter-of-factly. "Pulled a switch. Come back later with the real one, innit?" She tapped the side of her head. "Cunning, like."

Asbury glared at her, his face beginning to swell with bruises. "I needed the money."

"And your greed may have doomed us all. Jolly well done." St. Cyprian patted him companionably on the shoulder, eliciting another groan from the injured man. The giant fingers probed about the edge of the circle in a questing fashion.

Gallowglass had one hand on her revolver. "More than ten of them, innit?" she said, after a moment. The fingers scratched at the air about the circle like curious cats. They wouldn't be able to pierce the circle. But it wouldn't hold them back forever.

St. Cyprian looked at her. "That's what bothers you about this?"

She shrugged. "Just an observation. What's the plan?"

"This situation calls for a bit of ectenic surgery, I believe. The sooner, the better, if our friend here was telling the truth." God alone knew what Asbury had brought to the party. He'd have to find out where Asbury had gotten the skull, but later. If there was a later. Thinking quickly, he said, "We'll break the connections one by one. When it's weakened a bit, I daresay it'll retreat. And once it does..."

She cocked her revolver. "Simple, innit?"

"Yes, well, wait until I'm out of the way, please." He reached into his pocket and found the vial of powder. He tossed it to her. "Throw it over the skull and shoot. Keep its attention, if you can."

She gave a lazy salute. "Try not to get eaten, if you can."

"I wouldn't give you the satisfaction," he said. He took a breath, and stepped out of the circle. The fingers dipped towards him, smacking together in hideous fashion. He swept the ghost-knife out, cutting through their milky substance. The fingers retracted, and he felt, rather than heard, a moan of protest. It reminded him of an animal being refused food. The Asbury cousins twitched in their seats, as if whatever held them was quivering in rage. He reached the table and said, "Miss Gallowglass, if you please."

Behind him, he heard the crack of Gallowglass' Webley. A rain of dust fell across the table, revealing the squirming tendrils he'd seen earlier. Swiftly, he chopped through the closest one, freeing one of the cousins. He upended her chair unceremoniously and sent her toppling backwards, away from the table. A sub-dermal groan echoed through his bones as another connection was broken, and he shot a glance towards the skull.

The thing rising from it was taking on a firmer shape. It might have been a face, albeit one moulded by a child or a lunatic, and stretched to impossible size. It silently gnashed tombstone teeth in an idiot's leer. He'd seen worse, but not lately. The sight of it paralyzed him, for just an instant, but long enough to almost cost him dearly. It reached for him again, plucking at his legs and neck. He fell back against the table, chopping at the semi-solid digits. Out of the corner of his eye, he saw Gallowglass lunge forward and grab the back of another cousin's chair. She yanked it back, severing the connection, and spilling the unconscious man to the floor.

The bulging eyes of the spirit revolved slowly, seeking this new disruption. It was still uncertain, unfocused. That was their only advantage. St. Cyprian took the opportunity to break away from its groping fingers and lunge for a third cousin. The ghost-knife sang down, gouging the table. The floorboards rattled beneath his feet and Gialdini's whistle had risen to a screech of frustration. That left only one—the medium. The ghost-knife was warm in his hand, and pellucid matter clung to the blade. "Be ready to move," he shouted, as he hacked away at a questing finger.

The abominable face rippled towards him, jaws wide. It was speaking, a low rumble of sound rising beneath the whistling on the gramophone. His skull ached from the force of it, and he stumbled. It was like being caught in a turbine. He sucked the last erg of heat from his cigarette and expelled the smoke into its mad, yellow eyes.

It blinked, and the pressure eased. St. Cyprian caught hold of the medium. She thrashed in his grip, like a drowning woman. He thrust the knife home, piercing the tendril that snared her throat. It reared back, glistening stick-pin teeth oscillating in a narrow mouth. The tendril lunged for him, and he chopped through it.

Fingers thumped into him like clubs, and he gasped in pain. A monstrous hand climbed up his legs like a spider, squeezing his middle. Another reached down, as if to twist his head off. The spirit was still speaking, and he caught a ragged pulse of what might have been antiquated English—nonsense syllables, but recognizable for all that. Its yellow orbs bulged like straining balloons in its stretched features, inhuman and incomprehensible.

Desperate now, he sent the medium toppling to the floor with a convulsive heave as he was whipped off of his feet and hurled into the gramophone. It fell silent with a squawk, and he rolled aside as fingers snapped down, cracking floorboards. The substance of the hand wavered and faded, reduced to drifting motes.

Adrenaline and fear lending him speed, St. Cyprian backed towards the table. With no physical tethers, the spirit was anchored solely to the skull. It twisted like an animal, lunging wildly against the bars of some invisible cage, but dwindling as it did so. Without a source of nourishment, it was shrinking away, tumbling back into somnolence. He sliced away at any questing tendrils, keeping it at bay. Behind him, Gallowglass dragged a cursing, protesting Asbury from the circle. "Ready when you are," she said, over his groans of pain.

In a matter of moments, the great face had crumpled into a toddler's grimace, and then into the barest memory of a visage. The skull resembled an anemone, covered in twisting, tubular fingers, clutching at nothing.

St. Cyprian slid the point of the ghost-knife through an eye-socket and lifted the skull from the table. Carefully, hands shaking, he carried it to the circle, and tossed it inside. The smoky excess faded fully, retracting into the shadowed recesses of the skull. Something that might have been an eye glared out of the bullet hole in the cranium.

178

"Now what?" Gallowglass asked, staring down at the skull.

"Now, we wait. It'll settle down eventually, and we can properly contain it, or exorcise it, as the situation warrants." He pulled out his cigarette case, and selected a new one before offering it to Gallowglass.

"And then?" she asked, taking one.

"Add it to the collection, I suppose," he said. He struck a match and lit her cigarette. "It'll look dashed swell on the mantle, don't you think?"

Moving Pictures
William J. Martin

A long time ago, a young girl of twelve stood with her mother on the edge of a crowd of soon-to-be broken families. A brisk ocean wind, coupled with the arid grey sky only emphasised the April chill, and even that was nothing compared to the unspoken tension shared by everyone that was gathered here this morning. The year was 1917, and America was going to war.

Before them stood her father, clutching a briefcase while silently allowing his wife to adjust his tie. Similar scenes were going on throughout the crowd, wives patting down their beloveds as if their biggest worry was if they had packed enough clean pairs of socks. Susan watched as he swatted her mother's hands away, and the two adults playfully bickered like the besotted couple they had been for decades, before he gave her a concerned smile. His attention shifted to his daughter, and he knelt down to face her. A hand went to her shoulder, and the world crumbled into darkness.

The crowd that had surrounded them withered, whole families wasting away like young trees in winter. The great, steel ship that her father was soon to board melted into the clouds, before fading to black, only the cold, blue lights from the windows remaining before they too dissipated. Even her mother, who was still clutching her daughter's hand, softened, the lines and details of her face smoothed away until she became little more than a featureless mannequin. The young girl, however, didn't notice any of this. To her, everything was somehow just…out of focus. Everything except her father, who could not have been more defined. She found herself taking in everything about him. His wiry frame, which he still carried with absolute confidence; his slicked-back hair; even the way he was kneeling down, a sort of squat that had once been the perfect starting point from which to pick her up and sling her over his shoulders before racing around their backyard. She couldn't help but feel this would be the last time she would be able to see how her father was in the flesh.

"Susan."

The world seemed to quiver as he spoke, as if the sound wasn't coming from him, but rather what remained of the world around them.

"Susan." The world spoke again, and she feverishly nodded.

"I'm afraid your old daddy has to go away for now."

Her eyes widened.

"I'll try to come back as soon as I can, now."

He continued, but all she could hear were those words.

"Going away."

He was still talking but it was all a blur, his words suffering the same fate as the world. All that mattered was that her father, whom she loved, would leave, and she knew in her heart that this would be the last time she would hear his voice. She tried to focus on him again, just as she had a moment ago, but now all she could focus on were those two words.

"Going away."

They started repeating in her head, slowly, softly, gently building to push everything else out of the way. Even as he carried on talking, she couldn't make out the words; that single thought overwhelming her as the cold, blue light from the windows of the ship he would soon be boarding began to seep into the world around them.

"Going away. Going away. Going away."

181

She couldn't even hear him anymore, the constant pounding on her ears becoming too much to bear. She rushed forwards, trying to hide in the haven of her father's jacket pocket, only to push herself into an empty space. She looked around, the blue light building just as those incessant words continued to do.

"Going away. Going away. Going away. Going away."

A distant silhouette could just be made out in the distance, and she tried to chase after it, knowing it was the man that she would never see again. Yet, even as she tried to move, she stayed locked in place, now hovering in an endless blue void. She reached out for the tiny shadow, before it too was consumed by the void. She looked about herself, at the brilliant expanse of loneliness, before allowing herself to collapse.

"Goodbye, Daddy."

Susan Parsons shook herself awake, the last whispers of a nightmare fading in her ears. Once again, she looked around, fear gently subsiding. Pale moonlight drifted into her room, causing the numerous picture frames that lined the walls to gently glisten. Despite the warm summer air, she could still feel something of a chill passing through her nightie. She rose from the bed, her small frame lightly springing across the floorboards to shut out the light, early morning wind. Once there, she rested on her windowsill, surveying the vista that backed her house.

Beneath her lay a wild expanse of uncut grass, overgrown bushes, and countless wildflowers, all given a ghostly blue tinge in the moonlight. She looked further and, sitting atop the solid, milky line of the river, sat the warm, bustling horizon of America's own metropolis. She couldn't make out anything more solid than a few notable buildings, despite the boasts of her younger self about how she could see right into people's offices if the time was right. But it was impossible to mistake the sheer grandeur of a city that knew just how important it was. Susan allowed herself a little smile, even a sigh, as she noted what time it must be, and that she couldn't just sit there until the sun rose. Before too long she was back in bed, her dream lost in the backwaters of her memory. And soon after that, a shimmering, wraith-like mass of light curled out from beneath her bed, and drifted out into the night, leaving behind it the whispers of a loved one taken too soon.

The following morning, she emerged from her room feeling the way one does after crying to sleep. She strode throughout the halls of her home as if a great weight had been lifted from her shoulders, before sitting down to a hearty breakfast of bacon and eggs. Once upon a time they would be ready and waiting for her as soon as she woke up, but recently, her mother had apparently decided that having paid help was clearly beneath her. The hot summer sun permeated the house, white surfaces shining brighter and transforming the yellow wallpaper into a glittering gold.

While eating, Susan idly watched the routine she had learned by heart through her twenty years of observation. Her neighbours, Mr. and Mrs. Wright, left their house almost arm in arm, before splitting off to do their respective chores and hobbies. The small, bouncing form of Steven, the milkman's boy, chased after his father as they moved from delivery to delivery. Susan, content that nothing substantial had changed in her small town's morning behaviour, let her thoughts wander to what she would do that day. It wasn't long before the most attractive option of heading into the city beat off everything else. With smile and a final sip of her coffee, she rose, before setting off back to her room.

As she did, however, she came across the hunched over figure of Agnes, her mother, who appeared to be cleaning up a mess of glass shards. With a naïve charm, Susan decided to investigate.

"Good morning, mother." She announced, bending over to try and get a better look. "Are you all right? It can't be mice again, is it?"

"Ah, Susan, yes, there you are." She sighed as she rose to her full height, with all the grace of an aging ballet dancer. "No, thankfully, I'm quite sure that we keep a clean enough house to not need to worry about that. However—" She held up a picture frame, a large, diagonal crack across its cover. "Something disturbed your father in the night, I'm afraid."

"It must be those playful spirits at it again," Susan teased, trying not to look at the cold, stony face looking out at her from the cracked frame, "You know, the ones Mrs. Brown thought were—"

"No, Susan. Thank you for reminding me, but I am quite sure the cause is more likely a broken hook…although…" She sighed again, a hint of hope in her voice, "Who knows, my dear…who knows…"

Susan moved closer, drawing her mother into a soft embrace, which her mother gently reciprocated.

"I'm sorry I teased you." She muttered, before her mother moved away, pulling herself together with a sniff.

"Although, talking of spirits, a subject I hope you start treating with a little more respect, I'm afraid there's been something of a problem with Mr Pallister. I was reliably informed just yesterday that he couldn't host the get-together this evening, and so it seems that duty has fallen to us this week. I'll have to work with the maids for most of the day just to make the house presentable. I hope that man just found some of the closure he needed." She sighed, gently shaking her head in concern, before putting her attention back on Susan, "You will make sure to be back in the house before we get started."

"Oh, there's no need to worry, mother." Susan chuckled, "I certainly won't try and repeat what happened last February."

Agnes shook her head, an embarrassed smile on her lips. "Good. Now, go on, child, run along, and leave your old mother to work."

"Alright then. Have fun." Susan grinned, before giving her mother one more hug, and heading off back to her room. It was high time for a young girl of class such as herself to take a visit to New York City.

Though it may have changed over recent years, to Susan Parsons, the Big City would always feel like her hometown. The lights and sounds that have and continue to dazzle newcomers are nothing but a particularly beautiful nightlight to the girl who had grown up staring at it from her bedroom window. Today, however, the beauty was masked somewhat by the wet, grey clouds that had crawled across the sky sometime just before noon. Likewise, Susan's mood had dropped considerably since arriving. Despite the comfortingly bright attractions of Times Square and Broadway, the clouds, and the infernal chill which Susan recalled from the previous night, had caused the day to take on a dank, miserable atmosphere, one which managed to dampen Susan's enthusiasm for crowded, tourist-filled department stores. Eventually, after seeing nothing interesting in the shops, and a good deal of aimless wandering from street to street, she had managed to spend much of her time in the older, less glamourous parts of town.

Objectively, there wasn't anything inherently wrong with the little covered markets and cafés she had spent the day exploring, aside from the fact that, whether or not she was doing this on purpose, or if some unconscious thread was leading her on, but she found herself visiting a great deal of places that she hadn't visited since her childhood. Even when she decided to head back into the newer areas of the city, she only found herself bumping into more and more that reminded her of her lost father. They seemed to almost jump out at her, a twitch in the corner of her eye leading her towards old posters for her father's favourite brand of cigar; patches of shadow pierced by soft light emanating from the family-run café that Susan's family had used to visit regularly; a sudden, childish laugh in her ear as she stumbled across a small formation of rocks near the edge of Central Park which sparked memories of a young girl trying to climb them before falling into his welcoming arms…

She shook herself back into reality. *Silly girl. No business worrying about that.* She noticed the red light of sunset breaking through the clouds. She quietly chastised herself for wasting the day, digging up old memories when she should be out enjoying herself. This continued as she headed back towards the grand hall of Pennsylvania Station. Her head was down, and there was a constant, self-indulgent grumble under her breath. Indeed, she was so distracted by trying to ignore her own thoughts she completely failed to notice the awestruck young girl looking up in wonder at the sheer size of the train station—until she walked right over her, knocking the pair of them to the ground with a yelp.

"Oh, goodness, excuse me!" Susan bustled as she frantically began to pick herself up, "I'm afraid I am terribly sorry! I just didn't see you there, and I was so focussed on myself, I simply…" she trailed off, content that whoever she had walked into had probably got the message.

"Nah, nah. Perfectly alright." Came the reply. The girl that

Susan had just run into got to her feet, dusting herself off and picking up her small wicker briefcase. "My mistake, standing around when other people have got places to be." She laughed at her own expense, before giving Susan an excited smile. "Actually, truth be told, I'm not even supposed to be here. I just change trains here so I should be heading out of town in a minute. But honestly, how could a girl come all this way and see absolutely nothing of New York City, hm? And I've got to admit, everything's even bigger than I expected!"

Susan watched her unexpected acquaintance with an uneasy curl in her lips. She wouldn't have minded going back to feeling grumpy at herself, but this stranger's sheer, childish optimism was impossible to ignore.

"Of course," she replied, humouring her slightly, "Although if you really are changing trains, then you probably shouldn't be standing here talking to me."

The two of them shared a brief giggle, before they both started walking deeper into the station. There was a moment of awkward silence between them, until it became clear they were most likely heading for the same platform.

"I hope you don't mind me asking," started the other girl, as their train rattled to a stop, "but by chance you're not heading too far out into Long Island, right?"

Susan nodded. "I'm not. I live actually quite close to the river. Why?"

"Well, just as it so happens neither am I!" She laughed, before taking a seat by the window, Susan taking the seat opposite, "I've been told there's a good place to stay around there."

"I suppose there is definitely a place to stay around my neighbourhood." Susan laughed. "I'm sorry, but the hotel I assume you're thinking of, it's not exactly the nicest sort of flop house." Disheartened to see the other girl's unamused expression, she quickly chimed in on a happier note, "Say! I don't even think we've been introduced yet." She beamed, and offered out her hand, "My name is Susan, Susan Parsons."

"Megan." She replied, her initial optimism coming back into her voice, "Megan Travers."

"Well then, Megan. It's quite the pleasure to meet you."

From that point on, the conversation became more amiable. It turned out that Megan had quite a chequered past tucked away inside her wicker briefcase. Susan listened, enthralled, as her new friend told her about how she had left her small town from just outside Boston to escape her restrictive family and find love and fortune in the big city. Of course, she explained, where better than the biggest city of them all? Over the past couple of years, Megan had been slowly working her way down towards Manhattan, stopping in small towns, taking work for a while before moving on.

"That could be a movie!" insisted Susan, as they wandered closer to her home. The pair of them bathed in the cool blue of the moon, while the last hints of sun streaked the horizon with red.

"Never really had time for movies," Megan admitted, "or the money really. I'm sure if I managed to find a boy good enough, I'd have asked him, but, eh, I've never really focussed on that sort of thing. When you've got a goal, you can't take your eyes off it for a second."

"It seems you have the time now." Susan laughed, "New York is just across the water, and there's a movie theatre just a few streets away. I think you can afford to take some time out and see one."

Megan nodded, "Maybe." The pair of them drew to a halt outside Susan's house. "I'm guessing that's all for tonight then?"

"Not at all," Susan began walking towards the front door, "I'm sure mother won't object to a guest for dinner. If you feel like joining us."

"I honestly don't think I can accept—" Megan nervously started, before being dragged up the garden path towards the house.

"Oh, yes you can," laughed Susan, "I absolutely insist!"

Megan began to giggle, which turned into a laugh as she allowed herself to be taken inside. "Well, in that case, how on earth can I refuse?"

As it happened, Agnes was not as excited about the sudden new visitor as Susan had hoped. When the pair of girls came across Susan's mother, she was in the process of preparing for her scheduled weekly commune with the otherworldly.

"Good gracious, young lady, where have you been?" Agnes snapped at Susan, a clear sense of tired exasperation in her voice, "At least you didn't drag your heels even more. Who knows what sort of spectral connections you could have accidentally broken." She sighed, "At least you're here now. You'll find your dinner in the stove, but now it'll have to wait until—" It was at this point she noticed Megan, "And may I ask who you are, my dear?" Her voice was clearly tired; annoyance being reigned in to make sure she was polite to her guest.

Megan, who had until now been looking interestedly at the table, where a set of candles had already been laid out, waiting to be used, shrank away at the question, "Oh, I'm begging your pardon, ma'am. My name is Megan, I'm a friend of Susan here." she gestured towards Susan, as if her simply being there would lend weight to her story.

Agnes' face visibly softened, "Well, I have to admit, it

isn't the first time Susan has brought somebody home without bothering to tell anyone." She chuckled towards Susan, who was currently trying to appear very small, and hoping Megan didn't see her embarrassment.

"I'm afraid I can't offer you anything at the moment," she continued, "Thursday has something of a ritual in our household. I know, you must be absolutely starving, but I'm afraid the spirit world works on its own timetable."

Megan took a cautious step forward, as she was starting to turn as red as Susan had been just a moment ago, "Don't worry, I understand." She was very quiet, as if she was unsure whether or not to actually speak, "Although, if it's alright with you of course, I would hope that, if you're holding a séance, is it alright if I join in?" Her voice had slowly withered away until it was just a shy whisper, "I may have somebody I'd wish to talk to."

"Of course," Agnes replied, motherly softness filling her voice in a way that Susan hadn't heard for years. "As it happens, one of our group has recently left us, as much as we'll miss him. I'm sure you'll fit right in with the others, dear."

"Actually, I wouldn't mind joining in either." Susan added, to which Agnes gave a sage nod of acceptance. Almost on cue, there was a cheerful rapping at the door, at which Agnes excused herself and headed off, leaving the two girls on their own. The two of them moved to close the curtains, and continued to prepare for the séance.

Susan gripped Megan's hand, trying to focus on why she was taking part in this. Previously she had been sceptical of her mother's spiritual side, even while allowing her to practice these weekly séances with little success. But this time, something had changed. She hadn't thought of her father as

190

anything more than a framed photograph for years, but today she couldn't keep her thoughts off of him. In a sense, he had risen from the grave, creeping into her mind and waiting to be noticed. If there was anything to her mother's hobby, now was the time to find out.

The grandfather clock read fifteen minutes to midnight. It was about to begin. Six of them—Susan, Megan, Agnes, along with three of Agnes's friends, all of whom had known Susan since she was a child—all gathered around the table. Five candles stood in a circle, and inside them, a perfect crystal sphere. The clouds had parted, and the light of the moon was lightly flowing around the closed curtains. Susan felt the slight shift in her grip as Agnes rose to her feet.

"I welcome all thee who have gathered here tonight." She began, addressing each of the participants, "Tonight we few, humble mortals intend to contact the unending mysteries of the great beyond, in the hope of contacting those we have lost. As always, if a member of the group wishes to come forward now, they shall take the part of our medium. If there are no volunteers, then I shall take on that duty myself." She looked around the circle, each member respectfully shaking their head. Susan felt Megan squeeze her hand tighter when she was put under Agnes' gaze.

"It is settled." Agnes continued, sitting back down and assuming her role, "Now, I urge you all, if you have a loved one you wish to speak to this night, hold them in your thoughts, so I may try to contact them." The silence that followed was heavy with mournful thoughts, visions of the dead playing in everyone's mind. Susan thought of her father, of the way he talked; of the way he was always able to keep the peace when she and Agnes were on the verge of arguing; of the way he always jokingly treated her as adult, offering her a cigarette when he was about to have one himself. She created his image in her mind, and called out to it, hoping he would reply.

"If we are all ready," whispered Agnes, "we shall begin." She raised her voice, a booming authority conveyed through a slight shift in tone, "Our father, who art in heaven, hallowed be thy name," She continued, joined by the rest of the congregation, their heads bowed and eyes closed.

"...Lead us not into temptation, but deliver us from evil. Amen."

They collectively took a breath, and gazed into the crystal ball in the center of the table.

"Angels," began Agnes, "Spirits, heavenly forms from beyond our powers of understanding, we beseech thee, come to us now, hear our cries of loss." Susan felt the hair on her neck begin to prick, and in the half light of the candles it was clear that goosebumps were starting to appear on her arms. "Each of us here has lost, and lost before our time. We wish only to speak to our loved ones, one last time. Give us this chance to achieve fulfilment!" A soft whisper, almost inaudible, scraped past Susan's ears. Her eyes widened, hands beginning to shake with the fear of the unknowable soon making itself present.

"If there are any spirits in the room here, we bid thee, give us a—!"

A silence fell upon the group as a bright blue flame flickered into life inside the crystal ball. It flicked and twisted, growing steadily for a moment before burning gently, as if waiting for her to continue. "W-we welcome thee, good spirit," Agnes started, unsure how to handle this, "We ask thee, are you here to speak with any of us here?"

The flame seemed to turn, slowly, a dim core deep inside the light at the center. It peered at each member of the séance, silently judging before carrying on. Until it reached Megan.

As it faced her, Susan felt the grip on her hand tighten, causing her to gasp, but that was nothing compared to the ear-splitting scream which exploded out from Megan's lungs. The flame began to grow once again, its icy light quickly outshining the candles as it licked out from inside its crystal cage. As it did, Megan's scream became louder, and higher, until the very earth itself seemed to shake beneath them. The flame had engulfed the ball now, and had begun to sprout cold blue tendrils, all of which began to work their inexorable way towards Megan.

The fire's light grew, steadily filling the room with whatever force it carried. The pictures that covered the walls began to shine, the shaking house turning each one into a glimmering jewel. To Susan's horror, she noticed that it wasn't just the frames that were moving, but the pictures themselves. One after the other, each photograph sprang to life. Landscapes that had once been peaceful were consumed by dark clouds; portraits of dogs were now empty backgrounds, their occupants having chased each other across the wall. All except for one.

Susan looked to the photograph of her father to see him just as before. Even as every photograph in the room burst to life, he stayed still, hard features still belonging to a dead man. The contrast made him stand out in her mind, a lonely constant in a sea of chaos.

The light began to shift as the fire continued toward Megan. Despite the heat that Susan could feel radiating out from whatever this was, it seemed to leave no impression on the world around it. It pulled itself forward with cold singlemindedness. A tendril of fire snaked around Megan's arm, brushing against Susan in the process, and her mind was flooded with that same mantra that had plagued her the night before.

"Going away. Going away. Going away."

She tried to jerk her hand away, turning when she found it trapped in the stony grip of Megan's own. A number of burning tendrils had wrapped themselves around Megan's head, even more worming their way onto her hands, up her arms and wrapping around her chest. As Susan watched, some of the flames began to sear through her clothes before passing through and into her skin. Megan's mouth, still forced open in horror, became filled with a light, almost invisible against the blue as it emerged from her throat, before steadily increasing, becoming impossibly bright. As more of the flames moved to possess her, her eyes rolled back, a similar glow beginning to emerge.

Before long she was engulfed in blue, the heavenly light bursting from her face everywhere it could. Eyes, ears, even her nostrils blazing with piercing whiteness. It was almost painful to even look at, the shapeless mass of blue and white searing itself onto Susan's retinas, even while the utter spectacle made it almost impossible to truly pull the sight into focus.

Suddenly a firm hand gripped her shoulder, and Susan was aware of heavy breathing next to her ear. When it spoke, it was a familiar, yet coarse, rough voice that addressed her. The voice of something that had been through too much.

"Why didn't you listen when you had the chance?"

Susan's body shook.

She squeezed her eyes shut, and, fists clenched, ripped her hands free and putting them to her ears.

"NO!!"

She screamed, a whirlwind suddenly picking up in the room around them, before subsiding. There was a thud as Megan's unconscious body slumped onto the table. Susan didn't move for a moment, before slowly uncurling to look at the damage. Or…she would, if the room didn't appear entirely spotless. For a short moment, her fear seemed to be doing the same, until she noticed her father's picture, once again fallen to the ground.

He stared at her through cracked glass.

Susan was awoken by a swift rapping on her bedroom door. She grunted in acceptance, and her favourite maid entered. She wore a grave expression, and silently helped the girl to her feet. Susan asked her what was going on, if it was time for breakfast, even though the sun didn't seem to be high enough. It was clear the maid was making a conscious effort not to answer, as if simply opening her mouth would cause too much to spill out, a cascade that wasn't hers to release. Instead, she led Susan on.

"Mother?"

Agnes looked up from her seat in the front room. The grey skies of dawn tinted the room. She didn't reply.

"Mother, what's happened?"

This time, her mother was unable to contain herself, pulling her daughter into a rough embrace. Susan automatically returned the gesture. In response, Agnes only seemed to hold her tighter, a croaking sob rolling through her as she began to weep into her shoulder. Susan silently held her arms around her mother, head resting on her hunched shoulders. After a few moments, her eyes were drawn to the pale shape of an open letter lying on the table. The bottom edge was spattered with drying patches of wetness, and all she could make out were sparse words:

Dear Mrs. Parsons,
We regret to inform you that Colonel Steven
Ernest Parsons has been killed in action—
Susan looked away. Not the right feeling for tears, at any

rate. She buried her face into her mother's shoulder, just as she buried her father deep into the bottom of her heart. She felt the cold metal of a photo frame press against her back. A family, together in spirit, for the last time.

And then, suddenly, she was alone. The weight of her mother disappeared from between her arms, and she stumbled forwards into nothingness, body suspended in a fathomless void. Vague shapes and dull colours moved in the darkness, twisting around and circling her like ravenous sharks.

Whispers came. Words half-uttered flashed through the space around her, catching in her ear for an instant. At first they were hesitant, one by one flying past, merely examining her before they vanished just out of her reach.

"…whe…"

"…sen…"

"…los…"

She tried to follow them, twisting her body in all directions as she desperately searched for any tangible source of her assailants. The voices became bolder, whole groups of them starting to attack her at once. The distant shapes seemed to be doing the same; lights hardening into edges, shadows marking out curves. In the unknowable distance, abstract spots of colour began to merge, and merge again, the world rebuilding itself in a phantasmal fantasia.

And in the centre of it all hung Susan, slowly burning up under the sudden onslaught of light and noise. A constant stream of words forced themselves into her mind. The refulgent mass of colours blazed through her, uncaring. She screamed, any sound drowned out long before it reached her ears. Her hands moved to her face, pressing against her eyes with ever-growing desperation.

And still she hung, a lonely, pathetic shadow in a world of fire.

Suddenly the darkness returned, the inescapable noise replaced with the familiar bite of cold wind. Susan felt mud between her toes. She moved her hands from her face and looked around slowly. The remains of a church lay on the horizon, and the distant, rapid knocking of bullets drilling through flesh punctuated the scene. She took a step forward, almost slipping and falling into a rough crater filled with dust and red-stained water.

Her eyes widened as a mass of black matter in the base of the crater began to move. The broken shape of a man, uncurling with a hideous crack, began to emerge. Thick, dark blood, dripping from oil-stained skin, began to ooze down into the mud as it shifted. An emaciated limb strained to reach out towards her. Her father's voice rasped from the figure. His words were wet, gurgled through a body drowning in filth and its own bile.

"Why didn't you listen, Susan?"

She shook her head, taking a horrified step backwards, and once again falling back into the empty void. Hanging alone in the darkness, without even a whisper in her ear, she curled herself up, eyes pressing into her knees, tears finally starting to form.

"I'm sorry, daddy!"

The sun was already half way across the sky when Susan began to wake. There was an ache in her bones, and her muscles sang as she moved. Her eyes were covered in a thick dust, which took a few tries to scrape away. Clearly she had been crying.

Stumbling into the hallway, she made her way towards the front room, memories feeling like an overexposed photograph: Details were missing, and there was far too much light…

"You're awake then." Agnes said, after a moment of awkward silence, not taking her eye off her sewing.

Susan nodded, "Who's that for?"

"Mrs. Bush, from down Pottage Street. It's not glamourous but at least it gets us food on the table." There was another silence as Susan chewed on a particularly large bit of bacon. "You could always help out, you know."

"I will. Just after summer. I'll get a job working in a nice big department store in town, don't you worry, mother. They just don't start hiring until the leaves start falling."

"Still."

"Maybe we could invite Mr. Houdini around and try and see if he can disprove whatever happened last night. That should get us something."

"It'll get us more trouble than it's no doubt worth." Agnes muttered, quickly gasping as the needle pricked her finger.

"Oh, baloney! We can just send him a letter, ask Megan to come over again and—"

"Susan Parsons, you stop right there!" Agnes snapped, throwing her fabric down onto the table, "How dare you— here I am, doing a servant's work, while you go off spending your money on atrocious dresses and who knows what else! If your idea of chipping in is some get-rich-quick scheme involving that charlatan and that poor young girl, Megan...why, goodness knows how she feels! The least you could do is put some darn clothes on and apologize to her!"

Susan sat quietly, eyes following the pattern of the tablecloth a little too intently. "Alright then." She rose, swallowing another forkful of scrambled egg, before silently heading back to her room.

"She used to be such a sweet young girl..." Agnes sighed. She turned to the photo of her husband, "What happened to her, Steven?"

Megan was practically waltzing with herself as she left her hotel room in the inaccurately named Deluxe Royale. The night of blissfully peaceful sleep, despite her rough lodgings, was showing its effects. She reflected briefly on the previous evening as she made her way towards the lobby. Despite her clear head, she found herself unsure exactly what had happened to put her such high spirits. She had just begun putting a few of the pieces together, with a few more starting to form when she noticed Susan standing at the reception. A large smile burst onto her face, and she dashed forward, still clutching her briefcase, to greet her friend.

"Ah, hello there!" She tugged the other girl into a grateful hug, "Tell me, is it just as beautiful outside today as it looks from my room's window?"

Susan raised an eyebrow, "Uh, good morning, Megan. You… seem rather happy."

"Well, yes I think I should seem like it because I am! Last night was such an astounding, eye-opening experience!" She began to lead the pair of them out of the lobby, leading Susan with one hand, tightly keeping hold of her suitcase clutched with the other. "I knew coming down here would be a good idea, and look how right I was! Why, I pretty much doubt that I've felt this good in years!"

"Oh. Well, I've actually just come by to apologize."

"For what?"

"For last night?"

"Come on now, I don't see any reason for that! Like I said, last night left me feeling happier than I can remember!"

"I still feel as if I owe you some sort of apology."

"For what? We've been over this way more than we need to; I really don't feel like you've done anything worth apologizing for."

"Well, yes, I know that…but still…" Susan trailed off. For whatever reason, the…horrifying images she could remember from last night seemed to be completely alien to Megan. She didn't exactly want to bring up any specifics, mainly because she had no idea how to begin explaining it. She opened her mouth, then closed it when she realised that she was only going to repeat herself. The pair carried on through the suburbs, eventually stopping when they reached the local film theatre. They decided to stop for a moment, taking some respite from the hot summer sun in the shadow of the marquee.

"Hey…" Megan started, "Remember what you said about seeing a movie?"

Susan had never been very good at watching movies with people. No matter how much she wanted to enjoy it herself, she always ended up focussing on whether or not the person sitting with her was enjoying it. This was no exception. The theatre was mostly empty, save for a sparse handful of residents, most of whom Susan had known since she was small. She tried to focus on the movie, but she couldn't make herself really get into it. Instead, as always, she was far more interested in checking Megan's reaction every few moments to make sure it had grabbed her instead.

Harold Lloyd had just been bowled over by a team of college footballers when she noticed it. That damned chill, once again following her. Megan gasped, lightly gripping Susan's arm. She snapped to attention, hoping that for once she wasn't the only one who could feel it. With a quick sigh as she realised it was still just the movie, she began to cast her eye around the vast hall, hoping to find whatever was causing this unearthly chill. Though the décor was clearly gorgeous enough to warrant being looked at, it wasn't exactly out of the ordinary. She twisted herself, doing her best to be surreptitious in her efforts to get a look at every possible angle, almost climbing over the seat to try and look inside the projectionist's booth.

Then she noticed Mr. Pallister. The missing member of her mother's little congregation. Despite the darkness, there was something clearly wrong with him. His skin seemed bloated, almost giving off a pale glow in the light reflected from the screen. His clothes seemed similarly off, his suit clearly ragged and unwashed. He sat there, directly across the aisle from the two girls, staring into the middle distance. As though he was watching the screen, and not just the projection. Susan would have believed that he was dead were it not for his eyes. Though it was impossible to tell what they were seeing, Susan could sense that they were filled with something of a fierce intelligence. Even as Megan once again burst into laughter beside her, Mr. Pallister sat still, frozen while the world moved on without him, mind consumed by something Susan didn't dare to imagine.

She didn't realise how long she'd been staring until Megan began gently nudging her.

"Hey, come on, we've got to head out. The show's over. I can see the cleaners getting antsy at us."

Susan nodded, letting herself be manoeuvred to her feet, and led out by Megan, still unable to take her eyes off the still figure.

She didn't see him leave.

The pair of them slowly began to make their way back towards the Royale. Susan wasn't quite ready to go home, and she appreciated the company.

"I still can't believe that this is what I've been missing!" Megan beamed, "How do you suppose they even go about doing all of those things? How do they manage to get the camera just in the right position, and that's even before they start acting…"

She went on like this for a while, Susan adding in perfunctory nods and shakes of the head. Every time she attempted to get into the conversation, the image of Mr Pallister's ghostly aspect bubbled back to the surface of her mind. After a while, the excited outbursts and questions began to die down, and there was a moment of silence between the pair of them.

"Susan… do you know what happened last night?"

Susan hesitated, before shaking her head.

"I saw an angel, Susan."

"Excuse me?"

"I'm afraid I've lied to you a little bit." Megan blushed, moving to sit down on the sidewalk, with Susan joining her shortly afterwards. "I didn't come here to escape my family. I don't even have a family at all. Not anymore…"

Susan shuffled closer.

"Here, look—" She opened her briefcase, taking out three worn, battered photographs, "This is them." She handed them to Susan. "That's my dad, right there. When I was a kid he used to say he was the strongest man in the world," she chuckled, "although the way my brother was going, that probably wasn't going to stay true for too long."

Susan gave an empathetic smile, and Megan's face fell slightly, "They both went off to fight."

"It's alright. I know exactly how that feels."

Megan took the photos back, before showing Susan the last one: a short, stocky woman, with a warm smile.

"Then this is my mother. She died. Just last year. Doctor said there wasn't anything to do." "I had to watch her, Susan, I saw my beautiful mama waste away in front of my eyes." She leaned into Susan's chest, as Susan gave her another squeeze. "They were taken from me, Susan. My whole family taken from me. Leaving me all on my own."

Susan remained silent, her other arm going around to hold Megan in a tight embrace. They didn't move for a while.

"That's what I saw last night," Megan explained quietly, "I looked into that crystal ball of your mom's and an angel came out."

Susan's eyes widened slightly, the memory of Megan's face twisted and burning as an unearthly creature that was anything but an angel took hold of her.

"It spoke to me, you see. That's why I've been so high today. It told me I could speak to my family again, Susan. I can see them again! I need to! Otherwise it's like they've been taken all over again!"

She tucked her head into Susan's shoulder, softly repeating herself. "I can't lose them. I can't lose them again."

It was dark by the time Susan returned home. Even after consoling Megan until she felt alright on her own, Susan had absolutely insisted that she stayed a little while longer in case anything happened that required comforting.

The house itself was blank from the outside. Even her mother's window was without a warm candlelight that told the world that somebody lived here. Susan crept inside, closing the door as quietly as she could. Unlike the past few nights, the clouds hadn't yet started to break apart, and Susan was left to fumble her way to the light switch in darkness. She flicked it, restraining an irritated grunt when nothing happened. She would have to note that down in the morning. Flicking the switch back off, she continued feeling her way along the wall, making her way to bed.

She reached the hall light, and flicked it, again to no response. Then she heard a childish giggle rush past her ear.

She froze, turning for a moment, squinting slightly, as if trying to see anything in the pitch blackness, like a rabbit noticing golden eyes in the underbrush.

Then the lights flashed on.

Half of the pictures that had once lined the walls had been ripped away, smashed against the opposite wall left lying in torn and broken piles. The wallpaper had been brutalised, letters haphazardly carved into it across the length of the hallway. Susan took a step back, eyes widening as she read.

WHY DIDN'T YOU LISTEN

Susan turned and ran, scrambling up the stairs towards her bedroom. There was a crash as the rest of the photos dropped to the floor. Spurred on by the noise, Susan finally cracked, screaming as she tried to get away. A maelstrom followed behind her. Glass shattering, metal frames twisting and scraping as they hit the floor. The broken frames began to crunch against the wallpaper, tearing it further; wooden stairs creaking in anguish as everything came down upon them.

Everything began to converge, an ungodly howl rang in her ears with every step she took. She burst into her room, the roar simmering down into an incessant, childish laughter as she turned and slammed the door shut. It lingered on the air for a moment, before fading into nothingness.

Leaning back on the door, Susan finally sucked in a breath. She hauled herself to her feet, only moving after hearing the reassuring click of the lock telling her she was safe. Light poured in through her window, painting the room a dull red. Susan staggered towards the glass, kneeling down to take in the view that had soothed any number of her sleepless nights. The threat began to creep back into her memory, and exhaustion started to fill her body. She let her head sink down to the windowsill. Her eyes began to water, a quiet sob passing through her. She tore her eyes away from the horizon, covering her face moments before her sobs became something more. The only sound that echoed through the house was that of her muffled tears.

The sky was still dark when Susan's door opened again. The air was cold, heavy with the chill of night. Light from the distant city illuminated the hallway with a dull red glow. It was very much not how she had last seen it. Any sign of the visions in her mind, shattered frames and torn wallpaper, had vanished. The corridor was clean, as it should be. Susan shook her head gently, hoping to cast away lingering memories of her latest dream as she headed downstairs. She paused by the photograph of her father, back in its rightful place on the wall, new frame intact. With care, she took it off its hook, taking it with her as she went to take a seat on the front room table.

What's happening to me, daddy?

Megan stood on Susan's doorstep, clutching her suitcase. Her hands twitched as she reached up to quickly rap against the door. Her clothes were creased and unwashed. She looked like a far smaller, sadder version of the girl that Susan had walked into just the other day.

"I didn't want to bother you." She said, "I just saw that your curtain was open and, well, I figured I should at least try to say goodbye."

"What? What do you mean? Where are you going?"

"I can't stay here. I can't, I—" Megan looked at her feet, "I've already messed things up here."

"Megan, you aren't making any sense." She took a small step back, "Come inside. You're not going anywhere at this time of night anyway."

Megan thought for a moment, before shuffling inside with a weary sigh. "I'm not staying long."

"Just tell me what's happening." Susan closed the door behind her, before going back to take her seat.

"I shouldn't be here anyhow…" Susan patted the chair next to her, and Megan begrudgingly took it. "Normally it takes a little longer before…"

"Before what?"

"Before I get tied down."

"Tied down."

"Yes."

"And what do you mean by that?"

"I try to stay quiet. I try to not let people get close to me. Or to let me get close to people."

Susan's brow twitched, a hint of understanding starting to form. "You mean, what you said, about your moving around, about your coming here, to the city—?"

"Yes." Megan sniffed, her breath starting to shake, "Every darn thing I've told you about myself has been a lie." She sucked in a few short, wet breaths, "I never wanted to make it big, Susan. I just wanted somewhere to run to. I thought, if maybe I kept running then I would never have to lose anybody again. Wouldn't even have anybody *to* lose." She sniffed a few more times, wavering on the edge of tears. Her face glistened in the cold light of the moon. "Now I'm here, and I make a friend right on day one." She smiled, her next breath almost a hollow laugh, "It's only a matter of time. Something is gonna happen, I just know it, and then you'll be gone. It'll be like my family all over again."

There was a moment of silence. Susan worked over everything she had just heard while Megan stayed still, looking down at her briefcase. The moon passed behind another shadow, leaving them in darkness. They could only just see the outlines of each other's faces.

"That…Megan, sweetheart, that is absolutely no way to

do…anything!" She stared, dumbfounded. "You really spent all these years with nobody to talk to, or even anywhere to really go? Is this what you think your family would have wanted you doing?"

Cold light once again filled the room, glinting off the picture of Susan's father. She forced herself to ignore it. "Megan…you can't just spend your life running scared at the thought of the people you've lost."

"Quite right, dear."

Susan jumped, Megan turning her head wearily to see Agnes standing by the empty spot on the wall where her father's picture usually hung. "Nobody should live their lives consumed by their lost loved ones."

Susan turned her head away, and her eyes widened in fear, mouth opening into a silent gasp.

Her father sat across the table, figure comprised of pure, ice blue light. The air around him was silent, his stillness affecting even the dust that danced over his skin. Only the effervescent glow seemed to imply any sign of life. It seemed to fill the room, a consciousness going where its body could not. Motionless eyes were frozen in a cold stare, pointed directly at her. She looked at the two other women in the room, jerking her head between her mother and her friend, hoping, begging that they would acknowledge what she could see. To her dismay, and to her fear, they were both looking at her.

"You understand, dear?" Agnes continued, features cold in the light given off by Susan's father.

"M-me?" Susan carried on looking between Megan and her mother, hoping for some sort of answer. Megan had begun to shuffle in her seat.

"You say nobody should live by running away from their past. Well what have you been doing?"

"What are you talking about?" Susan snapped. Her father's brow furrowed, silent lips sinking into a frown. She turned to face him, her breath starting to come in quick, panicked bursts, "I-I haven't run away from anything! You say so yourself, I never even do anything, except spend money!"

"Exactly, my dear." The older woman sighed. "You say Megan here has no ties, running around with nothing to remember her by. Well, what about you?"

There was a moment of silence, the ghost of Steven Parsons watching over them all. Megan cleared her throat, looking up at her friend.

"She has a point, you know."

"What makes you say that? You don't even know me!"

"Exactly. But look at me. You invited me here after only a train ride. Then, yesterday, you spent all day with me, like I was all you had to care about."

Susan went pale. "That's not fair. I know people. I know everyone in this neighborhood."

"But do they know you?"

Susan looked at her mother, then Megan, then the apparition of her father, then down at her knees. "Stop it. Leave me alone."

After another moment of silence, there was a small creak as Megan started to get up from her seat.

"Don't—!" Susan began, gasping out the start of a plea that didn't need to be finished.

"Megan, dear," whispered Agnes, "Please stay awhile. It's the middle of the night, nobody's going anywhere except into town. At least stay the night."

Megan looked over at Susan, her face half in shadow as the light of the moon shone through the curtains.

"Okay." She begrudgingly nodded, "I'll stay. For now."

"Mother." Susan murmured, "You remember when

daddy…went away? Just before he left, do you remember if he said anything to me?"

Agnes thought for a moment, then nodded. "He did," She took a few steps closer, kneeling down next to her daughter, "He got right down and told you to live well. That he was going away to make sure you stayed safe. He wanted you to live a fine life, dear, with a good husband, friends, and even children of your own."

Susan's eyes flicked upwards, then over to the window. Her father looked back, disappointment having turned to sorrow.

"Why do people have to die?" She asked, wistful, still looking at her father's translucent figure.

"Oh, my dear, nobody dies." Susan looked down, more than a little sceptical. She glanced up at Megan, who looked much the same. "Yes, they may leave us after a time but…" Agnes picked up the photo of her lost husband, still glinting in the moonlight. "They stay with us, in their own ways. Through their words; through the memories they leave in all of us."

She placed the photo back down, taking a contemplative breath. "That's what we all do, when we gather round this table late at night, and I start waving my hands around and making a big scene." She chuckled, hands going to hold Susan and Megan's shoulders. "We see ghosts, yes." She turned to Megan. "But not spirits, not little sprites in sheets that fly around with hell in their hearts. We see the people we remember, happy, and hopeful. We see our memories come to life before our very eyes." She took her hands off the girl's shoulders, clasping them with a sigh as she once again looked at the photo of her husband. "The pictures move, and the dead live again."

There was another creak as Megan shifted in her seat. Both

Susan and Agnes turned towards her, both of them relieved to find the girl poking around inside her suitcase. She pulled out three photographs of her own, and looked at them quietly. A soft smile crossed her face.

"I suppose they do, don't they." she murmured, sniffing back another breath, which turned into a tearful laugh. "In that case, we're all haunted, in a way?"

Agnes gave a small, relieved sigh, "In a way, yes."

She passed the photo to her daughter, before moving over to Megan. Through tired breaths, the girl began to talk to the older woman, who was letting herself become engrossed with the history of her daughter's new friend. Megan began pointing to each the photos, explaining who this was, and who *this* was, getting more and more excited as time went by. She clasped her suitcase, and moved it down onto the floor.

Susan was left alone with her thoughts. She took the discarded photograph of her father, looking over to the spectral figure across the table. She looked between them, watching as the ghostly figure began to smile, watching as his daughter became the woman he had once hoped to meet. The picture stayed the same, but the face had moved.

She placed the photograph down, where it shone in the naked moonlight.

The French Communication
Aaron Smith

I tried my best to sneak into the cottage quietly, removing my shoes as I entered to muffle the sound of my steps, hoping he'd be asleep, but I should have known better. He could still hear everything; his ears had not been dulled in the least by age. When I turned on the small lamp by the door to avoid tripping over the furniture, there he sat, in his favorite chair, staring at me like a stern grandfather, though there was no blood relation between us at all.

"You had a good time tonight," he said. It was a statement, not a question.

"And now," I replied, "you're going to tell me exactly how you know I had a good time, because you can't resist showing off, can you?"

"You might learn something."

"Proceed," I sighed, and the observations and the facts connected to them rolled off his tongue like notes pouring from the piano of a jazz musician.

"The late hour of your return here is our first clue, for you would not have stayed out until this time of night, or, actually, morning, were you not enjoying yourself. The disrepair of your stockings, combined with the dirt on them indicates that you danced much of the night, to the extent that you found it more comfortable to remove your shoes while doing so. The disheveled state of your hair, despite your attempts to coax it back into place, is further evidence of the intensity of your physical activity. Drink flowed generously, I would assume, based on the fact that not only my eyes, but my nose as well can testify to the spot on your dress where spilled champagne has stained the material. The slight stumble you made when entering the cottage tells me that more drink passed your lips. And, while on the subject of your lips, I might add that the smearing of your makeup indicates that you shared a kiss with some young man. Putting all those bits of observation together informs me that you did, indeed, have what seems to pass as a good time among those of your age. Am I correct?"

I was suddenly embarrassed by my appearance, disheveled as he said I was, and replied, "I suppose so."

"Am I wrong?" he asked.

"No, no, it was satisfactory."

"Yet your voice is colored with disappointment."

"It was fun, but, somehow, it wasn't enough."

"Elaborate, please."

"I drank and danced so much because I didn't have anything to talk about with those people. Had I sat still and tried to converse, I'd have been bored out of my mind! And, yes, there was a kiss…but it was with some local farmer's son and his clumsy, dirty hands kept trying to go where they had no business being and I had to slap them away. I had a good time, to an extent, but it was a drunken, wild, pass the time and don't think too much sort of good time, and I want something more. Maybe this isn't the place for me."

"You are unhappy in Sussex? Is your pay insufficient?"

"No, not at all! You've been very generous. And kind, too, in your own eccentric way, and…and you let me do what I please, for the most part."

"I allow you the freedom an adult should have, for you *are* an adult, if a very young one. Yet I must keep somewhat of a watch on your activities when you are not at work here, for I promised your grandmother, on her deathbed no less, that I would keep you safe while in my employ."

"I know, and I'm grateful for that. I just…I do miss London, and often."

"That is understandable. I will admit that I also miss it, though in a very different way. But it is late and you are tired and I am too old to keep these hours often. The morning will bring light and we will both feel better. I suggest you retire now, and I will do the same."

"Yes, yes, I will," I said, picking up my shoes and walking toward my room.

"Goodnight, Miss Hudson," he called after me.

"Goodnight, Mr. Holmes," I said as I turned back and smiled.

I felt better in the morning, as my overindulgence in champagne had left no haze and the cool countryside air rejuvenated me. I glanced out the window as I made breakfast and saw that Sherlock Holmes had risen early and was out inspecting his beehives.

I was grateful to him for hiring me and hoped I had not been rude to him the previous night. His habit of observing every detail of one's appearance and behavior could be disconcerting, but I also found it comforting to know that some people do not grow weak and lose their particular skills as they pass into their sixties or seventies. Yes, the old detective moved slowly at times and often tired easily, but his mind was as sharp as ever and he made an interesting, if not always pleasant, employer and housemate.

He soon entered the cottage, tossed aside his beekeeping gear, sat down as I served him his food and coffee, and produced an envelope from his pocket, placed it on the table and said, "This was delivered while I tended the bees. It seems your wish has been granted, Miss Hudson, for a short time, at least."

"My wish?"

"You wanted a return to London, did you not?"

"Yes, but…but why?"

"A request for my advice and assistance."

"But your retirement! You know you mustn't exert yourself."

"Taking a train to London and conversing with an old friend is hardly exertion. It is true that I accept few requests for help now and I do enjoy the solitude of the countryside, but there are certain men who have been of great help to me over the years and I consider it fair that I should respond if they summon me."

"So who sent the letter?"

"Have I ever mentioned the name Wiggins?"

"No," I said. Holmes rarely spoke of his days in London, and I was glad of that, for I found his storytelling style to be dry and dull. Most of what I knew of his detecting career came from stories my grandmother had told me when I was a child and from the few accounts I had read from the work of Holmes' chronicler, Dr. Watson. Honestly, Holmes' work, as well as his reputation and fame, were of little interest to me.

"During my years of business in London," Holmes continued, "I was often aided by a band of street urchins I named the Baker Street Irregulars. For a shiny coin or a meal from your grandmother's kitchen, those boys would carry messages for me, keep a lookout for persons of interest to a case, or perform other tasks best done by those beneath the notice of most Londoners. Very often, knowing how to blend in with the streets is a valuable skill to possess, and the Irregulars had acquired that skill through hard experience due to the circumstance of being born at a low rung on society's ladder. Wiggins was once the leader of the Irregulars, and I placed more trust in him than in many men twice or three times his age. Perhaps due to my influence, he grew up to be a police officer and has risen to the rank of inspector at

Scotland Yard. It seems he is having difficulty with a case and wishes to consult me."

"What kind of case?"

"Something involving the spiritualist movement."

Holmes' voice dripped acid as he spoke those words.

"You disapprove of spiritualists?" I asked.

"I disapprove of any sort of person who cheats others by throwing superstition about."

"A lot of people believe in the afterlife. You don't?"

"I believe in nothing for which I can find no evidence, and I have yet to discover a ghost or phantom that does not leave physically measurable traces and therefore is not what the gullible assume it is."

"But what's the harm? Thinking their friends or relatives have gone to a world beyond this one brings comfort to people, doesn't it?"

"And it spits in the faces of science, logic, reason, and verifiable fact. When one person holds a silly belief and keeps it to himself, perhaps then it is harmless, but absurd ideas tend to spread like wildfire and burn reason out of the minds of many who never get so far as to examine those ideas analytically. Spiritualism does it on a small scale, and organized religion does it in a way that changes nations and destroys the innocent. In either case, chasing specters is an activity the world can do without."

"I see. And this Wiggins requires your presence in London? Wouldn't the telephone suffice for consultation?"

"Perhaps I desire a change of scenery as much as you do, Miss Hudson. It has been quite some time since I have walked those streets."

The trip to London was uneventful. Holmes spent most of it with his eyes closed and without speaking, though I could not be certain whether he was asleep or deep in meditation and considering what he knew so far about the reason Wiggins had written him.

As we neared the city, Holmes ended his silence and said to me, "I will require your assistance with this case."

The statement made me nervous and I responded, "I am not Dr. Watson. I have no experience with things like this."

"I do not expect you to be Watson. I may ask you to perform some small tasks, but mostly I will need you to do what you do so well at home: be sure that I eat at regular intervals, for I often forget food when my mind is occupied; and do not allow me to exert myself too much, for I do not wish to suffer a stroke or heart attack in the middle of this affair."

"I had hoped to have some time to enjoy London," I said, regretting the words as soon as they came, for I knew I was being selfish.

"And you will," Holmes replied. "When the case is concluded, I promise you three days to roam London at your leisure, day or night, as payment for your work, provided you do not do anything foolish or immature."

"And who will take care of you while I'm indulging my whims?"

"Wiggins, in his letter, assured me that you and I are welcome to stay at his home as long as we wish. Mrs. Wiggins will see that I am fed. If she raised their two children to adulthood, I assume she can deal with an old man for a short time."

Inspector Wiggins and his wife, Cecilia, welcomed us warmly to their modest home. The house was cheerful and clean, nicely decorated, though small, as one would expect on a policeman's wages.

The inspector was in his fifties, a handsome man just beginning to go grey and fat with age. Cecilia was still quite pretty, but wore the lines of years of worry around her eyes, probably the price paid by many a Scotland Yard man's wife.

Just after the main course of our first meal at the Wiggins residence and the casual conversation that accompanied it, Holmes said, "I wish to hear the particulars of the case now.

At Holmes' prompting, Wiggins put on his inspector's face and told his tale. Cecilia looked bored and excused herself to make coffee and tea, but I forced myself to pay attention, knowing that ignorance of the business at hand would make me look stupid in Holmes' eyes later, and I did not want that to happen.

"Ralph Harrison," Wiggins said, "is a friend of mine and a former colleague. Shot by a suspect, he retired due to now walking with a pronounced limp. He contacted me recently due to suspicions that his wealthy aunt, a Mrs. Carrington, has been the victim of fraud and lost a great deal of money. I share Ralph's point of view on the matter, but have thus far been unable to prove any wrongdoing.

"Mrs. Carrington's husband, a major, died during the Great War, leaving his widow heartbroken to the point that she spent a period of time in an asylum before being released to resume her life. Even after her mental state had seemed to have improved, she still could not let go of the idea that the major's consciousness continued to exist in the spirit realm. She was adamant in the opinion that he would not pass on to heaven or whatever waits beyond this life without communicating with his beloved. She spent years reading the various religions' statements concerning death and the fate of the soul, and sought out many mediums and other men and women who claimed the ability to speak with spirits, but she saw through their feeble chicanery and tossed them aside like rubbish before moving on to explore the next avenue of her quest.

"This pattern continued for years until Mrs. Carrington received a letter from a man calling himself Ogden the Otherworldly. I must confess I burst out laughing when I heard that rather pompous title, and I see that you, Miss Hudson, are about to do the same, while you, Holmes, remain as stone-faced and attentive as ever. Very well, I shall continue.

"Ogden, in his letter, promised Mrs. Carrington that he could help her communicate with her late husband. Not one to give up her dream, the widow agreed to see Ogden and invited him to her home one evening. Her nephew, Ralph, was there for the arrival of the so-called Otherworldly.

"From what Ralph told me, the affair began as one might expect, with Ogden arriving in a dramatic costume which included a cape of a deep purple color. Mrs. Carrington, her servants, and Ralph were told to sit and relax. The lights were extinguished and the room lit only by candles. Ogden then proceeded to summon, or at least put on the act of summoning, Major Carrington, and the details were enough, real or not, to convince Ralph's aunt of the spirit's authenticity."

"What were those details?" Holmes asked.

"According to Ralph, Ogden spoke with Major Carrington's voice and related memories that no one but the widow and her late husband would be aware of, intimate details of their life together, including using the pet name, Butterfly, which the major had used to address his bride-to-be during their courtship, a name she swore she had never repeated to another living soul."

"I see," said Holmes. "And what happened after the seemingly successful summoning?"

"More such events were scheduled," Wiggins answered, "with Ogden now charging money for his services. Large sums of money."

"That is all you know?"

"Yes, but I can tell you that Ralph is quite concerned that this Ogden is taking advantage of his aunt and will not stop until her finances are drained away to nothing."

"In the morning," Holmes said to Wiggins, "you will speak with your friend and arrange for Miss Hudson and I to dine with his aunt. It is imperative that this event take place at her home. Also, I should like to meet Mr. Harrison before going to the Carrington house, for I have questions to ask him."

"Very well," Wiggins said.

Ralph Harrison visited the next afternoon. His concern for his aunt's wellbeing was evident on his face and in his voice as he said, "Thank you for coming, Mr. Holmes. I am sure you will be able to end this dreadful situation." He sat down and leaned his cane against the side of his chair.

"Mr. Harrison," Holmes said, "will you please describe your aunt's residence to me: the size of the house, the number of floors, and the locations of the rooms relative to one another?"

"Yes, I will do my best. It is a very large house, not a mansion, but impressive, indeed. There are two full floors, as well as a cellar and attic. On the first floor are the parlor, kitchen, dining hall, library, and a vast hallway connecting all those. The second story contains a multitude of bedrooms; I am not certain of the number."

"The stairs to attic and cellar, where are they?"

"One may get to the cellar by way of a door in the kitchen, and the attic is accessed by a set of stairs at the end of the second floor's hallway, just past the door to the last bedroom."

"What is kept in the cellar?"

"Wine, of course, as well as a small workshop that belonged to Uncle Roger…I mean, Major Carrington."

"And the attic?"

"It is used to store the many things accumulated during the time my aunt and uncle lived in that house. I could not tell you exactly what those items are."

"Thank you," Holmes said, then turned to me. "Have you been listening, Miss Hudson?"

I nodded.

"Good," said Holmes. "Now please repeat to me what Mr. Harrison just told us of his aunt's residence."

I had no idea why Holmes would ask me to do such a thing, but I fulfilled his request and, when I had finished, he clapped his hands together once and shouted, "Excellent!"

The home of Mrs. Carrington was, as her nephew had said, impressive. It was among the largest houses I had ever visited, and was beautifully decorated, though I could not help imaging how much nicer it would have been if redone in a more modern style.

Mrs. Carrington was in good spirits and delighted to make the acquaintance of the famous detective, though Holmes assured her that he was comfortably retired and pursuing no more work in his profession.

As we ate a delicious meal prepared by Mrs. Carrington's personal chef, the small talk that had followed introductions was soon brushed away as Holmes turned the conversation toward his case—the case our hostess, of course, did not know about.

"I understand you have recently had a unique experience," said Holmes.

"Ah!" Mrs. Carrington said with a laugh, "Ralph has told you of the miracle of my reunion with Roger!" and she launched into her own telling of the tale of how she had spoken with her late husband on several occasions now, with the help of Ogden the Otherworldly.

When she had finished the story, she sat back and smiled.

"It must have been wonderful," Holmes said, "to hear your late husband's voice after so many years. I suppose you expected never to hear it again."

"Certainly not in that way, no. I could have heard it every day for many years…but I could not bring myself to do so."

"What do you mean?"

"One of the last gifts Roger gave me before going off to fight that stupid war was a phonograph recording he had made of himself reading some of my favorite poetry. I have not listened to it in years, nor have I read the journals I kept early in our marriage. The memories brought me too much pain. But now I know that Roger is all right, that his spirit still exists, so I am happy."

At that moment, Sherlock Holmes looked at me and an expression of concern came across his face.

"Miss Hudson," he asked, "are you unwell? You look quite pale."

It was a signal we had arranged before our arrival, and I gave the rehearsed response.

"I feel…I feel one of my dreadful headaches coming on."

"Poor dear," said Mrs. Carrington.

"Yes," Holmes said, "the girl suffers from these episodes on occasion. Would you have a place where she can rest for a time? A spare bedroom, perhaps?"

"Of course. There are several such rooms." Mrs. Carrington turned to her maid, who had stood waiting for instructions through the entire meal. "Emily, escort Miss

Hudson upstairs and see that she has anything she needs."

"Yes, ma'am."

When I was certain the maid had gone downstairs and I was alone, I rose from the bed and prepared to do as Holmes had anticipated I would have to. I was quite nervous, having never engaged in such acts of deceit and stealth before, but I understood the reasons.

I crept down the corridor and found the upward-leading staircase. I took out the pocket torch Holmes had lent me and ascended into the attic. At the top of the stairs and through a small door, I found a dark, dusty room cluttered with boxes. I opened several and found clothing, books, old curtains.

Shining the torch back and forth across the rows of piled rubbish, the light finally struck a small box adorned with a name: "Roger."

I first looked carefully at the outside of the box, taking note of things Holmes had instructed me to watch for.

I removed the lid and looked inside to find a square paper wrapper which contained, as I could tell when I felt it, a phonograph record. Under the record were several small books, the sort of diary many people carry about in their pockets or handbags to take notes or jot down sudden ideas. I picked one up, opened it, read a page, and immediately put it back in its tomb, for I felt as if I had just peeped into someone's most sacred and private memories. I must have been blushing terribly.

With the box's contents back where they belonged, I moved to the attic's small window and examined the latch that held it shut.

I almost laughed out loud, delighted and amazed by just how correct my employer's assumptions had been, but my nervousness at sneaking about returned and I climbed down from the attic as quickly as I could and returned to the bedroom.

I rested for a few minutes, as I did not want the excitement of my search of the attic to show on my face when I returned to the table. From downstairs, I could hear a burst of laughter from Sherlock Holmes, and the footsteps of the servants accompanied by the clattering of dishes being removed from the table.

I finally rose and walked slowly back to the first floor.

"Are you feeling better?" Mrs. Carrington asked.

"Yes, much, thank you," I said as I sat down at the table.

"Emily," our hostess called to the maid, "bring Miss Hudson a fresh cup of tea."

As Inspector Wiggins drove us back to his home, Holmes said, "Mrs. Carrington is utterly convinced that she has indeed communicated with the dead major, and I fear it will cause her great pain when I reveal the truth, but her absolute financial ruin must be avoided. False happiness is not worth going to the poorhouse for."

"Then you are certain," Wiggins asked, "that Ralph's suspicions are valid?"

"As Miss Hudson will now confirm! Tell us, my dear girl, what you discovered in the attic."

"It was just as you predicted," I said. "I found a box containing the recording of Major Carrington's voice, diaries written during the romance, and other trinkets of courtship. And the dust on the lid of the box had been disturbed rather recently, as I could tell from your description of what to look for."

"And the attic window?"

"Scratches at the latch, as if it has been tampered with."

"Ha!" Holmes laughed. "Ogden must have heard—as those

who share professions tend to gossip—of Mrs. Carrington's quest for communication with the long-departed Roger. Seeing an opportunity to succeed where others had failed, he or an accomplice broke into the attic and borrowed the diaries, which revealed intimate secrets such as the nickname, Butterfly, and the recording, which allowed Ogden to learn to imitate the major's voice."

"What next then, Holmes?" Wiggins asked. "Will you simply reveal the fraud to the poor widow?"

"Oh, no," Holmes said. "That would not be nearly enough. Ogden the Otherworldly will soon be humiliated, and for that we shall require the help of an old friend, a woman who was a client of mine many years ago. In the morning, arrangements will be made."

As we finished our breakfast, Holmes handed a folded note to Inspector Wiggins, who was about to leave for his shift. I could tell that the note consisted of several pages.

Wiggins opened it, read it quickly, and put it in his pocket.

"Is all clear?" Holmes asked.

"Perfectly," said the inspector, and he made his way out the door.

"Last night," I said, for my curiosity had reached a great height, "you mentioned enlisting the help of a former client."

"Indeed," Holmes said. "Among the other tasks I have given Wiggins is to contact a Madame Lavigne. A Frenchwoman, I first met her in the early years of this century when Watson and I were in Paris for a consultation with the French government on a matter of which I still cannot speak plainly. While there, Madame Lavigne contacted us and pleaded for our help. Her son had been abducted. We located the boy and returned him to his grateful mother. She promised that if we ever needed her help, she would gladly grant it.

Sadly, much like Major Carrington, Madame Lavigne's son perished in the war. So saddened was the mother—who was also a widow—that she could no longer bear to live in the city where she had raised her child, for every street brought some memory back to her, so she relocated here to London where she still keeps a flat. Considering her history of loss and grief, I expect Ogden would consider taking her as a new client. Wiggins will relate to her the details of our case and she will then, I hope, agree to assist us."

"But," I asked, "won't Ogden grow suspicious if he is contacted suddenly by a new client? If I remember correctly, it was he who walked into Mrs. Carrington's life; she did not seek him out."

"By the end of today, Miss Hudson, Ogden will have already been told, by Mrs. Carrington, to expect word from Madame Lavigne, for I convinced our hostess last night, while you were investigating the attic, that the poor Frenchwoman is as in need of Ogden's aid as she was."

It occurred to me then that perhaps Holmes was going too far, that he was just an old man hoping to relive the glory of his younger days, and that the solution to the problem was much simpler.

"Why all this work?" I asked. "Why can't we just tell Mrs. Carrington what we found in her attic. She might be angry at us for snooping, but she'll know she's been swindled."

"No," Holmes said, "she will not. Mrs. Carrington has fallen so far under Ogden's spell that only absolute proof will convince her of the falsehood of what he has told and shown her. She is adamant in her belief in his abilities and would only make excuses. Also, we must admit to ourselves, Miss Hudson, that what we found fits my theory, but is hardly evidence of the most solid and damning kind. Disturbed dust on a box of mementoes would mean nothing and Mrs.

Carrington would come up with some explanation of her own, that the maid must have been sorting through the attic or that an animal entered and unsettled the dust. As for the tampered-with latch on the attic window, she would insist that we have no way of knowing that it has any connection at all to the box. Perhaps she might even combine the two observations and use them against us by saying that a window likely to open easily because of a damaged latch would also be likely to let in the breeze that blew the dust aside.

"Also, if she believed us simply through our words to her, it would be a quiet revelation of the sort that causes heartbreak. The best cure for heartbreak, as I have seen on more than one occasion, is anger. If Mrs. Carrington sees herself as the only victim of the unscrupulous spiritualist, she will blame herself and sink deeper into the mourning that has consumed so many years already. However, if she is shown through Ogden's own words and deeds and the circumstances we will set into motion with the help of Madame Lavigne, she will, I hope, aim her wrath at Ogden instead of directing it inward, and that will be what is best for her.

"Do you understand now, Miss Hudson, why we must do this in a very particular way?"

I did understand, and I felt a bit guilty for doubting Holmes' methods.

"Yes," I admitted. "I would like to help in any way I can."

The rest of the morning and afternoon was uneventful, even boring. I wanted to go out and reacquaint myself with London, but did not feel I should leave Holmes, so I read, assisted Mrs. Wiggins with some household chores, and left my employer to his ponderings and meditations.

Inspector Wiggins arrived home in the evening and handed Holmes a package wrapped in brown paper. It was small and rectangular.

"All is accomplished?" Holmes asked.

"It is," Wiggins answered.

"Then we await a response. As we wait, I have much to do. I shall be in my room and am not to be disturbed tonight."

"Mr. Holmes," I interrupted, "you must eat."

"That will not be necessary yet," he said. "I haven't the time."

"You are too old to ignore the needs of your stomach! I know you often neglected food when you lived under my grandmother's roof, but you were much younger then."

Holmes glared at me, and I thought he was about to unleash a fit of anger, but he seemed to pull back the reins of his emotions and a calm look crossed his face.

"Thank you for your concern, Miss Hudson," he said, "but the matter of Mrs. Carrington's safety must come first."

And with that he stood and, leaning on his cane with one hand and holding the package in the other, slowly walked toward his room.

Late into the night, I could hear occasional movement from behind Holmes' door. It worried me, for I hoped he would not overtax himself. At some point in those dark hours, I thought I also detected an odd smell in the house, a somewhat sweet aroma, but with a chemical bitterness to it. I must have fallen asleep soon after, for the scent had faded away by the time I woke.

Holmes looked dreadful when he emerged from his room the next morning. His grey hair was disheveled and dark circles sat under his eyes.

"Are you ill?" I asked.

"Perhaps you were right," he answered, "in that I should have eaten last night. I shall enjoy the delicious breakfast

Cecilia has prepared, and then I shall return to bed for a few hours. Wiggins," he held up the package he had taken into his room the night before, still sealed or, more likely, sealed again, "I shall place this back in your capable hands."

The inspector took the package, as well as a set of keys Holmes drew from the pocket of his robe. I did not recognize the keys and I knew for certain that they were not for the doors of the cottage in Sussex.

Wiggins left for the day, Holmes went back to bed, and I began another dull day in the home of our hosts.

Evening arrived again and the four of us sat down to eat, but our meal was soon interrupted by the telephone.

Mrs. Wiggins answered the call, turned to us, and said, "Mrs. Carrington for you, Mr. Holmes."

Holmes, who looked much healthier after his long nap, rose from his chair and took the phone. We could hear only his side of the exchange, which consisted mostly of affirmative answers. When the call had ended, he joined us at the table.

"The pieces are all in place," he said. "Mrs. Carrington and Ogden have spoken and he has agreed to meet Madame Lavigne the evening after next at the Carrington house. There will be six of us present, not including Mrs. Carrington's servants. Ogden, Mrs. Carrington, Ralph Harrison, myself, and you, Wiggins, and Miss Hudson. There, for a small fee— for those who prey like sharks on the innocent and distraught tend to start with small bites and dig their teeth in deeper on each subsequent attack—Ogden will attempt to make contact with the spirit of the late Laurent Lavigne."

Mrs. Wiggins had made sandwiches for lunch on the day of the event we had been awaiting. I was already seated at the table when the door opened and Holmes emerged from his room. He walked slowly toward the table, pulled his chair out to sit, and suddenly gripped the back of the chair with trembling hands. His breath came out in staccato gasps.

"Mr. Holmes, are you all right?" I asked.

He didn't answer. The chair slipped from his grip and fell on its side. I watched in horror as the tall, slim, elderly man crumpled to the floor, just narrowly missing having his head strike the edge of the table.

I stood and went toward him, but Mrs. Wiggins was there first, knelt to see to him, and waved me aside.

"Give him room to breathe!"

"Is he all right?"

"He's feverish," she said as she felt his forehead.

Holmes opened his eyes, coughed once.

"Mrs. Wiggins," he said in slow, weak words, "would you be so kind as to help me to bed?"

He started to rise, his body shaking. Mrs. Wiggins supported him as he stood and they began to shuffle toward the guest bedroom.

I waited at the table, terribly worried, but certain Mrs. Wiggins was better prepared than I to judge the severity of Holmes' condition. I cooked for him, cleaned the cottage, and did small household tasks, but he had never fallen seriously ill while I had lived with him.

Mrs. Wiggins returned a quarter of an hour later.

"How is he?" I asked.

"Exhausted. I fear he has pushed himself past the limits of what a man of his age should do. He must rest and do nothing else for several days at the very least."

"Should we call a doctor?"

"That will not be necessary, provided he taxes himself no more."

"The séance tonight!"

"You and my husband will have to go without Mr. Holmes."

"But how will we know what to do?"

"You will have to use your best judgment. To try to cancel it simply because one guest cannot attend would surely alarm the man you are trying to expose for a fraud. My husband has known Sherlock Holmes for most of his life and has learned much from him. And you seem to be a smart young lady. Things will work out."

Inspector Wiggins and I arrived at Madame Lavigne's building an hour before we were due at the Carrington house. I was so nervous about the coming night that it did not immediately occur to me to wonder how she had traveled from her flat to the ground floor. No servant accompanied her, but we found her waiting in her wheelchair.

"Good evening," she said in her nasally, accented voice. She was very old, or at least weathered from a hard life, and unusually tall and gangly for a woman, as I could tell by the outline of her long, thin legs under the blanket as Inspector Wiggins lifted her from the chair into the car. The wheelchair just fit into the rear seat and we were on our way. Madame Lavigne said nothing during our drive. I studied her features and was fascinated by her homeliness: a beak of a nose with a dark mole on the tip, eyes with dark bags below them, prominent lips resembling the bill of a duck, and stringy grey hair. Her hands were covered in age spots and the fingers twisted and bent with arthritis. She wore a plain black dress.

"Madame Lavigne, it is good to meet you," Mrs. Carrington said as she admitted us to her home. Her maid, Emily, stood behind her with Ralph Harrison.

We all assembled in the parlor, with Madame Lavigne in her wheelchair in a shadowy corner, sitting silent.

Fifteen minutes later, the doorbell chimed and Emily went to answer it. She returned with a man of medium height who looked about forty. He removed his hat and bowed for us, his purple cape flapping behind him like wings.

"Ladies, gentlemen, I am Ogden. Madame Lavigne, I am honored that you have chosen me to bridge the space between this solid world and the realm of the deceased. Your son, a brave soldier and a good man, wishes you to know that even from beyond, he watches over you."

Madame Lavigne made a little squeal, a noise that might have been a mixture of shock and delight.

"Please, sir," she said, "I must hear him again! I must!" she reached under the blanket that covered her legs and produced an envelope, which she handed to Ogden.

Ogden looked inside the small parcel and a satisfied look crossed his face. He put the envelope in his pocket and announced, "Let us begin!"

"Emily, extinguish the lights," Mrs. Carrington commanded, obviously having been through the routine before.

The room went dark until Ogden struck a match and lit a single candle, which he placed on a table. He kneeled on the floor, stared up at the ceiling, and spoke in a slow, droning voice.

"Laurent Lavigne, I call to you through the veil that divides this world from the next. Come forward to the border between realms and communicate with me, and with your dear mother, and let her know you are not forever lost."

He fell silent for a moment and then spoke again, but the tone of his voice was different now and the accent, as well as the words, came out French.

"Maman, chère maman! Je voulais rentrer au foyer, mais je n'ai jamais eu le temps. Les coups de fusil étaeint trop terribles et bruyants, le sang…il était partout, partout et si…rouge. Je ne pouvais pas rentrer. Vous me manquez. Je vous aime."

It had been several years since I had studied French, but I translated, in my mind, the best I could and thought it had been, "Mother, dear mother! I wanted to come home, but I never had the time. The gunfire was terrible and too loud, blood…it was everywhere, everywhere…and red. I could not go home. I miss you. I love you."

Madame Lavigne shrieked. "Laurent, Laurent! It is you! My son!"

I thought it very odd that she responded in English after Ogden's words were in French. Ogden then switched languages as well.

"You see, Madame? He loves you. He reaches out to you from beyond the grave. I cannot quite make out his words now, but I see images, flashes of memory from happier times, from his youth."

"What," Madame Lavigne asked "do you see?"

"I see a happy child, a little boy, playing at the seaside while his mother watches over him."

And with that, Madame Lavigne began to laugh. The sudden, high-pitched cackle evolved into a deep masculine chuckle and the Frenchwoman stood, abandoning her wheelchair to assume her full height. The twisted fingers straightened and a hand went up to the head to tear away the stringy wig and toss it aside.

"What is this?" Ogden the Otherworldly cried out.

The rubber that had enlarged the lips and lengthened the nose of Madame Lavigne was pulled away next and I saw—and I felt very stupid for not realizing sooner—the familiar face of Sherlock Holmes.

The old detective stood there in his plain black dress, and would have looked ridiculous, perhaps, if not for the stern expression on his thin face.

"Inspector Wiggins, Mr. Harrison, seize the charlatan!" Holmes roared.

The two men approached, grabbed Ogden by the arms, and held him there.

Mrs. Carrington screamed, "Why? What is happening?"

"I am sorry," Holmes said, "but you would not have believed me otherwise. Madame Lavigne, you see, does not exist. Her son, Laurent, was never alive, and therefore cannot be dead and contacting us from some ghostly dimension.

"You, Ogden, were given several small pieces of information: the names of Madame Lavigne and her dead son, the story of the son dying in the Great War, and the London address of your victim. Once she promised to pay you for your services, you began the same method you used to cheat Mrs. Carrington of her money.

"You went to the Lavigne flat, entered when it was unoccupied, and searched for items that would give you fuel for your imitation of the late Laurent. You found photographs of a young man in a French army uniform and of a boy playing in the sand while his mother, whose face was not clear in the image, looked on. You also discovered a journal with yellowed pages and faded writing in a feminine hand in the French language.

"When you agreed to work for Madame Lavigne, I set Inspector Wiggins to several tasks. First, he took some of his wife's clothing and other items that would belong to a woman and placed them, along with some books in French, in a flat that I keep in London should the need arise for me to stay in this city again for a time. Second, he obtained several photographs from the files of a friend at the Times of London and added them to the flat's contents. Third, he purchased a small, thick diary, which he gave to me to fill with French writing, for which I imitated the handwriting of a woman, for there are obvious differences between the ways the genders write. I also used a certain chemical agent to cause the pages and the words written upon them to appear older than they actually are.

"There is no Madame Lavigne. Her son never died. And you, Ogden, are an imposter, a predator, and a fraud.

"Inspector, remove this man from my sight!"

"Just a moment," said Mrs. Carrington. She walked over to where her nephew and the inspector held onto Ogden. She stared at the purple-caped swindler for a moment, then raised her hand and struck him hard across the face. "Now, Inspector, you may remove this man from my home."

THE UNBEARABLE

Peter Rawlik

It was a cool wind that blew in off the ocean that day in
December when Edward Toth came home to Orchid Beach.
Everybody had thought him lost. He and his three friends, all
gentlemen adventurers and landowners in the area had earlier
in the year, headed west along the river. They had told
everyone that they were to survey the acreage Toth had
bought just south of the lake. It was wild, untamed land
populated with screeching wildcats and titanic alligators,
venomous cottonmouths and clouds of mosquitos that could
devour whole cows in mere minutes. It was a land of tall-tales
and bigger men, and when Toth and his friends failed to
return from their weekend camping trip few paid any
attention.

That had been early September, and when five days had
passed and still no word of their fate there was talk of sending
out a rescue party. Then the storm had come, the great
monster hurricane that swept in from the Caribbean. It was a
black cloud that came ashore and devastated the whole of
south Florida. Three out of every five houses in Lake Worth
had been destroyed, many of the coastal hotels had lost roofs,
inland the storm surge had driven the lake out of its bed and
washed away entire communities pinning residents inside
their own collapsing houses. Those that didn't drown, died as
the waves of debris rolled over them beating them with nail-
studded boards, shattered timbers and twisting barbed wire
fencing. In the aftermath, Edward Toth and his party were
forgotten, at least until he came home.

The cool wind had been coming from the southeast, and so
Miranda, the woman for whom Miranda's Refuge House had

been named, had closed the windows in that direction. It was for this reason that none of the patrons of the bar had seen the small ship sailing in from the south until it had reached the great pier that jutted like a dagger beyond the breakers and into the very breast of the ocean. The pier like the Refuge House and a number of other buildings on the island had suffered relatively little damage when the killer hurricane had rolled ashore. Miranda wasn't sure if the was because her husband, who had been a construction foreman on the island before he had died, had done a good job of being prepared for just such an event, or that she and everyone else had just gotten lucky. Alma, the woman she paid to read cards claimed that disaster had been avoided by appealing to *Aido Quedo*, the snake spirit of water and wind, a ritual she and several others had undertaken to spare the island the wrath of the storm. When asked why the mainland hadn't been spared Alma just shrugged and said that some sacrifices had to be made.

From the small ship a single man disembarked, he was a tall man, and despite his coat and hat you could tell he was thin. That coat was a beaten oilcloth duster that had once been tan but was now stained with unwholesome patches of green, brown and rust that suggested more than just normal wear and tear. On his head, an old slouch hat cast a shadow over the man's face that even the Florida sun could not penetrate. He came down the pier with a slight limp but whether that was an organic defect or caused by the heavy, black leather boots that he wore on his feet Miranda couldn't tell. As he came toward the shore the sea spray that had dotted his coat and hat caught the sun and scattered tiny glints of light in front of him, like heralds of an abyssal leviathan come to extract some terrible vengeance. He strode past the ruins of the dock house and then vanished behind the scrubby sea grapes that dotted the weathered beach dunes.

It was a moment later that the door to the Refuge House opened and the man in the oilcloth duster limped across the sanded oak floors and collapsed in heap at the polished teak bar. It wasn't until his gruff voice called out for a drink that Miranda recognized him. The coat and hat had stayed in place, not unusual in the cool Florida winter, and thus his face had remained hidden, but that voice, that scratchy, deep sound she recognized immediately. And she wasn't the only one. Old Man Tebeau, normally content to keep to himself and his bottle of Cuban rum, looked up from his book when the man spoke and gave the shadowy figure a once over. Likewise, Mister Jonathan Ewel who drank his whiskey out of a tin coffee cup sat that item down and stared at the man trying to make sure he was who he seemed to be. Even old Alma started at the sound of his voice, dropping her deck of fortune telling cards and then gasping superstitiously at the one that fell upright.

"The Sun, Miss Miranda," she announced in heaving tones. "You know what a bad omen that is for you."

Miranda had heard such nonsense before, and as always she chose to ignore it. Alma was paid for her skills as an entertainer, not a sibyl.

A bottle of scotch appeared in one of Miranda's hands and with the other she produced a small glass, cracked but still functional. The storm may have spared the island a direct hit, but it had made the luxuries of life a little difficult to obtain. Liquor was a necessity, but new glassware wasn't high on anybody's list. As she poured she sidled up opposite the man and took an opportunity to confirm her suspicion.

It was Edward Toth, but he was a shadow of the man he had once been. Back in August the man had been a healthy two hundred pounds of solid muscle, with a black van dyke that he kept well groomed. Now the man looked rake thin, haggard, and his van dyke had gone gray. There was a scar across one cheek that trailed up around his eye and then back to his ear. The upper half of that ear was gone, and the lower half was a ragged, chewed lump of flesh with a dark pit in it. Worst of all were the man's eyes. Up close the slouch hat did a fine job of hiding them. Even so Miranda could see that something was terribly wrong with his eyes. It was as if the shadows hid something darker, and then in the center of that darkness lay an abominable pit in which two distant stars battled to dispel the void around them.

Miranda gave him a moment with his scotch and then spoke plainly to him. "We thought you dead Mr. Toth."

He paused, his glass still in his hand and exhaled slightly. "It has been a long time since anyone has called me that. How long have I been gone?"

Miranda cocked her head sideways, momentarily confused by the man's question. She had heard stranger things come out of the mouths of men, and they weren't always spoken with madness. "More than three months. We're a week from Christmas."

Toth nodded. "It seemed longer. It seemed much longer, so very much longer." He took a shot. "Davis was right."

Tebeau leapt out of his chair, a feat that given his age was probably ill advised, and crossed the room. "Morgan Davis was your friend, the big game hunter from Australia." The old man's voice was cracked and dry.

Toth shook his head. "Davis was from New Zealand, a town called Brokenwood, but his home was the world. Where ever there was land to tame and game to hunt that's where Davis went. The man was never truly happy unless he had a gun in his hand."

"Where is he now?" prodded Tebeau.

Toth looked up from the bar. "Davis? Lost. He was the first." He turned to look at Tebeau but the hat still hid those horrible eyes. "The others, Park and Cook they lasted longer, but in the end I lost them too."

Tebeau's voice became more somber. "They're all dead then?"

"Dead? I suppose in a way they are. Dead to this world at least."

Ewel drained his tin cup and nearly threw it across the table. "Enough of this nonsense!" He was almost barking. "You're being purposefully vague." He took the room in four or five strides. "You and your friends went out for a little hunt and some boozing, stayed out camping too long and got caught in the storm. There's nothing mysterious about that. You made a stupid mistake that's all. A stupid mistake that cost your friend's their lives." He smiled wickedly. "The sheriff will have you up on a charge of reckless behavior."

Alma laughed. "Sheriff Reynolds is dead and we ain't have time to find a new one. Deputies scattered all over the county finding the dead and making sure they're buried—or..."

"Or what?" The word leaked out of Toth's mouth.

Miranda responded, a look of distaste on her face. "There are too many dead. They've taken to using mass graves, but off the coast there's not enough soil. They're building fires, cremating the dead, burning them."

Toth's back stiffened. "It's a terrible thing to be burned." As the words left his mouth he stood up from the bar and opened his coat. His pants were held up not by a belt, but by a length of rope. His shirt was torn to shreds and showed that the man had not just lost weight, but had become terribly rakish, and his skin hung off of his frame in thin, layered flaps. It was a horrific thing to look at, but more so were the scars that covered that flesh. They weren't the memory of cuts or punctures or any other kind of wound, but rather decorated the flesh in great uneven masses. It was like looking at a beach while the tide rolled out and seeing the varied gouts of sand dry out on top of each other, with each adding in a ragged and distinct layer. Edward Toth had been burned, not once, not twice, but multiple times, and his body bore the scars of it. Mangled and twisted flesh twined like roots across his chest, down his arms and up his neck. "Even worse when you are still alive."

He moved toward the door, but Ewel put a hand on his shoulder. "I'm sorry Edward. Really I am. Let me buy you another drink and you can tell us all about your time in the swamp, the last few months, dark days were they?"

Toth turned and placed his hand on Ewel's shoulder. "Dark days? No, just the opposite really." He stumbled his way back to the bar. "The sun was high that day, and hot. You know how those summer days are, where even at dawn the air is thick and heavy, and your lungs balk at processing that tepid filth that passes for breathe. It was a day like that. A day in which we started out with clear skies, but as the noon hour approached the storm clouds began to gather in the distance. We here on the island are insulated from those torrents, but on the mainland they are a daily summer event, evidence that some unseen cycle is at play in that wild backcountry. It is not Lake Okeechobee that is the source of the Everglades, but rather those daily influxes of swift and terrible storms that feed the swamp and the various rivers and streams that trickle out of it. The lifeblood of the Everglades is the very rain itself.

"It was our intent, Davis, Park, Cook, and myself, to just get the lay of the land that first day. We had followed a stream from the coast towards the hundred acres I had bought from Chapman back in July. The land was south of the lake, were

240

the dense pond apple swamp transitions into the great open swaths of sawgrass, bulrush and water lily that we call the Everglades. It wasn't always called that you know. John William Gerard de Brahm was one of the first white men to see the place that the local tribes called Pa-Hai-Okee. His 1773 map called the area the River Glades. It wasn't till fifty years later that the corruption Everglades found its way into common usage. Cook had read about de Brahm. He died in Philadelphia, derided for his queer beliefs and writings about the nature of the universe. Cook said the man had seen something in the backwaters of Florida, something that made him question the very nature of the universe, something that other people couldn't or refused to understand.

"Cook was like that. Read a lot. He was educated in his own way. I don't think he ever formally went to university but instead had visited various libraries and willing professors. He had spent time in New Orleans with de Marginy. He spoke and read French, and German too I think. He and Park used to get along splendidly. Park was a college man, a naturalist and handy with a pen when it came to sketching the local wildlife, either before or after it had been killed. That was where Davis came in. The man was never happy without a gun in his hand, and not just any gun. Davis favored his war-battered M1917 Enfield, a rifle that he had carried for more than a decade and seen him across five continents. At first he'd hunted men, but with the end of the war he shifted towards more acceptable forms of prey, the bigger and more challenging the better. Which in a way makes everything his fault.

"We were on my land, far from the river where we had left our boat when Davis saw the bear. It was a monstrous thing, easily over four hundred pounds with ragged and matted fur and a scar running down its face. An ear was missing. It was distracted, feeding on a patch of huckleberry. We saw it, but it didn't see us. Cook and Park tried to back out but Davis waved them still. Silently, he slid his beloved rifle off his back and into his hands. It was only when he slid the bolt back that the bear became aware of our presence. It reared up and roared. Davis waited. He was calm. He took a breath and held it. The beast charged. Davis pulled the trigger. The world filled with a burst of light, and the stink of gunpowder.

"He missed.

"He hit the bear, but the animal didn't drop as expected. Instead it turned screaming, and careened down the little spring fed stream that we had all been drawn to, leaving a trail of blood in its wake. I saw Davis smile, and then he spoke. 'Come on boys can't leave an animal wounded like that!' Then he took off gun in hand, his big feet splashing down the stream. There was no pretense at keeping quiet. As the rest of us fell in behind him, I caught a glimpse of the sky. The storm clouds weren't on the horizon anymore, but we weren't in any immediate danger. At least not from the storm.

"We followed him into the marsh, dodging clumps of sawgrass and rushes, avoiding the deeper pools as marked by the still water lilies. A flock of wood storks exploded out of our path, and a cloud of mosquitos fell in behind us. We tracked the beast for what seemed an eternity but in reality could not have been more than an hour or so. We came to rest in a small clearing. Cook was doubled over panting. Park had found the remnants of an ancient bay tree. Davis, more used to such pursuits, was standing still listening for some clue as to which way the bear had gone. I opened my mouth to speak, to tell him to give up, but he shushed me. Then he seemed to catch wind of something, a sound or a scent. He smiled and then bolted downstream leaving us behind to catch our breath.

"He came back moments later, but it was clear that something terrible had happened to him. His jacket was torn, his hat was missing, and his shirt bloody, but it was his face that gave me such a terrible fright. He had this look about him this terrible look. He was staring up at the sky and whispering. 'Too big. Too big. It can't be that big.' I thought he was talking about the bear. He bent down and picked up a length of stick. I heard him chamber another round. Then he put the butt of the rifle on the ground, and tucked the end of the barrel under his chin. Before I could say anything, before I could even understand what he was doing, he jammed the stick into the trigger and pushed. The back of his skull blew clear off. Cook and Park thought the sound was thunder. It was only when they saw Davis slump over that they realized that he was dead.

"I don't remember much of what happened next. I was in shock I suppose. Somebody picked up the rifle. I can remember the sound of the gun in someone's hand. Park was cursing. Davis' gun belt was empty, all the cartridges were gone, but I, and the others, knew that he always carried a full belt, and that we had only heard him fire twice. I didn't understand it at the time, didn't recognize it for what it was, but I should have. I should have known, should have put it all together. But I didn't. I didn't understand how the pieces were falling together. And the world I knew was falling apart.

"We started walking back, a solemn troop heading north. I checked my watch; it was past two in the afternoon. My eyes went back to the sky. There weren't any clouds, not above us, not even on the horizon. There should have been clouds. There should have been a storm. But there wasn't. There was only the sky and the sun. It took us a while to notice that.

"As we tried to make our way back to the spring, back to our boat, back to civilization it slowly became clear that a terrible change had taken place. As we trudged solemnly back along the slough that we had followed in the landscape around us became unfamiliar. The stream seemed to widen and then become little more than a wide, shallow puddle resting on top of the sickly green scum that covered the rocky marl beneath. As each step fell behind the other, the vegetation became sparser. The tall clumps of sawgrass thinned and then vanished. The few trees receded into the distance and were never replaced. We were left with only rocky marl with only the remnants of vegetation: thin, twisted, sticks bleached gray and brittle. It was not the way we came, and we knew that, but there seemed to be no other choice. We changed direction more than once, but never could make it back to the shade of the trees. We could see them, they were there, on the horizon, but we could never reach them. They were unattainable, no matter how far we marched, or for how long we could never get any closer.

"It was after six, or so my watch said, when Cook went mad. The sun was still high, in fact as far as I could tell, it hadn't moved in hours. I checked Park's watch and his said the same as mine. Cook began laughing, cackling about the irony of it all. 'They're all so afraid of the dark. Even Davis was afraid of the dark. But it wasn't the dark that got him was it? No, it was the sun, that unbearable, cyclopean eye staring down at us. Unbearable.' He laughed at that. 'Unbearable. Davis went after a bear and we've been left with the unbearable.' He sat down in the thin, tepid water that covered the marl. Park took him by the arm but he wouldn't move. The man was laughing, he was laughing hysterically. I marched on leaving Cook and Park behind. I hadn't gone more than twenty paces when I heard Park's pistol fire. After that I couldn't hear Cook laughing anymore. A few moments later Park jogged up behind me. Neither of us said anything, we just kept walking. And the sun, Cook called it 'that unbearable, cyclopean eye' it continued to beat down on us,

244

burning into our skin, into our eyes, into our brains.

"I have over the years heard tell of the horrible things men were forced to do in order to survive. Such tales always filled me with a sense of dread. What would I do in such a situation? Could I survive? Would I? Would I descend into a primeval state? Would I be able to return from such a descent? Now I know. I stand before you evidence that men will do unspeakable things to survive. The natives who live in the deep Everglades are known to eat the hearts of young palms, the soft interiors of sawgrass, and even the cottony heads of cattails. When available they will eat bass, sunfish and even gar. Alligators, frogs and turtles are fine meals, feasts if done properly. Park and I had none of that. But we still had the hunger, and satisfied it the best way we could. We built small traps for mosquito fish and similar sized fish, and slurped them down whole. Crayfish became sought after prizes, almost delicacies. I would tear the heads off and crunch down on the tails and claws, but Park would just crush them and eat them whole. Such things were plentiful in the queer landscape we found ourselves in, and we speculated on why such things were readily available. Park speculated that it was the lack of predators, specifically herons or storks. I have seen similar landscapes as to the one we traversed filled with a great flock of water fowl including ibis, herons, storks, flamingoes and spoonbills but in the place we had wandered into there was none of that. Not even vultures circled overhead waiting for us to die.

"On the third day there appeared on the horizon a small dark lump. It was not much, but it was the only feature that seemed to change, to grow closer as we continued our trek through hell. I knew it was the third day because I kept track using my watch. I marked the passage of time on the back of the case. Scratching a single line for each day that passed. We had thought perhaps it was a clump of grass, or a small palm tree, or even a scraggily willow. But as we neared it our hopes faltered and then turned to despair. The small lump grew larger and finally recognizable and we knew it for what it was before we were within a hundred yards. We should have turned away, but we couldn't, we had to know, had to see it for ourselves. There was a kind of doubt you see, a sense of unbelieving brought on by the incessant burning star that showered us in its terrible radiation. But there was no denying the truth once we reached the thing. It was plainly recognizable as the man we once knew as Cook. The sun had cooked him, given the heat and the water he may have been steamed, or even poached. It was an awful thing to see. Can you imagine it, a man prepared as you would a goat, or chicken, or even a rather large fish?

"The sight of it drove Park mad, or perhaps it was the hunger. He took out his knife and began skinning the body. Cutting through the clothes first, and then the soft meat along the shoulder and arm. He did it with some skill, learned I suppose from butchering deer or wild boar. As he did so he sang a tune,

> One, two,
> Buckle my shoe;
> Three, four,
> Open the door;
> Five, six,
> Pick up sticks;
> Seven, eight,
> Lay them straight:
> Nine, ten,
> A big, fat hen;
> Eleven, twelve,
> Dig and delve;

Thirteen, fourteen,
Maids a-courting;
Fifteen sixteen,
My lips she's licking
Seventeen, eighteen,
I'm tired of waiting
Nineteen, twenty,
My stomach's empty

It was on the tenth refrain of that horrid rhyme that I took out my knife and stabbed him in the back. I lowered him to ground and let the blood run out over his shirt and into the water. As his life drained away, he motioned for me to come closer. I lay my head down on his chest and into my ear he whispered 'Thank you.' I left him there with Cook, and I never looked back.

"After that I was by myself, trudging across that vast empty landscape that despite the presence of water, was as much like a desert as any I could recall. The sun beat down on me lake the gaze of some unbearable, inescapable titan of myth. I was watched by that unmoving, burning eye and from it I could find no respite. Even in my sleep, which came only when I collapsed and curled into a tiny ball with my coat and my hat covering my head, even then the light found its way into my eyes, and disturbed my dreams. They were nightmares of pure brilliance, of a sky full of stars in which I could see further and further. There was only light, no shadows, no perspective, no wavering heat mirages. I could see it all. As time passed it became impossible to tell the difference between the waking world and sleep. The two became one and the features of the real world fell away until I had nothing left but the light and a great white plain.

"It was a place of nothingness. Not the dark, for that at least would be a shadow of something. In that place there was nothing but that queer unblinking orb that radiated down upon me its hate and despair. It had bleached away the world and everything else in it. There was no land, no water, no plants or animals. There was only I, a lone and lonely gunslinger crossing the vast bright plane on a quest for freedom. In time I even forgot my name. It was better that way. I lived only to walk. In my madness, my white-washed delirium I dropped my coat. I did not even notice until my skin began to blister. It took days to work my way back and find it. By then I had been burned not once but a multitude of times.

It was after I filled the inside of my watch case with tiny marks that I saw the cloud. It wasn't a cloud at all, not really, but I have no other words with which to describe it. It was a dark spot in the distance, and one I could not keep my eyes off of. It was elevated and hazy. I knew instantly that I wasn't hallucinating. And knowing this I reached inside for any reserves I had left and quickened my pace. In hours the water had returned, and for the first time in days I had freshwater to drink. The marl came a few hours later, and with it the tiny darting shadows that indicated life. There wasn't much to eat, but what there was found a way into my mouth.

"As I had lost the wilderness, so did it return. With each passing step a semblance of normalcy crept back into my view. Submerged vegetation wrapped around my feet and made walking hard, but I welcomed it. Clumps of sawgrass were replaced by vast stands of it, and I reached out and touched it with my hands, reveling in the sensation as it cut into my flesh. A day later and there were stands of cattail ten feet high or more, and I took shelter in them, letting their shade provide me with a miniscule of relief from that unbearable, burning star.

"On the third day since I had sighted the cloud it began to rain. It was a sun shower at first, but then the clouds gathered and grew thicker. They darkened and with them came wind and lightning and for the first time in recent memory I knew darkness. In those first few moments I was overjoyed, and I danced as if I had gone mad, but then the cold came, and the wind, and with it came debris. A whirlwind of sand and leaves and sticks assaulted me, and I retreated into a stand of cattails for shelter, wrapping them around me as if I was a bird trying to build a nest. I slept with the wind howling and the rain battering me, but I didn't care. Something had changed, and or that I was grateful.

"I awoke to the sound of men yelling. I was being manhandled, pulled aboard a small fishing boat. Later I found out that I was in Florida Bay, somewhere northwest of Key Largo. I was floating in those shallow waters, and to all those who had rescued me I seemed a miracle, for neither shark nor crocodile had molested me. I spent a day on that boat before they took me back to shore. The captain and crew of the Seahorse were most accommodating, and though their supplies were both plain and meager they shared them with me without hesitation.

"Once back on shore in Key West I was a guest of the local constabulary until arrangements with my bank could be made. Afterwards, I booked passage on a small private trade ship heading up the east coast. That was three days ago, and as you have surely noted I have just come home. This is the first drink of liquor I have had in ages, the Keys being stricter of their enforcement of prohibition than Orchid Beach. It is also the first time I have told my tale of loss, madness and survival. To be honest both have left me feeling less than amicable."

With that he pulled out his watch and flipped it open as if to check the time, but Ewel had become infuriated during the telling of the tale. "You expect us to believe that nonsense

Toth? Its pure fantasy, and I've heard it before. Davis himself recited a similar story. He said it took place in Australia almost thirty years ago. Oh you've updated it for your own purposes but it's still the same story, a school girl's delusion that is all." He grabbed the man by the wrist. "He's made it all up to protect himself, to hide his crimes. Can't any of you see that?"

Toth dropped the watch and it hit the bar. It spun widdershins while Toth himself turned sunwise. Ewel continued to paw at the man, and one wild grab knocked the man's slouch hat off. Miranda caught a glimpse of what was under there, but Ewel saw it full on and in doing so removed his hands from the man and instead clutched them to his chest. Toth said something to the angry man, and then pulled his hat and coat tight to his person, and leaving his watch on the bar, stalked out into the day. Ewel crumpled to the floor and in minutes was dead of apoplexy.

No charges were ever brought against Toth, indeed no complaint was ever filed. No one in the town of Orchid Beach ever saw the man again, though it was assumed he lived in it for the rest of his life. Under orders of his attorney the Toth residence was rebuilt and the property expanded. Visitors were discouraged and tradesmen dealt with by a stern, blind Haitian woman and her mute son. That was till at least 1944. After that callers to the property went unheeded, and in 1946 his attorney announced that Mr. Edward Toth had passed away and that the property was being held in trust for the family. The acreage on the mainland, south of Lake Okeechobee had long since been seized by the Federal government for one drainage project or another. Occasionally, on some older maps one can find reference to a place called Toth's Slough, but that seems all the evidence that remains of his strange adventure.

As to the watch and what was said by Toth to Ewel, those too are curious stories in their own. The watch, damaged by immersion in saltwater, was of little use as a timepiece, though the gold of its casing had some value despite the thousands upon thousands of scratches that marred its once beautiful finish. Miranda left it where it had fallen and placed a bell jar over top of it. It stayed there until the bar itself was shut down in 1952. An inventory for that year suggests it was transferred to the Orchid Beach Historical Society, but an assessment of items salvaged after Hurricane Andrew did not list the pocket watch amongst the items salvaged from the flooded archives.

Miranda and Old Mister Tebeau never mentioned what they glimpsed under Toth's hat. Nor did they ever repeat what was said between the two men. People tried. They plied them with drink and the offer of cash. One man tried to write a book about Toth. But the two kept their silence. Tebeau died first, at age ninety-three, in bed with his sixth wife. Miranda died that same year, hit by a car crossing Highway A1A. Even then, decades after her squalid bar had closed down, people still remembered who she was. The funeral was hold in the big hotel off Poinciana Street, and more than a thousand people lined up to pat their respects. She may not have been rich, but she was Orchid Beach royalty.

But Alma, who kept reading people's cards well into the 1970s in a squalid, two-room apartment on Dixie Highway used to talk about the old days with her niece Winifred Cotton. Miss Cotton was not the most reliable of historians, and she herself died from drinking rubbing alcohol in 1978. But before she passed she spoke to local author David Eyman, and told him what her Aunt Alma said about that day and what was beneath that hat.

"As my aunt told it, Mister Toth's hat came off and he

251

hissed at Mister Ewel. 'I see you Jonathan Ewel! I see you and yours and the petty things you've done with your children in the dark. I see you and all your wickedness.' And Aunt Alma knew what he said was true, not because she had known about it, and not because Ewel had died right then and there, but because she saw what was hidden beneath that hat. Mister Toth's eyes were gone, there weren't nothing there but a great gaping hole of darkness where his eye sockets should've been, and there in that terrible darkness burned a single hideous orb. It was a tremendous and infinite thing that gazed out upon everything, and saw the truth of the world. An unreasoning, unforgiving white star, a three-lobed burning eye that had poured itself down onto Toth in the queer place it had found in the Glades. 'I see you Ewel, I see you all.' Screeched Mister Toth as he walked out the door. "Be grateful you all live in the dark.' It was a terrible thing to glimpse said Aunt Alma, truly unbearable."

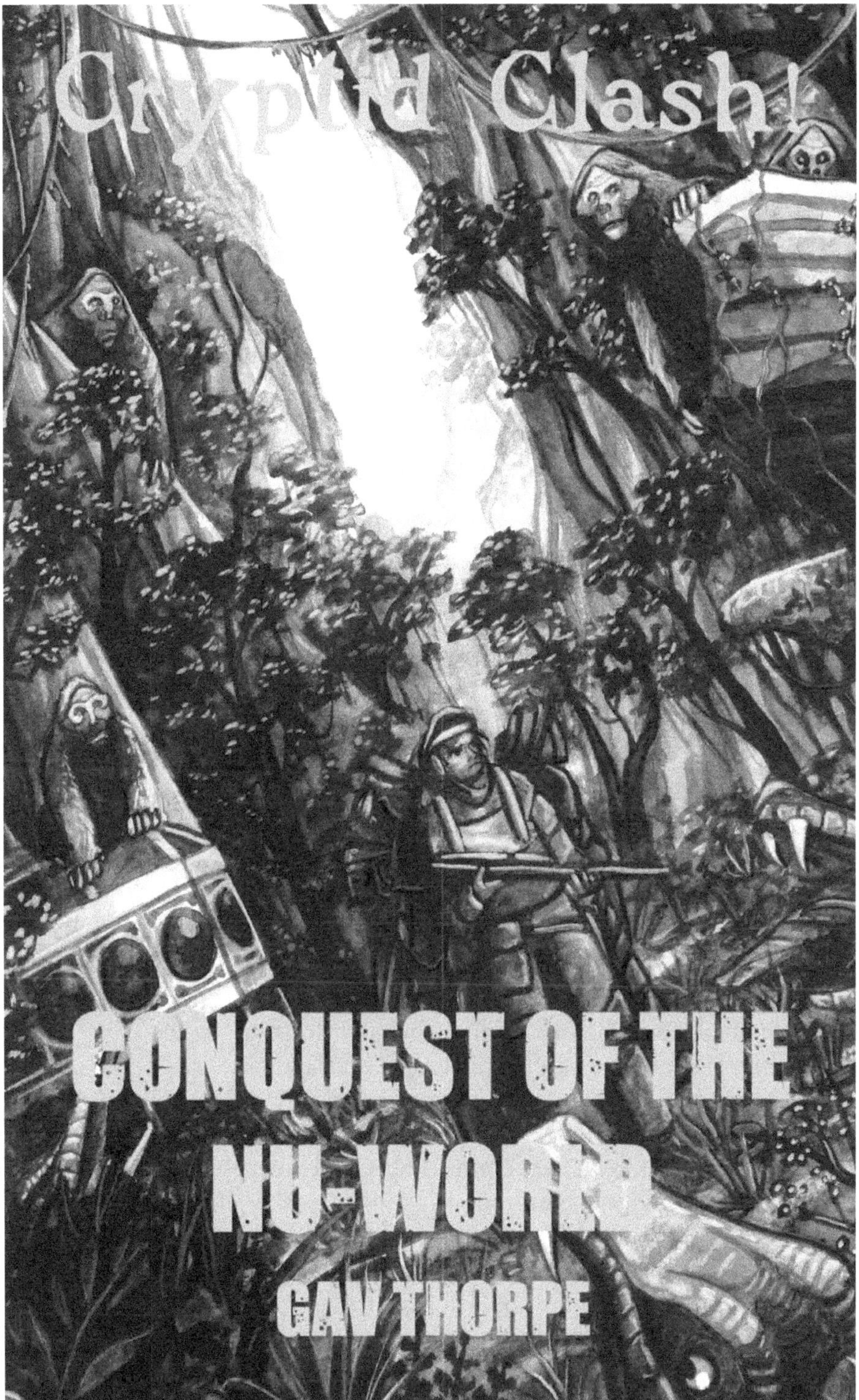

Cryptid Clash!
CONQUEST OF THE NU-WORLD
GAV THORPE

Conquest of the Nu-World

Gav Thorpe

"A myth," said Doctor Tanzi, shaking his head in disbelief. "Superstition. Folklore. The ban-manush."

Ninety-eight light-years away, the terraformed colony planet Goloka has gone silent. Azavedo Explorations dispatches a team of mercenaries and middle-management to investigate.

There is something in the forest. The colonization process should have filtered out apex predators. Humanity should be at the top of the food chain.

And yet, there are two greater hunters stalking them...

Cryptid Clash! features horror, urban fantasy, and military sci-fi luminaries such as William Meikle, Gav Thrope, David Annandale, C.L. Werner, Nikki Nelson-Hicks, and Josh Reynolds.

The Q-Jump terminal, a u-shape four hundred metres across fashioned from the most advanced superconductors and t/s indent technology, flashed a brilliant white, and where one moment had been vacuum and tiny particles of dust there was now a gleaming cylinder. The portalcraft opened up, shedding foil skin in shimmering leaves, casting aside its monomolecular wire frame to reveal a far sleeker ship, a dart-like gunboat designed for atmospheric transit.

The descent of the *Laphroig* through the thickening atmosphere of Goloka set the grey hull vibrating. At the controls, monitoring the craft's artificial sentience, sat Kelvin Dagworth III. He tapped his fingers pensively on the brushed chrome dashboard.

"Any luck with the comms?" he asked the man in the co-pilot chair, Tigran Sargsyan.

"Nothing, just the descent beacon," replied the Armenian. He was more relaxed than his commander, slouched as far as the drop harness allowed. "I'll keep trying."

Strapped into the drop-seats behind them, the assembled

254

passengers of the *Laphroig* made for an unusual crew for the Incursion-class vessel. Kelvin looked back at them with a forced smile and their idents flashed through the periphery of his data-contact.

Kelvin had supplied them all with clothing and boots for rough terrain—jackets and expandable smocks, fatigue leggings, full calf boots, survival belts and portable packs. Hopefully it would be unnecessary preparation, but he had learned from bitter experience that if he didn't, some expert or executive would be trekking through the pre-settlement wilderness in nothing more than a suit and tie. Nobody was getting sunburn, hypothermia or a broken ankle on his watch.

Closest was Doctor Tanzi Dewan, a native of Bangladesh. He insisted on being called Doctor Tanzi in jocular manner, his overly self-effacing manner painful to watch. An expert in xenocolonial expansion, he had been dispatched by the board members of Azavedo Explorations to assess the biological viability of Goloka following the interrupted reports from Dr Krebaum. He sat with his eyes closed, head bowed, fists gripping the crash harness tightly.

Next to him was Hugo Melo, boasting a top-of-the-line athletic build bought from the bodyshoppers of Taiwan rather than earned in a gym. His pinched face looked incongruous atop the broad shoulders and thick biceps his management salary had afforded him. He was also representing the board of Azavedo Explorations.

What didn't show up in the feed, and thus remained unknown to Kelvin, was that Hugo had been commissioned to take over the running of the colony should it be found that the Krebaums and Carlos had gone off-plan. He was hoping this would be the case, as a planetary administrator role would distance him from certain financial indiscretions that were at risk of coming to light back on Earth.

Melo was the money man, given executive control of the expedition, though operational command was Kelvin's alone. The two of them had not seen eye to eye since they had met four days earlier, pre-jump, but Dagworth had survived worse clients.

On the opposite side, Carlos' accountant, Xhang. Of all of them, she looked the most comfortable in a drop-seat. She turned her head and met Kelvin's gaze with an impassive stare from hazel-coloured eyes that contained the glint of a datalens—implant, not peripheral, pretty hi-spec for an accountant.

Kelvin had seen that look from plenty of private contractors over the years, and the fact that Xhang shared it with him was something—a display of trust? It was clear she wasn't really an accountant, the way she held herself and knew her way around a gunship spoke to a military background. The crates she had loaded aboard were also more than just a few money transfer records…

It had been too late for Kelvin and Tigran to object, unless they wanted to pass on the contract altogether, so the two of them had agreed in secret to ignore the merc in the room. As Tigran had pointed out, it was just their job to get the whole strange bunch safely to Goloka, after that what they got up to was very much their business and nobody else's.

Take the money, don't fret. Tigran's mantra.

At the back by the systems monitoring station was their occasional engineer, Jeremy Baines. They'd travelled a good few jumps together, occasional partners on a job, but both unwilling to formalise the relationship with a business pact. It had been luck that Jeremy had been around for the short-notice mission, saving Kelvin the hassle of settling in with an engineer brought in by Azavedo Explorations.

"Don't look so worried, doc," exclaimed Alonse DeVere, one of the three declared private contractors sat in the primary combat stations at the aft of the dropship; the other two being a degendered that called perself Honeycomb, and 'Senior Contractor' Sarette MaKwayi. Hailing from Belligerent Solutions (PTY) LTD, the three PCs wore grey combat fatigues and black webbing, sidearms in holsters at their waists, though their main weapons were stowed in the hold—Kelvin had strict rules about firearms under his command, and felt the weight of his own pistol at his hip. It had been three years since he'd had to fire it.

"Why would I be worried?" asked Tanzi. "We're just dropping through an uncultured atmosphere at over ten thousand miles per hour, Mister DeVere, to land at a work-in progress station on a partially complete pre-stage one world, whose inhabitants have ceased transmitting for seventy days. No reason to be worried at all, is there?"

Alonse laughed and patted the Hazer '58 on his belt.

"This ain't just for show, doc."

"Probably just a downed transmitter," Sarette said with a shrug. "Nothing to worry about."

Even she wasn't convinced.

A lot of people think that a colony world looks like a primeval paradise; this was mainly due to the constant and highly misleading Q-Jump commercials that played in their heads throughout the early 20s and 30s. The problem with building a new planet from primordial swamp upwards is that it takes millions of years, and that does not give a timely enough Return on Investment for most shareholders.

Rather than grassless jungles and volcanoes, Goloka looked, for the most part, almost exactly like the highlands of Northern Bangladesh. In fact, following the metalled road from the landing zone toward the colony encampment, Doctor Tanzi might well have been transported back to the farmlands outside the village where he had grown up.

"The air," he told the others as they took a water break. "The air doesn't taste the same."

"It doesn't taste the same as anywhere on Earth," Kelvin reminded him. "Higher CO_2 levels here than back home to accelerate the flora growth."

They were all a little short of breath, for the same reason, except for Honeycomb, who, as well as per heavily modified androgynous battle-form benefited from extensive organ enhancement inside per reinforced exterior. With per long-barrelled MPHG the degendered looked more like a robot warrior from a fictioncast.

With them came the STaLKer—Sentient Transport (Light Kit)—carrying the contractors' supplies and ammunition

257

packs. Its gangling legs seemed too weak and uncoordinated to sustain its bulky body, but the autonomous intelligence unit kept it striding alongside them over the even ground of the road. Occasionally one of the private contractors would take out their digimap to check where they were, but the causeway ran pretty much straight for thirty kilometres between the landing zone and the outpost.

They had arrived only a couple of hours (Earth rotational) before dusk, and the twilight caught up with them quickly, turning the trees and hillsides into mauve shadow. Kelvin called a halt, intending to camp for the night, but Hugo Melo had other plans.

"We keep on," said the administrator. "It's only another three hours to the station."

"We don't move in the dark," Kelvin countered. "It's my call."

"I don't think so," Melo insisted, sticking his thumbs into the belt hooks of his trousers, artificially moulded muscles bulging beneath his sweat-dampened shirt. "This isn't an operational decision."

"Worried about the hourly rate, money man?" said DeVere.

Kelvin glared at Melo, but it was obvious the board's representative wasn't going to back down. He looked to Sarette to back him up but the private contractor was talking to her two associates, showing no interest in the debate.

"Let's just go," Tigran told his partner. "A couple of hours and we'll be having showers and a soft bed. Better than sleeping out."

Kelvin considered digging in his heels—if Melo got his way now he'd push even further later. The decision seemed made already though; the others were continuing up the track without him and Hugo.

"Fine," Kelvin muttered as he turned away, hitching up his pack a little more on his shoulders.

The air was humid and cloudy as they carried on, slicking everything with a sheen of moisture beneath the overcast darkness.

Down to the microbes in the soil, Goloka had been modelled on a DNA sweep of the Low Hills of Sylhet, a full ecosystem replicated on a world nearly a hundred light-years from where the genetic samples had been sequenced. Fauna could be heard in the thickening woods, arboreal and aerial, cawing and crying at the approach of the humans. It put Doctor Tanzi in mind of his childhood, sounds he hadn't heard for fifteen years, not since moving to New Yemen to study. His frequent and repetitive remarks on this pushed the patience of the others to their limits and more than once Kelvin had to intervene, changing the subject to cool things down.

They were about an hour further on, still ten kilometres from their destination, when Sarette called a halt.

"Where's Baines?" she snapped, the light of her helm-lamp flashing from one face to the next.

"Jeremy?" Kelvin hadn't even noticed the engineer had gone, so engrossed had he been in his surroundings.

"I think he went to take a leak," said DeVere.

"When?" Sarette jabbed a finger toward Honeycomb. "IR sweep, find him."

The augment nodded and strode back down the road, eyes gleaming as per gaze swept back and forth through the trees. Soon pe had disappeared from view as well but the tick-tick-tick of per signal on Sarette's monitor indicated nothing was amiss.

"Shall I get the drone?" asked DeVere. He made to move toward the STaLKer, but Sarette shook her head.

"If Honeycomb can't find him, he's lost."

"We'll set up camp here," declared Kelvin, worried about Jeremy but glad of the opportunity to re-establish his authority as expedition lead. "A base of operations to conduct a search."

This time Melo offered no argument, shaken up by the unexpected disappearance of the engineer, and they started unpacking the reflective bivouac shelters from the STaLKer, only to be stopped by the buzz of Sarette's communicator and the neutral voice of Honeycomb.

"Found something."

"Something?" Tigran said nervously. Sarette waved for him to be quiet.

"Report," the senior contractor said, motioning for DeVere to follow her as she took a few paces back down the road. There was no further sound, the communicator switched to a private channel between the contractors, but Sarette's shoulders slumped at the news she was given.

"What is it?" demanded Hugo, moving after the soldiers.

Kelvin noticed Xhang, who had said nothing through the entire episode so far. She was alert, like the rest of them, but not nervous. Kelvin moved a little closer to her and unclipped the cover on his holster.

"Everything all right?"

"Clearly not," came her curt reply.

"If you have an undocumented firearm, please tell me now," he said quietly.

She turned a blank look toward Kelvin, her impassive stare a challenge and denial at the same time. Satisfied that she had made her point, Xhang returned her attention to the pair of soldiers at the end of the circle of light cast by the STaLker's body lamps.

"The safest place is behind me," she said quietly.

Kelvin wasn't sure he had heard her right, but did not have time to inquire further as Honeycomb emerged from the gloom and joined the other two private contractors. She was carrying something in a bind of camouflaged sheeting.

"What have you found?" Hugo demanded, striding up to them.

Honeycomb turned on him, per mirror eyes catching the light from the STaLker to appear like two circles of bright yellow. Pe held out per hand, the cloth open to reveal...another hand, crudely severed at the wrist, tendons and flaps of ragged skin hanging free.

Hugo turned away, retching. DeVere laughed.

"Jeremy was my friend," growled Kelvin, squaring off to the merc. DeVere controlled his fit of bad humour and nodded, the apology unspoken but sincerely meant. Kelvin looked to Honeycomb for answers. "Is that all?"

"The smell of urine. Trails in the mud and blood where he had been dragged away."

"Do you think…?" Tigran didn't want to ask the question because he knew the answer would be no. He steeled himself against this truth. "Is he alive?"

"No shouting, nothing," said DeVere with a grimace. He snapped his fingers. "Whatever got him was quick."

"I'm authorising full ordnance load-out," Hugo said shakily, pale in the harsh glare of helm and STaLKer lights.

"About time," said DeVere, a little too triumphantly for Kelvin's liking. "Time to earn some danger money."

"Wait," said the captain. "This is still my expedition."

"Something killed Jeremy," said Hugo. "We have to find it and kill it before it attacks again."

"It's gone. Shooting up the forest isn't going to find him," Kelvin replied, reluctantly forced to take the counterview. Like Tigran, he desperately wanted Baines to be out in the trees somewhere, maybe hurt and unable to call for help. But DeVere was right, that seemed highly unlikely.

"There isn't anything in the fauna sweep that could do this," said Doctor Tanzi. His hands quivered as he accentuated his thoughts with broad gestures. "Even if a stray Bengal Tiger was caught in the cross-section, seed-systems scan for dominant predators and remove them. The community is supposed to fulfil the apex role."

"That makes no sense," said Hugo. "Something bit off Baines's hand!"

The exec staggered away again, one hand clutched to his mouth, reminded of what he had seen.

"We have no clue what we're doing, what we're looking for, where it might be," said Kelvin. He nodded to Sarette. "Break out your big guns if you want, but we have to continue on to the station. Maybe they'll be able to help us."

"That would be the station that we haven't had a signal from since we landed, right?" said Tigran, less than enthused by Kelvin's proposal.

Nobody had any better ideas.

ALL THE PETTY MYTHS

Curated By M.H. Norris

All the Petty Myths
Midnight
M.H. Norris

An exclusive preview from award-winning mystery author M.H. Norris' new series, *All the Petty Myths*. Look out for the full story in the collection of the same name, out soon from 18thWall.

Dr. Rosella Tassoni looked over the auditorium full of half-asleep freshmen and quickly remembered why she *usually* only agreed to lecture upper-level courses.

"Since the beginning of time, man has told stories. When a written language came along, these were written down. Some would surpass their own cultures, becoming what we know to be legends. Today we call the study of those legends mythology. Every culture has their own distinct legends, yet many share a similar foundation. Max Müller considered these legends 'a disease of language,' but clearly they're something more. I prefer Tolkien's explanation for legends in his essay 'On Fairy-Stories,' originally delivered to students very similar to you. 'The history of fairy-stories is probably more complex than the physical history of the human race, and as complex as the history of human language.'"

Rosella clicked the slide over before reading the quote. "What are the origins of, as Tolkien would call them, 'fairy-stories'? 'I am too unlearned to deal with this question in any other way than with a few remarks…It is plain enough that fairy- stories (in wider or in narrower sense) are very ancient indeed. Related things appear in very early records; and they are found universally, wherever there is language. We arc therefore obviously confronted with a variant of the problem that the archaeologist encounters, or the comparative philologist: with the debate between independent evolution (or rather invention) of the similar; inheritance from a common ancestry; and diffusion at various times from one or more centres.'"

Turning away from the screen she studied the crowd. "Tolkien is considered one of the greatest fantasy writers in the history of mankind. His books are still widely read and have even inspired Academy-Award-winning movies and a popular MMORPG."

That comment helped her pick out the gamers in the audience by their grins. She could tell a couple of them were thinking about playing that as soon as class was over. In fact, the way one boy's head shot up, she couldn't help but wonder if she looked at his screen if she would find Middle-Earth.

"But, more than that, he was one of the great philologists, with an intense knowledge of language's history—and the mythology that has always clung to it. *Gilgamesh*, after all, is our earliest surviving written record. Tolkien acknowledged Müller's quote though and had this to say, 'Max Müller's view of mythology as a 'disease of language' can be abandoned without regret. Mythology is not a disease at all, though it may, like all human things, become diseased. You might as well say that thinking is a disease of the mind. It would be more near the truth to say that languages, especially modern European languages, are a disease of mythology.'"

That caused her to chuckle. "I prefer to agree with Tolkien on this. After all, that quote is how I earn my living, in a sense."

As she walked across the stage, clicking through slides, she eyed one of the students. He slipped into the back of the lecture hall, border-lining the time that it was socially acceptable to arrive late. Which was, also, the time it was polite for Rosella to be late. She'd earned her doctorate. At least according to the old myth—Rosella preferred to be on time to speaking events, not in the mood to waste not only her time but the time of those listening. The student quickly opened his laptop and tried to look attentive, but his shoulders were tense yet his face portrayed a different story. His face appeared to be relaxed but his clenched jaw told her he was stressed and a little over focused on the task at hand. Not only that but she could see his wire from here. He must be new, he was too tense. That or he hadn't been warned that she was pretty good at reading body language. But seriously, Quantico was slipping if they thought that act was covert. She assumed he was wired simply to test him in the field, in a safe situation. Baby's first op.

"Some stories are to teach a lesson, it's the reason we have fables and how Aesop became a household name. Others are fun stories to tell around a campfire or a childhood sleepover or to be turned into the next Disney movie."

"Others take a darker side, or rather people choose to let them." Another click another slide.

"Serial killers, immortalized in this day and age by the influx of crime dramas which seem to occupy most major networks. People are obsessed with the idea of the forensic sciences."

Now she had their attention.

"Sometimes, the two meet. Killers think they can hide behind the myths. Forensic Mythology if you will."

A student in the fourth row raised her hand and Rosella nodded to her. Being called on by a guest would at least give her a good story.

She was one of the ones who'd perked up at the mention of *Lord of the Rings Online*. Her Mac was plastered with stickers—a TARDIS design that went out with the sixties, a *Metropolitan* press badge reading Smith, and Mara Jade holding a pink lightsaber aloft; it was clear this girl knew her science fiction and fantasy. Her straight posture and over-eager expression let Rosella know that this was probably one of her friend's better students.

"So, you're saying that most urban myths aren't true?"

Rosella smiled. "That's not my job to figure out; that was more something Margaret McConnell studied to learn, and I direct you to her books. I prefer to leave that to other people to argue over. I have to sort the very real killer from the myth."

Another hand, this time from a boy who had looked bored until she had said "serial killers." Then his attitude changed rather quickly and the combination of that, along with the book by Temperance Brennan in his bag, made her wonder if he knew how much was real and how much was fiction. Though at least he was reading one of the more accurate adaptations. Nodding to him, she was partially curious what question he'd come up with.

"How do the two manage to come together? Mythology's just stories. Forensic Science is an actual science."

It was a question she often got. With a nod she clicked a slide. "Most people wonder how I manage to see the two combined. Who here has gotten one of those annoying chain emails, the ones that say if you don't pass it on you'll bad luck or meet an untimely demise?"

Hands all over the auditorium went up. They usually did when she asked the question.

"A few years ago in Dallas, Texas, one of those went around. The thing was, people who didn't pass it along met said untimely demise."

She clicked a slide and showed a set of three victims. Each one had received a single bullet wound. A tarot baring the reverse chariot was laid beside them. "All of our victims had received that email within twenty-four hours of their death and for a while that was our only tie-in. Forensic science—the wound delivered at point blank, the presence of the card. Fornensic mythology—the email, and the card itself. When reversed, the chariot tarot card means bad luck."

"Did you catch the guy?" Someone near the back asked without raising their hand.

"Eventually. He managed to kill five victims before we were able to nail down his location. But when killers use something like these superstitious emails or urban legends, they often use them as a mask to hide their crimes. Some people are so focused on the legend coming true that they refuse to see what's right in front of them—a human being."

"So the myths aren't true?" The over-eager girl repeated her earlier question.

"Once again, I didn't say that. It's not my business to prove or disprove them. Though I will say those annoying emails are probably the creation of someone who had too much time on their hands and more than enough access to the internet."

That earned her a few chuckles.

"Forensic Mythology is an emerging sub-classification of the forensic sciences. And while many of my colleagues don't think it's practical, I do know that it has helped to save lives and bring peace to victims."

Another hand went up and she nodded to the person about halfway back. "But why mythology? What made you think to combine it with the forensic sciences?"

Rosella launched into her traditional lecture, smiling at how once again, she had managed to get the students to steer the conversation to where she wanted to go. Of course, they didn't realize that that's what just happened.

The rest of the class passed quickly and soon enough students were packing up to rush off to their next class, a hot date, a procrastinated study session, or one of the seemingly endless things students could do. Finally, the tardy student from earlier made his way up, carrying a copy of her latest book in his hand.

"You know, you can drop the cover now. A tip, when your body language sends mixed signals, a trained eye is going to notice."

The kid's face dropped and he shrugged. "They said you were good. Does that mean you won't sign my book? I actually really enjoyed it."

Rosella let out a chuckle. "I'll sign it. I'm assuming somewhere in that bag there's a file for me?"

"A case came up and my superior wanted you to take a look. He thinks it might be up your alley."

"Your superior knows that, officially, I'm not here." Rosella let out a sigh, the extremely long to-do list she had made for this trip to DC suddenly seeming unattainable.

"According to him, it's right up your alley Also, he said something about covering your hotel here and rescheduling any appointments you miss to take a look."

She turned to Professor Alicia Walter, an old friend of hers. "I might have to take a raincheck on that coffee.

www.ingramcontent.com/pod-product-compliance
Lightning Source LLC
Chambersburg PA
CBHW071427260626
47170CB00008B/2616